THE SWORD OF BHELEU

Garth saw nothing but the bonfire and the glowing sword. He would take that sword; he would burst into the chamber and snatch it red-hot from where it stood. Then he would flee.

Flee? An overman flee from humans? No, he would wield that splendid blade until it shone as red with blood as it did now with heat! Somewhere a part of him knew this was insane, but it was brutally suppressed by the unearthly power that dominated him.

Boldly Garth marched up onto the holy pyre and wrenched the sword from its place. His hands smoked with the heat of the hilt, but the overman paid no heed.

"I am Bheleu; I am the God of Destruction!" cried the monster in Garth's body.

By Lawrence Watt-Evans
Published by Ballantine Books:

THE LORDS OF DÛS

Book One:
The Lure of the Basilisk

Book Two:
The Seven Altars of Dûsarra

Book Three:
The Sword of Bheleu

Book Four:
The Book of Silence

The Cyborg and the Sorcerers

The
SEVEN ALTARS
of
DÛSARRA

Book Two of *The Lords of Dûs*

Lawrence Watt-Evans

A Del Rey Book

BALLANTINE BOOKS • NEW YORK

A Del Rey Book
Published by Ballantine Books

Library of Congress Catalog Card Number: 80-70659

ISBN 0-345-31495-6

Manufactured in the United States of America

First Ballantine Books Edition: June 1981
Second Printing: March 1984

Map by Chris Barbieri

Cover art by Darrell K. Sweet

Dedicated to
Roy Thomas and
Barry Smith,
for stirring
my interest in
heroic fantasy.

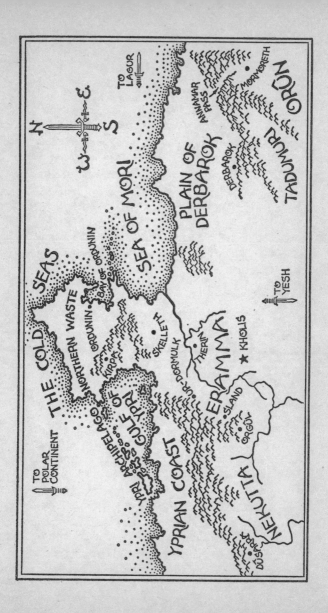

CHAPTER ONE

The rider paused at the top of the low ridge; the plain that lay just beyond was spread out before him under the pale stars of late summer. Directly before him there was an interruption of the flat earth; jagged silhouettes rose in black humps, huddled together within an uneven stone ring. The circle was broken at the point nearest him, and a single shattered wall rose to mark what had once been a substantial gatehouse; beside that wall flickered an orange flame, as warm as the stars were cold.

Although he was still too far away to discern any details, he knew that this was the town of Skelleth, and that the single light was the watch fire of the guardsman at the ruins of the North Gate. He had been here before, and knew that of the five gates in the crumbling city wall only this one was guarded. It was guarded against him and his kind.

There was no sign of life other than the lonely fire, and even had the man posted there been fully alert—as he undoubtedly was not at this hour—he could not have seen the rider or his party at such a distance in the dark. Their approach was undetected.

The mounted figure sat for a moment, his face invisible in the darkness and the shade of his trader's hat, studying the panorama; he glanced up as a night-bird flew overhead, and his eyes shone a baleful red with reflected starlight. His hollow-cheeked face had no nose, but only close-set slit nostrils; ragged black hair hung almost to his shoulders, but there was no trace of a beard on the leathery brown hide of his jaw. He was inhumanly tall and correspondingly broad. He was, in short, not human, but overman.

1

His long-fingered hand, with its oddly jointed thumb and opposable fifth finger, grasped the guide-handle of his mount's harness, an unnecessary precaution; his warbeast was trained to obey verbal commands or the pressure of its rider's feet, and moved with such feline smoothness that there was no danger of dislodging its master. The creature was blacker than the night sky, and as silent; its golden eyes and polished fangs were the only discernable features. It stood the height of a man and, from its stubby whiskers to lashing pantherlike tail, measured a good eighteen feet. Its triangular ears were up and alert, but it gave no warning growl.

Accordingly, the overman raised his arm in the signal to advance and led his companions over the final ridge and down onto the plain. His warbeast moved with silent catlike grace, its great padded paws disturbing not a single stone; the rest of the party was not so circumspect.

There were four in the party, all grown overmen, but only the leader rode a warbeast; his three followers made do with yackers, the universal beast of burden of the Northern Waste. Each rode upon one of the ugly creatures and led another heavily laden with the goods they hoped to trade in Skelleth. There was something slightly ludicrous in the stately dignity of the overmen as they perched stiffly upright upon the broad backs covered with ropy, matted brown hair, and guided their beasts with finely tooled silver bits in slobbering black-lipped mouths full of uneven yellow teeth. The yackers' hooves rattled on every pebble, it seemed, and there was a constant snorting and rumbling from the six shaggy, drooping heads.

They were travelling the ancient Wasteland Road, which led straight to Skelleth's North Gate; as the last yacker reached the foot of the ridge, the leader turned his warbeast off the road, heading west instead of south.

"Hold, Garth!" called the second in the procession.

The leader tapped a signal with his heel and the warbeast halted. "What is it?"

His companion drew up beside him and asked,

"Where are we heading? Is that not Skelleth?" He pointed to the flickering watch fire.

The third overman pulled up beside them as well as Garth replied, "Yes, of course that is Skelleth, and that is where we're going."

"Then why have we left the road? These yackers are quite slow enough as it is."

It was the third overman who replied, "Larth, did not Garth explain our situation to you?"

"I remember nothing that explains our turning away from our destination."

"Then you remember nothing. We are to enter the town in secrecy."

"It was not you I asked, Galt."

"Galt, however, speaks correctly," Garth said. "The Baron of Skelleth does not want overmen in his town; most especially, he does not want me there. When last I saw him he ordered his guards to kill me on the spot. Fortunately, they did not cooperate. However, if we can present the Baron with a peaceful trading caravan in the market square, not as a possibility but as an accomplished fact, I think he can be made to see reason and accept us."

"So we are to sneak in like thieves?"

"Why else are we travelling by night?" Galt's tone was sweetly reasonable.

"It is not dignified!"

"And what would be dignified?" Garth inquired.

"To ride directly in by daylight, and demand as our due that we be allowed to trade."

Galt snorted. "That might be dignified, but it would also be stupid, perhaps fatally so. Garth says there are more than thirty guardsmen in Skelleth; true, they are mere humans, and none too well equipped by his account, but there are only four of us, and we are not exactly well armed either."

Garth added, before Larth could reply, "It would not do for friendly traders to be bristling with weapons; we cannot risk incidents involving bloodshed. That is why I required that you three be unarmed, and I will conceal my own weapons before we begin our dealings with the people of Skelleth."

"Quite correct." Galt nodded in agreement. Larth continued to look unconvinced.

"Still," he demanded, "why have we left the road?"

His answer came from the fourth and youngest overman, who had not yet spoken, showing the proper deference to his elders; he could not, however, refrain from replying, "Because there's a guard on the road, stupid!"

Larth's voice was emotionless as he said, "Galt, restrain your apprentice."

As all knew quite well, that flat tone was indicative of building rage; Galt did not hesitate to order his underling to shut up.

When Larth had calmed somewhat, he asked, "How do you know that we can find another entrance unguarded?"

"I don't know for certain," Garth said. "But when I was here before, they guarded only the north; the West Gate opens on a road that leads only to the Yprian Coast, which has reputedly been deserted for centuries, so what need to guard it? Therefore, we will enter through the West Gate. We will reach it by circling wide around, well out of sight and sound of the guard at the North Gate. Now, if we are to reach the market square before dawn we must move onward, so let there be no further debate." His warbeast, in response to a signal undetectable to the others, strode onward.

"Very well," Larth said. It took rather more to get his yackers moving once again, but a moment's prodding eventually registered with their dim brains and they resumed their plodding and snuffling. Galt and his apprentice were not far behind.

There was still an hour remaining before first light when the little caravan reached the West Gate—which was, as Garth had expected, unguarded. It was also in such a state of total ruin that only the fading trace of an ancient road leading through the rubble showed where it had been, and it was only under protest that the yackers could be compelled to make their way across the jagged bits of broken stone. Garth's war-

beast paid this minor inconvenience no heed whatsoever.

Once inside the wall, there was little immediate im-
provement in their surroundings. On either side of the
road stood nothing but ruins. Gaping holes half-filled
with rubble showed where cellars had been of old,
sometimes rimmed with uneven remnants of walls of
stone or wood or plaster, and between these pits were
the broken pieces of buildings that had had no cellars
and now lay in heaps upon bare earth.

Galt commented, in a careful whisper, "Hardly the
awesome fortress that our ancestors described."

Larth, in a rather less cautious mutter, replied,
"Who can tell in this darkness? It looks deserted;
Garth, are you sure this is Skelleth?"

"Yes, I'm sure; only the central portion is still inhabited. When the wars ended so did the town's reason for existence, and so did the supply trains from
the south that kept it going. It's been slowly dying
ever since. That's why I think the people will welcome
trade, even if it's with overmen."

"I hope so." Larth's voice sank into an incoherent
mumble.

The party moved on, and around them the buildings became less ruinous; on either side stood sagging,
abandoned houses and shops—derelict, but still upright. Rotting shutters hung from bent hinges; broken
doors stood open, revealing only blackness. Then, as
they approached the surviving center, more and more
doors were closed, even barred, and fewer shutters
missing or broken. Before too long the only openings
on either side were other streets, rather than empty
lots where buildings had been razed or had fallen in.
Everything was dark, however; the people of Skelleth
were clearly all still abed.

Finally the street debouched into the market square
that occupied the town's exact center; it, too, was
dark, silent, and empty. Garth was pleased to see that
the Baron's mansion, which occupied the entire north
side of the square, was as dark as any other building.
He stopped his warbeast in the center of the market
and motioned for Galt to join him. When Galt obeyed,

he whispered. "This is the place, trader; that is the seat of the local government. Where would you suggest we set up?"

Galt studied the square carefully, and finally pointed to the southeast corner. "That looks good."

Garth nodded. "Then you three set up there. It occurs to me that a warbeast will not be a welcome sight in Skelleth, and I am going to put Koros and my weapons somewhere out of sight. I would suggest that you do the same with the yackers; just tie them up in an alley somewhere, where they won't upset the merchants. Koros, I think, had best go somewhere further out; I'll find a ruin somewhere on the West Road."

"As you wish."

"I'll be right back. Just remember, keep it peaceful."

Galt nodded. Garth turned and rode back along the route they had just come, while the others made their way to the southeast corner of the market and dismounted, stiff from their long ride.

Galt studied the location with a practiced eye, then indicated a spot in front of a tightly shuttered shop, just beside the mouth of a narrow street. His apprentice immediately hauled a bundle off one of the yackers and began spreading blankets on the ground designated. Larth stood nearby, peering apprehensively about in the gloom, and Galt found himself grateful that Garth had made sure the party was unarmed; Larth was plainly nervous enough to have drawn sword at the slightest sound, which would simply not do.

Of course, that was Larth. He himself was not so easily bothered, nor so easily commanded. The dagger in his boot was simply a sensible precaution, and none of Garth's business.

Leaving Larth to his anxiety, he began hauling bundles off yackers. In a matter of moments the ugly beasts were unburdened. Galt whispered to his apprentice, "Tand, you start spreading out our wares. Get Larth to help you if you can, but don't start an argument. I'll be back in a moment."

He gathered up the lead ropes from the six harnesses and began coaxing the yackers down the narrow street, out of the market. The beasts were not actively uncooperative, but it was still difficult to manage all six of them, so that he was several minutes at the task.

Finally he managed to get them arranged in a circle, their lead ropes tied together. Although they could still move about, they were far too stupid to move all in the same direction; this arrangement should keep them more or less in the same place for quite some time. It did block the street, but Galt hoped that wouldn't matter much. It didn't look like a major thoroughfare. Besides, that meant that the overmen could not be taken from behind by enemies coming up this street; even if they got past the yackers, the inevitable noise would serve as a warning.

The yackers were a new problem for him. Though he was a master trader, all his previous experience had been gained on expeditions to Lagur, since that was the only place the overmen of the Northern Waste currently traded. There were no yackers used on such expeditions, since all trade with Lagur went by sea.

Once the beasts were taken care of, he returned to the square. He could hear the sounds of furs being unpacked; either Tand was working incredibly fast, or he had gotten Larth to help him, judging by the noise.

Then, just as he was about to turn the corner into the market, the sounds stopped abruptly. So did he. Something was happening, obviously. Peaceful, peaceful, he reminded himself; he fixed his most nearly human smile upon his face and strolled forward as casually as he could.

Larth and Tand knelt motionless amid heaps of furs and carved whalebone, staring off to their right. Following their gaze he saw a ragged human farmer, pulling a rickety cart half-full of squash, standing motionless in a street opening into the eastern end of the market. The farmer's mouth hung open and his eyes were wide, the whites palely visible in the first light of morning—light which had crept up while Galt was securing the yackers without his noticing it. It appeared very much as if this man had never seen an overman before, and quite possibly he hadn't. Larth and Tand were also staring, and it occurred to Galt that it might well be that neither of them had ever seen a human being before.

This, Galt knew, was the decisive moment. Secrecy was gone. Now, if their mission was to succeed, they needed to convince the humans that there was nothing out of the ordinary about overmen trading in their marketplace. Garth had hired him as an expert on dealing with humans, and he knew that humans could be convinced of anything if only approached properly.

He waved gaily, broadened his smile, and called, "Greetings, good sir! Would you care to see our wares?"

The man turned his gaze from the others to Galt, but his mouth remained open and his eyes wide.

Galt gestured at the heaps of trade goods. "We have fine furs, such as are rarely seen in these lands; we have fine carved implements of use in any home. Come and look, friend!"

The man's mouth slowly closed. He swallowed, and looked back and forth between the overmen. His eyes roved around the market square and found no one else and nothing out of the ordinary—except the party of overmen. Galt judged him to be recovered from his shock and considering the situation. He would not turn and run, because that would mean abandoning his cart; it had been a stroke of luck that the first human to find them had been so encumbered. He had two sensible options; he could behave as if the overmen belonged there, or he could raise an alarm. It was Galt's job to convince him the former was the better course.

Still smiling, he called, "It costs nothing to look, sir, and should something catch your eye, our prices are reasonable." They certainly were! This trip was not expected to make a profit, nor break even, but only to establish an opening; accordingly, he and Garth had agreed that they would refuse no serious offer—though they would haggle, of course; that was expected, and suspicion would be aroused if they did not —and would even give away goods free if it seemed advisable. "If you haven't brought any money, we might trade for those fine vegetables."

That decided him. The man found his voice and called, "Wait a moment, and I'll come look." He began moving again, wheeling his creaking cart into the square.

As he did, a shuttered window in the second story of the building the overmen had chosen to set up in front of opened, and a head was thrust out. "What's all the yelling? It's not yet dawn!"

Galt doffed his hat politely and called up, "My apologies, good lady; it was thoughtless of me to bellow so."

The head, which was indeed female—Galt hadn't been certain—turned to look at him. There was a moment of silence save for the creaking of cart wheels as the farmer positioned his wares. Then the woman asked, conversationally but in an unsteady voice, "You're an overman, aren't you?"

"Yes, good lady, my companions and myself are overmen, come to trade peacefully. We have fine furs and jewelry that would surely please one as lovely as yourself; Tand, hold up that white fox for the lady."

Tand was still motionless with surprise, but picked up his cue with only the briefest hesitation and stood, displaying an excellent fur.

The woman noticed Larth and Tand for the first time but paid them little heed, looking instead at the stacks of furs. There was a pause, and then she said, "I'll be right down." Her head vanished from the window, and Galt's false smile relaxed into a genuine one. The danger was past. They had been accepted.

When Garth returned several minutes later he found a small crowd clustered around his companions, bickering cheerfully over quality and price.

CHAPTER TWO

Garth glanced apprehensively at the door to the Baron's mansion as it swung open for the first time that morning. So far whatever gods there might be had smiled upon his little caravan; they had had no trouble on the road from Ordunin, nor with the merchants and farmers who had so far entered the market. The reactions of the villagers to a quartet of overmen sitting calmly in their midst amid displays of furs and carved whalebone had varied from simple acceptance to astonishment and horror—which could usually be soothed by a few quiet words and perhaps a gold coin or two. The fact that those already there appeared unconcerned had been a major factor in preventing general alarm or even a riot.

Unfortunately, Garth knew the Baron of Skelleth and his guards would not be so easily swayed. His previous visit to this northernmost outpost of humanity had ended messily, and the Baron had ordered his death, more for being an overman and uncooperative than for any specific crime.

Of course none of Skelleth's pitiful guardsmen were likely to try and tackle four overmen; Garth thought it unlikely that the village's full complement of three dozen would have been a match for his party if he hadn't insisted his companions be unarmed. They were on a peaceful trading mission, and he was determined to see that it stayed peaceful. For far too long had the overmen of the Northern Waste been dependent upon the sea traders of Lagur, who missed no opportunity to exploit their monopoly; if Garth succeeded in opening a land trade route through Skelleth the monopoly would be broken, and his people would have their first chance at a decent life since the bitter Racial Wars of three centuries earlier—and incidentally Garth would be honored and wealthy, which would be enjoyable.

The door was open now, and three guardsmen stepped through, blinking in the bright summer sunlight; Garth recognized one of them. The tall one in the steel helmet was Herrenmer, captain of the guard.

The unknown pair took up their posts, one on either side of the door. Herrenmer, having stationed his men, took a casual glance around, his duty done for the moment. His gaze fell on the overmen and Garth saw him tense. He spoke to his men, but Garth could hear nothing over the noise of the market; then all three started across the square toward the outlanders, Herrenmer in the lead, all three with hands near their swords.

Garth put down the wolfskin he had been showing to an overweight woman and said, "Larth, keep an eye on my goods while I speak to these men." He stood and stepped forward to meet the soldiers.

The trio stopped a dozen paces from the displays; Garth stood halfway between. There was a moment's pause, then Herrenmer demanded, "What are you doing here?"

"We have come to trade."

"You know that the Baron wants no overmen in Skelleth."

"I was aware that he wanted no armed overmen adventurers, an attitude I can fully understand, since such would tend to disturb the peace of your town; but surely he can have no objection to four unarmed traders, whatever their race or nation!" Garth had carefully thought out this little speech in advance, and was pleased to see that it had the desired effect, leaving Herrenmer momentarily confused and speechless. He pressed his advantage.

"I have heard the Baron himself express dismay at Skelleth's poverty and lack of trade; surely, then, he will be glad to have a whole new people eager to deal with Skelleth. We have gold and furs and other goods to trade for our needs, which will make Skelleth's merchants wealthy when sold in the south, where we dare not venture. Surely the Baron cannot object to that, for where the merchants are wealthy the government cannot fail to profit thereby."

"I know nothing of that; it is not my concern." Herrenmer paused, considering, then went on, "I will speak with my lord further about this." He turned and strode angrily back to the mansion; his two men followed, and when Herrenmer vanished through the still-open door, slamming it behind him, they took up their posts once more.

Garth watched them go, then turned back toward his companions. Before he could take a step, however, he heard his name called. He stopped and looked about for the source.

A waving hand caught his eye, and he recognized a man approaching across the market. "Greetings, Saram," he called.

"Greetings, Garth," the man replied.

Saram was heavily built, of medium height; he wore his hair short and kept his full black beard neatly trimmed, though he claimed it was not from vanity but practicality. When last Garth had seen him, he had worn the mail shirt and short sword of the Baron's guards, with iron studs in his leather helmet marking him as a lieutenant; now he wore a ragged but clean tunic of gray homespun and went bareheaded. Only the leather pants and heavy boots remained the same.

He drew up within convenient speaking distance and remarked, "So you have returned as you promised." His tone was casual, but his green eyes flicked warily about, missing nothing.

"I have," Garth answered politely. Saram had done him considerable good when last he was in Skelleth by refusing to attempt to kill him.

"The old man said you would." Saram's eyes focused on Garth's face as he spoke.

The overman shrugged, his face impassive, and said nothing.

"I had my doubts, but here you are. Where is your

warbeast? I was sure you'd bring it if you came."
Saram glanced idly about.

"It's hidden nearby. I saw no need to frighten your
townspeople."

"Wise of you, no doubt. And you brought friends
with you this time."

"Companions, rather; I am not myself adept at the
ways of buyer and seller, so I brought the master
trader Galt, his apprentice Tand, and my double-
cousin Larth." He pointed out each of the other overmen as he named them; young Tand and stolid Larth
did not notice, but Galt nodded in acknowledgment.

"Pleased to meet them all, I'm sure. Gods, what
are those?" This last was in response to glimpsing the
yackers, just visible from where he stood.

Garth was startled. "Yackers. Don't you know
them?" He glanced down the alley at the great beasts
of burden, which stood quietly meditating, safely out
of the bustle of business.

"No. I never heard of them." Saram stared at them
momentarily, then turned back to the overman and
said, "Garth, I have a message for you. The old man
wants to talk to you."

Garth replied, "I don't want to talk to him."

"No? He claims to have a proposition for you."

"I am not interested; when last I made a bargain
with him it resulted in nothing but deaths and diffi-
culties."

"Just as your agreement with the Baron did him
little good," Saram said smiling crookedly, "Yet you
expect him to listen to your explanations about your
renewed presence in his domain."

There was a moment of silence. Then Garth said,
"Your point is made. I will hear the King out. Where
is he?"

"Need you ask?"

"No. A moment, then." He turned and called to his
companions, "I have an errand; Galt, you take charge
here." Then to Saram he said, "Come on," and the
pair ambled off across the market square.

Their goal was an ancient tavern called the King's
Inn, though no one knew of any connection between

the inn and any recognized monarch; it stood on an alley that had once been but a few steps from the village market, but which had been cut off and left to die when the first Baron of Skelleth erected his mansion across the north side of the square, leaving no opening to the streets beyond. The alley, now accessible only by a winding route through the maze of byways that made up most of Skelleth, had sunk into a state of decay and filth unequaled throughout the known lands; yet the King's Inn remained an island of comfort amid the surrounding squalor and retained a steady clientele. Among its regular patrons, so regular in fact that he had never been seen outside its walls, was a strange old man, so very old that none remembered a time when he had not been there daily, crouched silently over his corner table. This man Garth knew as the Forgotten King, having been given this title for him by the Wise Women of Ordunin, but the townspeople had no name for him at all. Until the overman first came, some three months earlier, few ever spoke to him, fewer received an answer, and none sought him out; but in recent days, since being expelled from the Baron's guards for insubordination, Saram had spent many hours sitting at his table, trying to coax him into conversation and receiving only a few cryptic words for his trouble. Among those few words were instructions that when—not if, but when —Garth returned, Saram should bring him immediately to speak with the mysterious ancient.

Saram led the way through the stinking streets, fortunately dry from the recent lack of rain, and Garth followed, his reluctance concealed by the casual stroll he affected. The slanting sunlight had not yet made its way past the upper story of the inn in its slow daily crawl down the building's sagging half-timbered facade; the ordure that lined the alley was still hidden by shadow, but its smell was not so easily to be concealed and not for the first time Garth marvelled that humans could live with it. He held his breath as he and Saram picked their way to the door and wiped their feet on the stone step before entering.

The tavern's interior was a welcome change from

the filth of the alley; not so much as a speck of dust marred the ancient floor, worn by centuries of shuffling feet into a subtle wooden landscape of low hills and gentle valleys that showed clearly that its furnishings had not shifted nor its patrons changed their habits in many a long year. Each table crowned a hillock, each chair rested in wide grooves cut by the dragging of its legs. The great barrels of ale and wine that lined the western wall loomed above flooring so stained and worn that Garth wondered how it still held—he had no way of seeing the thickness of wood beneath, but only that this most popular part of the room had a good two inches less floor remaining than elsewhere. The slate hearth that stretched along half the eastern wall before the vast cavernous fireplace showed little wear, being harder stuff than the soft floorboards; curiously, the ancient stair that crossed the back wall had only the slightest indentation in each tread. Plainly, it was as a tavern rather than an inn that the establishment survived, since those stairs were the only access to the rooms upstairs.

Though every inch of the room was clearly old, worn, and well-used, none could ever think it deserted for it was spotlessly clean, save for the oft-scrubbed stains left by centuries of spilled wine. The morning sun had not yet climbed high enough to pour unchecked through the polished and age-purpled windows, yet the brass fittings on the barrels gleamed dully, the stacked mugs of pewter and china and glass glistened on their shelves, the blackened hearth shone dimly. The only spots of uncleanliness were two drunken farmers adorning opposite sides of a small table near the door, clad in dirty gray homespun, with greasy hair and smudged faces, who slouched forward muttering to one another. The innkeeper, though a plump middle-aged man wearing a well-stained apron, gave the impression not of disarray, but like his tavern, of well-worn comfort. The room's only other occupant, sitting alone in the corner between chimneypiece and stair, seemed somehow beyond such mundane concerns as cleanliness.

It was this lone figure that Garth and Saram were

interested in. The innkeeper watched apprehensively as the pair entered and crossed the room, and twice opened his mouth to protest their presence, but each time lost his nerve and remained silent. When they had seated themselves across from the old man, he gradually relaxed and returned to his task of polishing mugs that already showed a flawless silken sheen; but he polished the same mug for a good fifteen minutes with short, nervous strokes, and cast frequent glances at the overman who had intruded upon the peace of his place of business.

For a moment after they had settled in their chairs neither Garth nor Saram spoke; they considered the strange figure across from them, who sat motionlessly, seemingly oblivious of their presence.

The old man whom Ordunin's oracles had called the Forgotten King wore tattered yellow rags from head to foot, and despite the summer warmth he kept them wrapped tightly about him, his cloak closed and his hood up, so that its shadows hid much of his face. A long, scraggly white beard reached down across his sunken chest, and what could be seen of his hands and face was skin as dry and wrinkled as that of a mummy, with as little evidence of anything between skin and bone. His eyes were lost in darkness; in all their conversations with him neither Garth nor Saram had ever seen his eyes, and only on the rarest occasions had either so much as caught a glimmer of light from them. The shadows gave the illusion that he had no eyes, but only empty sockets; perhaps that, more than anything else, was why generations of tavern-goers had seen fit to leave him sitting alone and un-molested.

Garth studied him, but saw nothing he had not seen before. Garth was a typical member of his species in most respects, and as such he was not particularly good at recognizing human faces or reading emotion in them; still, there was something about the Forgotten King's face that made him uneasy. He shifted in his chair, which creaked beneath his weight. He was out of proportion with his surroundings in a tavern designed for mere men; he towered above the others, his natural height of near seven feet augmented by a woolen trader's hat that not only shaded his red-eyed, sunken-cheeked horror of a face, but hid a steel half-helmet. Peaceful mission or no, Garth was given to caution; despite his orders to his companions and hiding most of his armor and weaponry with his warbeast, his flowing brown cloak concealed a sturdy mail shirt, and a stiletto lurked in his right boot-top—the latter a precaution that was incidentally rather uncomfortable, as its hilt, though safely hidden by his leggings and the sparse black fur that adorned his leathery hide, chafed when he walked.

He studied the old man, but said nothing.

Beside him Saram glanced from the overman to the King and back again, his finger poking idly at a small circle of mismatched wood in the table-top—a circle that was the sawn-off shaft of a crossbow bolt Saram had fired at Garth, on the Baron's orders, during Garth's previous stay in Skelleth. The overman had used the table as a makeshift shield, and the barbed quarrel had proven impossible to remove, so that the innkeeper had cut it off and sanded it down to blend with the oak.

After a moment, when it appeared that neither Garth nor the old man was willing to speak first, the ex-soldier cleared his throat and said, "I have brought Garth here, as you asked."

The old man nodded very slightly, but gave no other sign that he was aware of the presence of others at his table.

There was another pause, this one briefer than the first. It was broken when the overman finally announced, "I am here at your request. Speak, then, and tell me what you want of me. I have business to attend to."

The old man spoke, in a voice like the rustling of long-dead leaves. "Garth, I would have you serve me further."

The overman suppressed the shudder that ran through him at the sound of that voice; he had heard it before, but it was something that one could not truly remember—or want to remember. He replied,

"I have no desire to serve you, nor any person other than myself."

The Forgotten King raised his head slightly and spoke again. "There are very few in these waning years of the Thirteenth Age who are fit to serve me. I do not care to wait for another."

"That may be; I do not deny that you may have uses for me. But why should I serve you? You offer me nothing, and I have little cause to trust you after the outcome of my last venture in your service."

"What would you have?"

"I would have nothing of you but to be left alone. When you promised me fame, my service yielded nothing but a dozen deaths and much trouble to no purpose."

"I did not slight you."

"Is my fame then so great? I see little evidence of it, old man."

"Did you then fulfill your service to me with a single trial?"

"No. I saw my folly after the single trial and went home."

"Yet you have returned, upon my advice."

Garth paused. That much was true; it had been the Forgotten King who pointed out the possibility of trade through Skelleth and its potential benefits.

"What of it? I did you a service, and you paid me with a simple suggestion I should have thought of for myself—but did not, I admit. We are even, then. I have no wish to serve you further. Hire Saram, here!"

Saram was startled out of his silence. "I? Oh, no; I am no adventurer."

The Forgotten King ignored Saram and said, "Is there then nothing that you seek, Garth? Are you content with your lot?"

There was a moment of silence; Garth contemplated the shadowed face while Saram looked back and forth, and neither could see where the old man's gaze fell. Finally the overman admitted slowly, "No, I am not content. I still seek what in truth I sought before; I want to know that I am not insignificant, not merely a meaningless mote in an uncaring cosmos. I sought eternal fame because it seemed to me that that was as close as I could come to making a real difference, and my nearest approach to immortality. I see little point in wealth or power or glory that will last only so long as I live. What, then, can you offer me? I no longer feel that the promise of undying fame will suffice to comfort me; can you offer more?"

"Under the proper circumstances I can give you whatever you want. If you fear death, I can promise you life to the end of time. If you seek to give your life a significance beyond the norm, then we are at one, for it is to work a fundamental change in the nature of our world that I seek your aid."

There was another moment of silence; then Garth asked, "What is this change you seek? You speak around your purpose. When I served you before you had me fetch you the basilisk and would not say why you wanted it; was it for this same mysterious goal?"

"My goal is unchanged." The harsh monotone of the old man's voice was likewise unchanged, but his head sank slightly, deepening the shadows that hid his face.

Garth sat back, considering. He had concluded, after much thought, that the Forgotten King's use for the basilisk—a use for which it had proven inadequate—included the old man's own death. He had no idea why the ancient would want to die; had he perhaps wearied of his long life? Nor had he any idea why a single old man should have difficulty in dying should he choose to do so, yet it was indisputable that he had survived whatever he had done with the basilisk. Perhaps, Garth thought, he had somehow misinterpreted previous events, for how could one lonely old man's suicide have cosmic repercussions?

That assumed, of course, that the old man spoke the truth. It was possible that he was indeed under some sort of curse of immortality which he hoped to break with Garth's aid—and dead men are under no obligation to fulfill their promises, so that he would offer whatever the overman wanted, knowing that he would never have to pay.

Then again, it was possible that the old man—who was very probably a wizard of some sort—really was attempting some world-shaking magic. That did not mean that his purposes were anything Garth sympathized with.

"What is this goal? Why will you not tell me? It could be some monstrous evil, some affront against nature and the gods."

"I seek only to fulfill that purpose the gods have given me, Garth; I swear this to be true."

"You still do not say what it is."

"Nor will I."

"And yet you ask me to serve you in this, without knowing?"

The old man said nothing, but nodded very slightly, once.

"I must consider this carefully. I will speak with you again when I have decided." Garth rose and strode from the table; Saram stirred, but reseated himself, and when the overman had left the tavern and the door had closed behind him, he turned back to the Forgotten King.

"It seems you offer a bargain only a fool would accept, full of vague terms and mysteries."

The Forgotten King said nothing, but Saram detected a faint shrug of his sagging shoulders.

CHAPTER THREE

As Garth rounded the last corner and came in sight of the marketplace, he saw Galt standing talking to someone. His fellow overman towered over the surrounding crowd, readily distinguishable, but at first Garth could not see who it was he was speaking with; then, as he began threading his way into the throng, he caught the glint of sunlight on a steel helmet and realized that Herrenmer had returned, presumably bearing the Baron's decision. He hastened his pace; the villagers, awed by his size and terrified by his face, parted before him, so that a brief moment later he was at Galt's side.

"Ah, Garth, it would seem that the local government wishes to speak with you and you alone. I offered myself as your representative, but was refused." Galt spoke smoothly and quickly, in a light tone, but Garth recognized a note of tension in his voice and saw that Herrenmer's hand was on his sword hilt. Behind their captain stood a full dozen guardsmen and, though no weapons were actually drawn, it was plain that a confrontation had been brewing.

"Oh? I apologize for my absence, Captain Herrenmer, but one of your townsmen wished to speak with me in private."

"The Baron also wishes to speak with you, overman; immediately." The man's voice shook slightly.

"I will oblige him momentarily. Larth, I leave you in charge. Galt, you come with me, in case we need to discuss business." The other overmen nodded; Garth took a step toward the mansion, but was halted by Herrenmer's hand raised in restraint.

"Wait a minute; I was told to bring you, not this other monster."

"But Galt is the business manager for our party. Should we need to discuss exact terms I will want his advice."

"If it will ease your mind, Captain, I will promise not to speak unless spoken to." Galt's voice was honey-smooth.

Herrenmer looked from one hideous face to the other, from Garth's crimson eyes to Galt's golden ones, and at last shrugged and led the way across the square.

The Baron's audience chamber was much as Garth remembered it, a fairly spacious room hung with old tapestries, with three small windows high in the northern wall behind the Baron's seat providing the only light. The Baron's seat was a simple oaken chair, and the Baron himself sat slouching in it, a small, slender man wearing a richly embroidered scarlet robe, with a circlet of gold on his brow. He fingered his thin black beard for a moment, then spoke.

"So it's true; you have returned."

This being self-evident, no reply seemed necessary, but Garth did not care to antagonize the Baron further with insolent silence; he replied simply, "Yes."

"I had not thought you would have had the gall to do so, despite your boast to that scum Saram, yet here you are. You have even brought others of your filthy race."

"We have come on a peaceful trading mission."

"So I am told. Are you aware that you are under sentence of death here, on charges of trespass, espionage, and crimes against the state? And that all your stinking species are enemy aliens?"

"I was aware that you were not eager to have us here. I hope to convince you that it would be to your advantage to welcome us."

"And how do you plan to do that?"

"In two stages: firstly, I will convince you that a regular trade between Skelleth and the Northern Waste will be very much in your own interests; and secondly, that killing me or otherwise thwarting me would make that trade impossible."

"Very well, then, I will listen. Why should I allow you monsters to trade on my lands?"

"Because we have much gold, from hidden mines in the northern mountains, with which to pay for what we want. Surely, much of this gold will find its way to you, in the form of taxes and tariffs. You told me once that you were not happy with your inheritance and hoped to improve your lot by war and plunder; would it not be equally satisfying to make yourself rich by peaceful means? Or even if it is the blood and glory of war you seek, will not our gold help to finance such an ambition? The terms of our former agreement, which you apparently feel I violated but which I feel I merely interpreted differently from yourself, included a statement that all overmen crossing your lands would pay what tribute you might rightfully demand; we will honor that, so long as such tribute does not make our trade prohibitively expensive. Surely you cannot refuse such an opportunity!"

"Dare not tell me what I can or cannot refuse, overman! Still, you make it sound very tempting. If your gold is as plentiful as you imply, I could indeed find uses for it." The Baron mused for a moment and then went on, "But then, to your second point, your own life; why should I not accept trade arrangements with your people, but still put you to death? I could easily demand your life as the necessary tribute; would not overmen give up a single life for a new trade route?"

"Perhaps they would under certain circumstances, but they will not give up my life, for I am the hereditary Prince of Ordunin, and the life of a reigning prince is not within your rights to demand." Garth was relying on the Baron's ignorance of the culture of the overmen of the Northern Waste in this, for in fact the title he claimed, though genuine, was strictly a ceremonial honor with no real significance beyond the privilege of speaking first in the City Council, a privilege it was customary to waive.

There was a moment of silence as the Baron considered this. Then he shifted his gaze to Galt and demanded, "You! Who are you?"

"I am Galt, my lord, a trader out of Ordunin."

"And who is this?" He pointed at Garth.

"That is Garth, Prince of Ordunin, a lord of the Overmen of the Northern Waste." Galt spoke casually, his pale blue cloak draped across one arm, his wide-brimmed hat shading his yellow eyes, looking completely at ease and unconcerned. Long years of experience had taught him that such a pose was most desirable in almost every sort of dealings with humans, be it trade, diplomacy, or less formal activities.

"You will swear to that?"

Galt blinked, and smiled a lipless smile. "If you wish."

"I do."

"I swear by my head that this overman is Garth, hereditary Prince of Ordunin, son of Karth and

Tarith, known to me as such for many years and so recognized by all my people."

"There were more of you, were there not?"

"Yes."

"Will they so swear?"

"Undoubtedly. Larth is Garth's double-cousin, and Tand has known him since childhood."

The Baron turned back to Garth. "Why did you not let me know this before, that I might have treated you as your rank deserved?"

"Why should I tempt you with a prince's ransom?"

"Are you not doing so now?"

"No, for I am not alone this time, and furthermore my people are now aware that Skelleth is no longer the mighty fortress that repelled our ancestors' attacks. Even should you take all four of us captive, there would be no ransom but fire and sword. As you surely realize, paying out ransoms sets a bad precedent."

The Baron scowled and slumped back in his chair. After a thoughtful pause he said, "It seems that you have the better of me in this matter; to indulge my whims would be far too costly, so I must let you live and go free. However, if you are in truth the reigning Prince of Ordunin, then there are other demands I may make. You seek for your people the free use of roads and rights of way that I happen to have proprietary rights upon. Our two nations are technically still at war, however, so that I cannot under ordinary circumstances grant such permissions as you seek without being untrue to my own oaths as vassal to the High King at Kholis; this is true though it would obviously be of great advantage to me personally and to my realm, and though our war has been unfought these three hundred years. Had you considered this?"

"Not in detail," Garth replied; he hesitated, and then continued, "I am not fully conversant with the laws of Eramma and I assumed that reasonable beings such as ourselves could find some way around such an obstacle."

"And I think we shall, Garth, I think we shall." The Baron grinned. "There are conditions under which I may make a separate peace, without the in-

tervention of the High King; specifically, I can accept
your surrender and your oath of fealty to me as a vassal prince."

"What?" Garth's reply was startled from him.

"Yes. You see, that would finish off the war very
neatly, and remove any obstacles it might create. Under the terms of my own commitment to the High
King I cannot surrender myself to you unless defeated
in battle, but there are no such constraints upon you.
Were you my vassal and loyal servant, our two peo-
ples would no longer be at war." The grin widened.
"Furthermore, as my vassal, your underlings would
of course have full access, free of tariff, to all my
lands. They would of course be required to pay the
customary taxes, and tolls for the use of some high-
ways, but only at the same rates as my human sub-
jects. In short, your goal of establishing open trade
would be achieved."

Garth was too shocked to speak. After a pause, the
Baron said, "Come, now, overman, is this so unreasonable? You offered any reasonable tribute; is a simple oath of fealty and the consequent obligation
unreasonable? The hundred barons of Eramma do
not think so."

Garth stammered, then fell silent. He gathered his
wits and replied, "I cannot give you an immediate answer. I cannot make such a commitment without con-
sulting my City Council." His initial astonishment was
fading, to be replaced with a growing outrage; how
dare this mere human even consider making himself
lord over overmen? Still, it would be well to remain
diplomatic; perhaps some lip service could be paid to
such an arrangement briefly, until a more sensible
agreement could be worked out. It was a matter that
did, indeed, warrant the consideration of the City
Council.

"Oh? Your Council? Very well. I had hoped to
conclude this matter here and now, but I suppose I
can tolerate some delay. Where is this Council?"

"In Ordunin." Garth stopped himself from adding,
"Of course."

"Of course. In that case, it seems to me that the

sooner you are on the way back to Ordunin, the better. I will give you twenty-four hours to be out of Skelleth on the Wasteland Road, and I will have you swear, here and now, that you will present my proposal to this Council as soon as you reach Ordunin, and that you will present it fairly and reasonably, as I have presented it to you. Agree to these terms, and your companions may remain and trade in peace."

Garth suppressed an impulse to lash out in rage. His expression, as always, remained blank and calm. It required an effort, though, for him to say, "I do so swear that I will present your proposal fairly to the City Council immediately upon my return to Ordunin."

"Good! I think our business is done then; begone! I would talk to this trader." The Baron waved him away peremptorily.

Garth bowed, giving no sign of his fury, and departed, the Baron's guards stepping quickly out of his way.

The Baron watched him go and smiled to himself. The overman would meet his terms, he was sure; he would swear the oath of fealty, thinking that he was committing himself to a few demeaning ceremonies and light taxation, service in name more than fact. It would be thoroughly delightful then to spring upon him the actual reason for his oath—an oath that included the obligation to provide his lord with all the military force at his disposal. It would be a simpler matter to pick a fight with that half-wit lord of Ur-Dormulk, who would march his army to Skelleth expecting an easy victory only to be met, not by three dozen half-trained farmers, but by warbeasts and overmen. Never again would that fat fool laugh at Doran of Skelleth! Never again would he be ignored and ridiculed, seated at the foot of the High King's table at the decennial meetings in Kholis!

A hundred overmen in full armor, a hundred warbeasts, would make him the most powerful baron in Eramma. *That* was the tribute he intended to exact from this absurd commerce!

When the door had closed Garth away from sight,

he bestirred himself from his daydreams of power and glory and waved Herrenmer up to his side. He whispered a few words in his captain's ear, then turned his attention to Galt.

"So, trader, you seek to bring wealth to our two lands. What would you consider a fair tax upon your receipts?"

As Galt roused himself to begin negotiations, Herrenmer slipped from the room; the overman paid him no heed.

A moment later Garth was halfway across the market square, returning to his two companions, when he heard the clink of mail and the thudding of booted feet running behind him. He turned to see Herrenmer hurrying after him.

"Did you seek me?"

The guardsman caught his breath, then replied, "Yes. I am to accompany you until you are outside the walls."

"I have twenty-four hours."

"I know; nonetheless, I am not to let you out of my sight until you leave Skelleth."

Overmen do not show anger in their facial expressions, a natural concealment that is ordinarily an aid to survival, since it permits them to utilize the element of surprise more readily even in a state of unreasoning fury. Perhaps the only drawback is that it leaves them inexperienced in reading the faces of other species, such as humans. It was definitely for the best at this particular moment that Herrenmer took Garth's impassive expression for a mild contemplation of the situation; had he known the seething rage that was building he would have had his sword drawn and been calling for reinforcements. Instead he shrugged, and looked away from the overman's hideous face, preferring to watch the ragged farmers and peasants rather than gaze at that leather-hided skull.

Garth had been annoyed by the Baron's apparent ingratitude in response to the promise of vast wealth he had done nothing to earn; he had been further irritated by his lack of trust in demanding that Galt— Galt, and not Garth—swear to Garth's identity and title; he had been appalled and infuriated at the suggestion that he swear fealty to this petty human tyrant, and disgusted that the Baron was so insistent upon haste. He had stood for it all and resisted the temptation to fling the dagger in his boot through the man's heart, or simply to tear him limb from limb, only to have this final insult thrust upon him. He was to be escorted from the town like an outlaw or some other undesirable!

It robbed him of all privacy and dignity, and as such it was the pebble that sank the barge. He could not quietly accept this!

He would not go slinking back to Ordunin like this, cast out of Skelleth until he declared himself servant to a scurvy madman, sworn to beg the City Council for permission to degrade himself and his people! He would defy the Baron somehow.

Unfortunately, it would not do for him to do so openly; the Baron was essential to the development of peaceful trade. If Garth killed him or otherwise seriously harmed him, it might well bring down the wrath of all Eramma upon not just himself, but all overmen, as untrustworthy brigands. It might even be enough of an incident to start up the long-dead Racial Wars again. A subtle poisoning might escape detection and do no harm to the prospects of peaceful trade—but it would also be thoroughly unsatisfying. He wanted the Baron to know what his effrontery had done.

Was there perhaps some way he could exploit the Baron's madness? As he had seen on his previous venture, and as all Skelleth knew, the Baron periodically lapsed into fits of depression so intense that he was unable to move himself at all, even to eat, so that he had to be carefully tended, like an infant, until the spell passed. Between these depressions his moods ranged from the alert intelligence he had displayed today to surly silence or screaming rage; Garth had seen all these moods, though not enough to see whether there was any pattern to them. He had also heard it said that there was an annual cycle, and that the Baron was at his worst in the spring.

He considered all this as he continued across the

square to where Larth and Tand sat; Herrenmer stayed at his side, but said nothing. He stood over his seated companions, who were engaged in quiet conversation, having no customers at the moment.

"I have been ordered to return to Ordunin; there are matters I am to present to the Council there."

The two looked up, startled. After a second's pause Larth asked, "Should we pack up, then?"

"No; the Baron requires no departure save my own. You two and Galt will stay until you have completed the disposal of these goods and the arrangements for future caravans. I leave Galt in charge; Larth, you will handle my share of the goods and proceeds and deliver it to Kyrith."

"Kyrith? Your wife? Will you not be in Ordunin?"

Garth glanced at Herrenmer, standing well within earshot. "Do not concern yourself with my whereabouts."

"Are you to leave immediately?" Larth asked.

"I have until tomorrow, but there are other matters I must attend to, and I will be home by year's end, most likely."

He actually had no idea when he would be home, but as it was still summer and the year was reckoned to end with the vernal equinox, it would almost certainly be before that. He had as yet no idea where he was going; he only knew that it would not be Ordunin. The Baron had required him to leave Skelleth, and to swear that he would speak to the Council immediately upon reaching Ordunin—but neglected to make sure that he would in fact go to Ordunin.

Garth had no intention of going back to Ordunin under the present circumstances; another annoyance to be credited to the Baron. He would have said as much, and explained the entire situation to his companions, had Herrenmer not been so close at hand, spying for his master.

He stood for a moment longer but thought of nothing more worth saying, and neither Larth nor Tand volunteered any more questions; then he spun on his heel and strode off toward the King's Inn at a pace that left Herrenmer half-running after him.

At first he did not seek out the Forgotten King's table, but merely sat alone near the front window, gazing out at the garbage that lined the alley and the back wall of the Baron's mansion while he poured mug after mug of good cold ale down his throat. Herrenmer attempted to sit at the same table, but Garth picked him up by the neck with one hand and forcibly seated him elsewhere, despite his protests. The captain did not care to argue further, and instead sat where he had been placed, glowering at the overman. He was joined by Saram, who had still been at the shadowy table in the back corner, and the two men discussed that morning's events, Herrenmer providing the facts of the overman's audience with the Baron while Saram embellished them with comments on the Baron's crafty nature and underlying insanity, and the probable benefits of allowing northern gold into the village.

It was well after noon when Garth finally made his decision; he would not undertake to swear his allegiance to any master, but he had no doubt that the Forgotten King's service would be less galling than that of the Baron. He would, accordingly, arrange a new bargain with the old man, the fulfillment of which would undoubtedly take him off to some foreign realm and provide him with something to do other than return to Ordunin. Something might come up that would show him a satisfactory solution to his current quandary.

As time had slipped past, sunlight had crept across the floor and slanted into the depths of the fireplace in the eastern wall, and several other patrons had drifted in, to find themselves congenial company and comfortable seats or merely to drink a pint and drift out once again. Garth paid none of them any heed as he rose and made his way to the corner where the old man still sat, unmoving, as if mere seconds had passed since the overman had departed, and not half a day.

Herrenmer saw his charge rise, and rose himself to follow. He found, to his astonishment, that his feet refused to obey him; he could stand, and move freely to either side, but when he attempted to take a step to-

ward the overman's retreating form, it was as if his
boots were glued to the floor's ancient planking.

He stared at Garth's back, then looked beyond to
the yellow-cowled figure that sat, still unmoving, in the
corner. A tattered edge of the old man's hood flapped,
though there was no wind in the tavern, nor any open
door or window that might admit a breeze; Herrenmer
caught a glimpse of light glinting from a hidden eye.
He could not see the eye itself, but only that single
fleeting sparkle in the shadowed socket; he felt a chill
sweep him from head to toe, and he told himself that
he really had no interest in approaching the strange
old fellow. He reseated himself at his table; after all,
he reassured himself, there was only the one door.
He could keep an eye on Garth perfectly well from
where he was, and need not worry about him slipping
out another way.

An involuntary shudder ran through him, and he
decided that he would just as soon not even watch the
overman's conversation; he would watch the door. He
turned his attention back to Saram, who had watched
the whole brief byplay with intense interest, but now
resumed regaling his former superior with the unlikely
tale about his current mistress that Garth's move had
interrupted.

Neither Saram nor Herrenmer noticed that someone
else had also observed the captain's curious hesitation,
and now watched with interest the overman's conversation with the mysterious yellow-clad figure. A dour
old man wearing clothes the color of drying blood,
this observer sat near the fireplace, ostensibly drinking
his luncheon; his eyes, however, flicked swiftly about,
missing nothing that happened in the taproom, but always returning to the mismatched pair in the back corner, their conversation just within range of his hearing.

Garth himself was oblivious to the whole thing; he
had been facing the wrong direction. He seated himself across from the Forgotten King and gazed for a
moment at the ragged hood that shaded the ancient
face; its color was scarcely visible in the sheltered
gloom, and the overman wondered how yellow could
look so dark. From where he sat he saw no motion, no

glint of light, but only shadows and the old man's wispy beard trailing from his withered chin.

"Greetings, O King," he said.

"Greetings, Garth." As always, the hideous voice was an unpleasant surprise.

"I have considered your proposed bargain."

The old man made no reply, but Garth thought he might have nodded slightly.

"I would know more about what services you would require of me."

There was a contemplative silence for a few seconds, then the old man replied, "I require certain items. I do not at present recall exactly which."

Garth, not yet over his anger at the Baron, felt a twinge of annoyance at the old man's vague reply. "Listen, I do not care to waste my time prying words from you. I will not bind myself to your service, but at present I seek a way to divert myself while I consider what manner of reply to make to your Baron of Skelleth. What are these items, and where are they to be found? Would you have me fetch them?"

The King was again silent for a moment, and Garth's irritation grew; finally, the old man said, "You are to bring me whatsoever you find upon the seven high altars of the seven temples in Dûsarra."

"Dûsarra?" The name was unfamiliar.

"A city in Nekutta, far to the west."

"And will I find upon these altars that which you need for your mysterious cosmic purpose?"

"You will find the solution to your problems with Doran of Skelleth; let that suffice for the present."

"What? Will one of these altar objects provide some magical means of dealing with that madman? You are being deliberately vague."

The old man shrugged.

Garth sat for a long moment, thinking. It was plain that he would coax no further explanation out of the Forgotten King, and the task set was exasperatingly cryptic. Still, such a quest would undoubtedly be an interesting diversion, and the old man had said it would provide a solution to his problems—presumably some means of coercing the Baron into behaving reasonably, or else a means of carrying out a satisfactory vengeance without destroying the fledgling trade. He had never caught the old man in an actual lie, and there could be no doubt he had knowledge beyond what was natural.

And what else was he to do? He could *not* return to Ordunin under the present circumstances. Until he could come up with some way out of his oath to the Baron he had nothing better to do and nowhere better to go. Running some fool errand halfway across the world would be a welcome distraction. That was all he had expected until the King had made his final statement, and he had thought it sufficient; the old man's words, curious as they were, could only make it more tempting.

However, they also somehow made Garth uneasy.

"I will do it," he said. "I will find this city you speak of, and rob these seven altars, and we will see whether my problems are solved thereby."

The Forgotten King smiled behind his beard.

Beside the fireplace, the old man wearing dark red nodded to himself.

Three days later, in a windowless chamber bright with golden tapestries and gleaming lamps somewhere in the black-walled city of Dûsarra, the high priest of Aghad sat, sipping bitter red wine and studying an ancient text. With a rustle of draperies and robes one of his subordinates entered, and stood waiting until such time as her exalted master should deign to notice her.

The wait was brief; the high priest lowered his book and demanded, "Yes, child?"

"Darsen of Skelleth sends a message." The underling held up a narrow strip of parchment such as could be wrapped on the leg of a carrier pigeon.

The high priest held out his hand, and the acolyte surrendered the note. He read it, then crushed it in one great brown hand.

"We must see this prospective visitor. Go tell Haggat to ready his scrying glass."

The acolyte bowed and vanished through the curtains with another swift rustle; the high priest picked up his book once again, glanced at the page, placed a thin strip of embroidered velvet upon it to serve as a bookmark, then closed it and slid it onto a shelf beside a dozen others.

Fifteen minutes later the priest strode into another windowless room; this one was draped in black and deep red, its somber gloom scarcely softened by the light of a single immense candle. A plump middle-aged man in a loose black robe stood within, holding a great crystal sphere in his hands; the acolyte knelt beside him, her face hidden in the shadow of her hood.

"She has told you what I wish to see?"

The man nodded, and held out the sphere.

The high priest reached out and took it; he cradled it in his hands and gazed into it. The other two maintained a complete silence.

Deep within the globe's interior, the flickering reflection of the single candle's flame twisted and shaped itself into the form of a sunlit path, a narrow road through grassy countryside; as the high priest watched, a figure appeared, riding down this golden strip of light. Mounted on a huge catlike black beast, clad in helmet, breastplate, and flowing brown cloak, the figure was that of a red-eyed overman.

The priest studied this vision for long minutes, then handed the sphere back to its master.

"This overman may be useful, perhaps very useful indeed. You, Haggat, will inform me of everything you can learn relating to him. You may have this acolyte as your personal property, to aid you in this and as your reward. Understood?"

The man nodded; one hand fell and pulled aside the acolyte's hood, then stroked her night-black hair possessively. The other hand balanced the crystal sphere, which flashed and glittered strangely. Despite the dim and uneven light, fear was plain on the girl's face as she looked up at her new master.

The high priest turned and left, thinking intently; although not the focus of his contemplation, he found himself aware that he considered Haggat to be very pleasant company. A man with his tongue cut out could not chatter on aimlessly as so many did.

He pulled his mind away from such distractions, and considered seriously what would be done with this thieving impertinent overman.

CHAPTER FOUR

The sun was sailing low in the western sky, as vividly red as Garth's eyes, turning the narrow wisps of cloud into a ruddy web of light and shadow. The overman admired the uncanny beauty of the scene; the colors seemed brighter, more fiery, than the sunsets of the Northern Waste. He mused as to why this should be so.

His mount seemed unimpressed. It kept its head low, its catlike ears spread, clearly displeased with its surroundings. Garth could hear, very faintly, the crunching of volcanic cinders beneath the warbeast's huge soft paws, a rather remarkable circumstance. Ordinarily the beast moved as quietly as any lesser feline, its padded feet as silent as the moon.

No wonder, then, that it disliked this strange new country! The sound of its own footsteps was alien, a constant reminder that it was far from home and all things familiar.

Ahead of them, dead black against the crimson-flushed western sky, there reared up yet another mountain range. Already, in the fortnight's journey from Skelleth, they had crossed one chain, the highest and most rugged Garth had ever seen, through a narrow pass, and made a detour around the southern end of another, lesser range. Now they were approaching a third such barrier, this one actively volcanic, as evidenced by the red-lit smoke that twined across the sunset clouds, and by the thin coating of fresh ash and cinder that lay across the countryside, clear proof that there had recently been a minor eruption.

According to the rough map the Forgotten King had provided, his goal, the city of Dûsarra, lay somewhere in the foothills of this range, but as yet he saw no sign of it. He wondered that people would live in such a land, with the shadow of fiery destruction looming over them, but there was no question that they did; for some time now the road he travelled had wound through farmland, elaborately irrigated and lush with unfamiliar crops. He had noticed that the farmers' houses were all roofed with tile or tin, rather than the more customary thatch; plainly, straw was too easily set ablaze by vagrant sparks drifting on the breeze that blew steadily down from the mountains, a warm, dry wind that brought with it strange new odors, scents he had never known before.

He had come this far without incident, which pleased him. After agreeing to undertake this journey it had been a matter of an hour or so to obtain an assortment of bags and pouches, to carry whatever he might find, and a week's supply of food and water, which he had augmented on the road by hunting and minor thefts from untended fields and wells. Thus equipped, he had allowed himself to be escorted out the North Gate, whereupon he circled around to the West Gate where he had retrieved Koros and his weapons and other supplies. He had then circled further, to the southwestern highway, a branch of which he was still following. Unlike his previous quest in the Forgotten King's service, which had led across barren, deserted lands inhabited only by barbaric little tribes, this journey had wound through league after league of settled, civilized countryside, more than he had known to exist upon the face of the world; he had dodged a double dozen of villages, and given a wide berth to a huge walled city indicated on the old man's map as Ur-Dormulk, all before even crossing the first mountains that marked the border between Eramma and Nekutta. Five times now he had set Koros free at night so that the warbeast could hunt its own food, and each time he had worried that it might not be able to find any meat to its liking except human flesh in the form of sleeping farmers, as there was not much wildlife to be found in such thickly-settled regions. Fortunately, Koros seemed to have managed, preying on stray goats and sheep when nothing else was available; Garth was grateful that it remained true to its training and avoided killing anything humanoid—when it could be avoided. It had, on occasion, eaten people when nothing else edible could be found, and it had eaten those it happened to kill in self-defense, but as a rule it knew not to.

It was an extremely useful animal, the finest product of a thousand years of selective breeding and magical shaping, but its voracious appetite could be very inconvenient. Ordinarily it was supremely obedient, but its loyalty decreased as its hunger increased, and Garth knew that five days without food, as opposed to the usual three days it went between meals, would render it willing to devour anything that moved, including its master.

It had fed last night on a pair of plump goats, and usually when recently fed it was as placid as a pampered housecat; today, though, the harsh landscape and crunching cinders seemed to upset it, and it growled softly, low in its throat, as a new twist of smoke drifted up the western sky.

Garth watched the smoke, and suddenly realized it had risen from a point between peaks; he stared at the jagged black shapes and thought he made out the curve of a dome amid the irregular constructions of nature. The shadows still obscured all color and detail, but the longer he looked the more convinced he became that there was, in fact, at least one man-made structure in these somber hills. He called the word that Koros recognized as a command to halt, as even the smooth grace of the warbeast's stride jogged him sufficiently to make it difficult to focus at so great a distance.

Yes, there was something there. He could not be sure what, as the sun was now slipping below the highest peaks, making it harder than ever to distinguish anything. He looked about, to rest his eyes, and noticed a farmer, a hundred yards away, leaning on a hoe and studying the overman and warbeast.

"Ho! Farmer!" he called.

The man did not move.

"Come here! I would speak with you!" He motioned.

The farmer looked about, as if to see if the overman meant someone else, though there was no other living being in sight, only the man's own twenty acres and the empty road stretching away in either direction. Then he shrugged and came, dragging his hoe casually, to stand a dozen yards away.

"Farmer, is that Dûsarra?" Garth pointed at the spot where he had seen the dome.

The farmer followed the direction of the pointing finger and said, "I suppose it is." His accent was strange to Garth, harsh and guttural, but his words were plain enough.

"How far is it?"

The farmer shrugged. "Couldn't say. You're an overman, I know, but what is that you're riding?" He studied Koros closely, from the glittering three-inch fangs in its jaw to the tip of its lashing tail, and from its glossy black-furred shoulder to its huge padded paws. A good eighteen feet long, the monster resembled nothing so much as an overgrown panther, though proportioned differently in order to support its greater bulk. It had a cat's golden slit eyes and triangular ears, stubby black whiskers on its muzzle, and a long slender tail. No panther had such fangs, though, and both legs and face seemed oddly elongated; it stood nearly as tall as the farmer himself. Pure black throughout, with no touch of color nor single gray hair, its muscles rippled smoothly under its fur; it clearly had no trouble at all in carrying the full weight of the armored overman and his supplies.

"It is a warbeast."

Koros growled.

The farmer suddenly seemed less sure of himself. He had assumed that any animal that served as a beast of burden, however formidable it might appear, must be docile and harmless—but no peaceful ox nor temperamental cart-goat ever made a noise like that. He thought better of previous actions, and said, "Dûsarra is ten leagues distant, my lord, along this same road, three leagues past the crossroads at Weideth."

"Crossroads?"

"Yes. It's of no importance, though; for Dûsarra you ride straight through on this same road, making no turn."

"What is Weideth?"

"The village at the crossroads; a small town, with no wall. You'll have no trouble there."

Garth was less certain of that than his informant seemed to be. This man seemed to accept an overman and warbeast calmly enough, but would an entire village?

"Is there no way around it? I do not wish to be seen."

"Around? No, my lord, not that I know of; the terrain thereabouts is very rough, and Weideth lies in a narrow pass, astride the road. It's a wonder they don't charge a toll, in truth."

"I see. My thanks, man."

The man bowed and stepped back, and when Garth made no further comment nor move to stop him, he turned and departed at a brisk pace.

This village, Garth thought as he urged Koros forward once again, was a nuisance. He did not dare risk losing his way at this point; he would have to ride through and hope he did not create too much of a commotion. Ten leagues to Dûsarra, and that three leagues past Weideth, the man had said; that meant he was seven leagues from the village. Seven leagues was two or three hours ride, perhaps a trifle more if the terrain was bad; if he kept riding he would pass through the village well after full dark, and reach Dûsarra in the middle of the night, while if he stopped and made camp he would arrive at midday tomorrow. Midday was scarcely a good time to try and slip unobtrusively through a village, nor was it a good time for reconnaissance in Dûsarra. He was not tired, and

Koros was well-fed; he should have no trouble in completing his journey without further delay. If he were to be a thief, then he would arrive as a thief in the night; he spoke the command for a trot and the warbeast strode on, the only sound the soft crunching of cinders.

The moon was near full, making it easy to follow the road even after the sun was well down, though it was not actually necessary to see it since straying to either side would mean passing through the tall grass of late summer, easily two feet in height, that flanked the way. Besides the pale light of the moon, Garth noticed as well a dim red glow flickering about the mountaintops that grew as he approached—volcanic fires, of course. He began to share Koros' dislike for this country; such eerie lights seemed threatening. A volcano active enough to light the clouds at night could well be active enough to bury its surroundings in ash and lava, yet here he was riding ever closer.

It was more than two hours after he spoke to the farmer, well after the last trace of daylight had faded in the west, with only the white moonlight and the red glow of the volcano to see by, that he was first spotted by one of the sentries. Garth did not see the young woman, nor would he have paid her much heed if he had, but she saw him, and studied him closely before slipping from her hilltop post and running back to Weideth with her report.

The Seer of Weideth was finishing his final cup of wine and seriously considering retiring for the night when the sentry burst into the village's single nameless inn—which also served as the public meeting house and in rainy weather as a makeshift marketplace—with her news. She looked about wildly for someone to report her discovery to, but the village elders were all long abed; for want of a better audience, she directed her shout at the Seer.

"There is an overman on the East Road, riding upon a creature like none I have ever seen!"

The Seer smiled at her melodramatics. "Have you, then, seen every sort of beast there is? There are frequently overmen on the north and west roads, and they do not all make do with horses and oxen."

"Yes, but this one is on the *East* Road, and wearing armor!"

The Seer started to dismiss her with a wave. "Overmen do not use the East Road," he began.

"This one does! If you will not listen to me, I'll find someone who will!"

His hand fell, and for the first time the Seer looked directly at the girl's face. He realized that she spoke the truth; a part of his talent was knowing the truth when it was spoken, and this young woman—she could have seen no more than eighteen years—was not merely excited or mistaken. There was an overman on the East Road, which no overman had ridden in three hundred years; an overman had come out of the east.

"The prophecies say that death and destruction lie in the east," he said.

"So I have heard," replied the girl sarcastically, her hands on her hips.

"We must wake the elders."

The sentry nodded. "They will know what to do."

"Yes. We cannot let an eastern overman reach Dûsarra."

It was several minutes later when Garth turned a corner in the winding road, which for the last three leagues had twisted its way through the foothills and now led along the bottom of a narrow defile, and caught a glimpse of Weideth. It was only a very brief glimpse, however, for the village he had thought he saw vanished almost instantly, leaving only another few hundred yards of highway that stretched out from his warbeast's feet and turned right out of sight behind a hill up ahead.

He blinked. There was no village. There was no sign of a village; there was only the road.

He stopped his mount with a word and studied the road. There was nothing there. After a moment's consideration, he arrived at a few possible explanations for what he thought he'd seen—a neat row of cottages

on either side of the highway, a widening of the gorge
into a respectable valley. It could have been a trick of
the moonlight, though it had seemed too detailed for
that. It could have been a mirage caused by some unknown effect of the volcano, letting him see a village
that in fact lay somewhere else. It could have been a
hallucination caused by volcanic gases; he had heard
of such things. It could be that he was more tired than
he had known, and his mind or his eyes were playing
tricks in consequence.

Or it could have been magic.

This last possibility seemed actually the most likely,
and it did not bode well; still, there was nothing he
could do about it sitting where he was. He signalled to
Koros, and the warbeast strode forward. Nothing unusual happened; the barren hills continued on either
side. When they had traversed halfway to the next
turn without incident, Garth relaxed. There seemed
to be no danger.

If it were magic, Garth mused, what sort of magic
had it been? Had an entire village been transported
away in an instant? That seemed unlikely. Perhaps the
village had been a mere illusion. If so, had it been
intended for him, or for someone else?

As it neared the bend in the road, Koros hesitated;
it seemed unsure whether to follow the road around to
the right, or to proceed straight ahead up the side of
the defile. Garth turned its head right, and it resumed
its steady forward progress.

This served to distract Garth momentarily; it was
not typical of the beast's behavior. It usually knew to
follow the road unless directed otherwise. Ah, he told
himself, it meant nothing; the creature was tired. Perhaps he *had* just imagined the village in his own fatigue. As he had just been thinking, perhaps the village
had been an illusion.

Or perhaps this deserted gorge was an illusion, and
it was the village that was real.

That thought had a disturbing plausibility, and
Garth stopped his mount. The village of Weideth was
supposed to be around here somewhere, yet he had
seen no trace of it except perhaps that single fleeting

glimpse. It was at a crossroads, and Koros had hesitated as if uncertain of the correct path—as if at a fork or crossroads.

But why, assuming that he was in fact in the middle of Weideth, was such an illusion created? He looked down at his mount, and at himself; the warbeast's fangs gleamed in the moonlight, and his sword slapped his thigh as he moved.

He was not, he admitted to himself, the sort of character whose appearance inspired confidence in strangers. No doubt the villagers had some sort of magician amongst them who used illusions of this sort to render the town invisible to any travelers who looked dangerous.

If it *were* an illusion, he reminded himself.

That could be tested, he decided; he ordered Koros to stand and guard, and dismounted cautiously.

He still seemed to be in a rocky, empty passage through the hills, not a village—but there was no reason the illusion should be less effective on an unmounted overman than upon one riding a warbeast. He stepped carefully off the road, and reached out to touch a convenient boulder.

It was there, all right, and felt very much like stone. He ran his fingers across it. Yes, it was smooth stone. He flattened his palm against it, and slid it downward a few inches.

One of his thumbs slipped into a crack; he looked more closely. Yes, there was a crack visible; he must have missed noticing it in the moonlight, if it had actually been there all along. What was under his thumb felt very much like mortar. He ran his hand sideways; the crack was dead straight and perfectly horizontal. He reached over further, where there appeared to be nothing but open air.

His hand struck something; he felt it carefully.

It was glass. It was a small square pane of glass held in lead, and beside it was another, and another. He blinked.

He was standing before a small house built of cut stone, his hand touching a casement window; other houses stood to either side. Behind him Koros growled uneasily.

He whirled. He stood near the middle of a village, just as he had seen it. What had appeared to be a turn in the highway was indeed a crossroads. That meant that he had been diverted from his route; he had turned north instead of continuing westward.

He growled in annoyance. He did not like this. He did not like magic. He did not like the necessary conclusion that there was somebody with unknown preternatural abilities actively trying to deceive him. His hand fell to his sword hilt as he looked about, and he mentally commended himself upon travelling well-armed since leaving Skelleth—armor was uncomfortable, but prudent.

The village was still and silent; the only sound was his own footsteps. The houses were all shuttered and dark—except for one. At the crossroads stood a building rather larger than the average cottage, with a signboard hung above its door; whatever message the sign might bear was invisible in the darkness, but the place was probably an inn or public house, and light showed through its curtained windows.

His magical antagonist might be working at some distance, or might be hidden in darkness somewhere—but it seemed more likely he or she was in that single illuminated room.

What, then, was he to do about it?

He had two choices; he could ignore the incident and be on his way, or he could confront whoever lurked behind those curtains. If he ignored it he would be leaving a potential danger behind him, able to attack from the rear, and sitting on his route home. That would not do.

He reminded Koros to stay where it was, loosened his sword in its scabbard, and marched to the inn. The door stood slightly ajar; he kicked it open and stood aside, lest an ambush be prepared for him. Nothing happened; he stepped forward again and looked within. A sudden wave of vertigo swept over him; he blinked, and looked through the door.

He was looking into his own home in Ordunin, the

rambling stone and wood house that he had built with his own hands. For a moment he froze in astonishment, but the incongruity suddenly seemed unimportant. He was home!

He stepped inside and looked about. Through the large window to his right he saw the wide plank terrace and the spectacular view of the bay beyond; sunlight sparkled from the waves and poured warmly into the room. He listened, and could hear the ocean's roar very faintly; nearer at hand a bird sang somewhere.

He noticed that he still wore his helmet and breastplate, his sword on his belt and axe on his back; such precautions were surely unnecessary here in his own domain! He reached up to remove the helmet, but paused; how had he come home? He had no memory of the journey, and he had not intended to come here; returning home meant that he would have to speak to the Council, in accordance with his oath to the Baron. Something was peculiar about this, and until he recollected what it was, it would do no harm to keep his armor and weapons on. He was not particularly uncomfortable—though a trifle overwarm—and he could bear to take such a simple precaution.

There was a sound somewhere further inside the house; that would be one of his family, of course. It would be a pleasure to see them all once again. He wondered what the date was; he seemed to have forgotten, yet he always kept track of such things, to know when to expect his wives to be in heat. He would have to ask. He called out, "Ho! Who goes?"

A door opened and an overwoman entered; Kyrith, his favorite wife. Her scent reached him, and warmth spread through him; she would be ready any time.

By human standards she was far from beautiful; she was as tall and flat-chested as any overman, and her face as inhuman; to Garth, she was a fine, handsome creature. Her golden eyes were warm and inviting; her black hair was long, for an overwoman, and Garth reached out to run his fingers through it. Her scent was entrancing.

She smiled, and caught his fingers; he smiled back. He felt his body reacting to her odor; that smell was the only sexual stimulus that affected an overman, and it was irresistible. He reached out both arms for her; she smiled, and poked at his breastplate.

"Shouldn't you remove your armor?" she asked.

He growled playfully, reached up to remove his helmet, and stopped. Something was wrong. Something was very, very wrong.

Kyrith was mute. The *real* Kyrith was mute, at any rate; she had fallen years ago while skiing, a fall that sent slivers of ice through her throat. She had lived, with only a slight scar, but her voice was gone forever. This was not her. The whole thing was an illusion.

He thrust the false Kyrith away and drew his sword; the illusionist had made a fatal error in giving Kyrith a voice, but there was no doubt that his or her magic was effective. Not only had the image of his home been perfect, but the sounds and smells, and his memory had been befuddled as well. Garth dared not take any further chances.

"Show yourself, magician, or I will lay about with this blade until I find you!"

His home vanished, and he was in a small village tavern; a fire burned low on the hearth, and a chandelier held a dozen stubby candles, casting their wan light across a dozen empty tables and five human beings.

One was an old woman who lay sprawled on the floor where he had flung the false Kyrith; she wore a hood and cloak of pale blue that spread about her in disarray, revealing her bony blue-veined legs and wrinkled face. Her hair was long and silvery-white. She made no move to rise, but lay where she was, watching Garth with terror in her expression.

The other four sat clustered about a table. There was a young woman in brown leather helmet and tunic and black skirt, a bow leaning against the back of her chair and a quiver of white-fletched arrows slung on her shoulder. Beside her sat a man of indeterminate age, his face hidden beneath a gray hood, his gray cloak hiding all but his hands—muscular hands, one of which clutched the handle of a pewter mug.

The remaining pair wore pale blue robes that matched that of the woman on the floor, and both were likewise old; one was a man with steel-gray hair and gray-streaked black beard, the other was another white-haired woman, shorter and thinner than her fallen comrade.

There was a moment of silent consideration, and then Garth demanded, "Why have you beset me?"

There was an uneasy silence; no one answered him.

"Is this the way you treat all travelers? Or is it because I am an overman? Because I wear armor? What do you want of me?"

The old woman at the table said, in a high and broken voice, "We meant you no harm!"

"Then what did you mean? You have twice attacked me with your illusions; why?"

"We did not attack you; we sought only to have you pass through our village without seeing it."

"You diverted me from my path; I am not bound northward."

"We did not know that; we thought you must be, for it is to the north that overmen are said to dwell."

Garth considered that for a few seconds; it did have a logical ring to it. "You attempted to deceive me when I entered this tavern."

"We sought only to remove your weapons, so that we could deal with you more easily."

That accorded with the facts. Garth relaxed slightly. This handful of humans was no threat to him, save for their magic, and he seemed to have beaten that; only one even bore arms, and that one a mere girl.

"Which of you conjured those illusions?"

The man in the gray hood, silent heretofore, spoke up. "It is a joint effort; no one of us is essential."

Garth considered this, and chose to doubt it; such a claim was good tactics, and more likely tactics than truth. "Who are you all, then?"

"I am the Seer of Weideth, and these three are the village elders." He indicated the other man and the two old women.

"Who is she?" He pointed at the girl with his sword.

"She is just the one who saw you coming in time to warn us. She is no one of importance."

"You call yourself a seer?"

"Yes."

"Can you read the future, then?" Garth had heard of such talents, and had in fact dealt with an oracle, the Wise Women of Ordunin, who seemed to know something of events yet to come; he could see many uses for such an ability.

"On occasion. I'm afraid I'm not much of a seer, if the truth be known. I do have knowledge and talent beyond the ordinary, but I have little control over it. I am the last and least in a long line of Seers in Weideth, and I spend more time studying the prophecies of my predecessors than making my own."

That explained why he had failed to foresee that Garth would not be deceived by the illusions, and therefore Garth decided to believe it. He had the impression that the man was being reasonably forthright. Perhaps a similar frankness on his own part would enable him to resolve this episode in short order and get on his way once more. He wanted to reach Dûsarra before morning; before midnight would be nice.

"Listen, then; I mean no harm to you or your village. I intend no evil toward any person or community outside the village of Skelleth. I bear no ill will for your mistaken attempts at self-defense. Let us end our dispute peaceably; I will not harm you, but will go about my business. In exchange you will refrain from bothering me further with your petty magic. Is this not fair to all, and a desirable conclusion?"

The Seer said to his comrades, "He speaks the truth as he knows it."

There was a moment of silent consideration as the elders looked at one another; the larger woman clambered to her feet, then found a chair and seated herself. Garth lowered his sword, but did not sheathe it.

It was the sentry who first spoke, saying, "But what about the prophecies?"

The male elder nodded. "There is that."

"What prophecies?" Garth said. "I am not an unreasonable person. Explain your meaning, and perhaps I can accommodate you."

The humans all turned toward the Seer, making plain that they felt it was his place, as Seer, to explain. He obliged.

"There are two prophecies that led us to be especially wary of your coming, overman. The first, made long, long ago, said merely that death and destruction lie in wait in the east, and shall come out of the east in their time. The second, made by my immediate predecessor—who unlike myself, was one of our greatest Seers and prophets; there seems to be an alternation—well, his was an elaboration upon the first, and says that when an overman from the east comes to Dûsarra he will unleash chaos and catastrophe upon the world. You see, therefore, that we do not wish to see you proceed westward from our village, since that road leads only to Dûsarra."

Garth considered this. It sounded vague to him, and he was reluctant to pay it much heed; he had business in Dûsarra.

"Does the prophecy give my name, or a more exact description?"

"No."

"Does it say that *any* overman from the east will bring disaster, or that there will be one specific one?"

"It implies one specific overman, but we prefer not to take chances; you are the first overman to come up the East Road in a very long time, the first since the prophecy was made."

"I have come from the Northern Waste, though, not from the eastern lands. I have no intention of unleashing anything."

"I never heard of the Northern Waste; still, it must lie to the east, or you would not have come on the East Road. Your intentions may prove to have very little to do with what actually occurs."

"Still, I do not think I am the overman prophesied, and I intend to go to Dûsarra. I would advise you not to try to stop me, nor to obstruct me when I return on my way home."

"We will not bother you once you have reached

Dûsarra; it will be too late by then. Anything we might do after that would be pointless revenge, and we are not so foolish as to attempt it. However, I beg you to reconsider. Do not go to Dûsarra! You may not be the overman we were warned of, but why risk it? You are a good man . . . Ah, I mean a good person. Do not chance bringing destruction upon yourself and others!"

"I regret that I cannot oblige you. It seems that we will not be able to part as friends after all, and in that case I must ask this young woman to surrender her bow to me; I have no desire to be shot in the back. I will leave it, undamaged, on the road west of the village. I must also insist that no further distracting illusions be used; I know where and who you are, now, and would take it very ill should you attempt to divert me."

He reached out for the bow; reluctantly, her eye on the sword in his other hand, the girl gave it to him.

"My thanks. I take leave of you now, and wish you all well. I truly hope and believe that I am not the overman your prophets spoke of." He nodded politely, and backed out of the inn, sword in hand. No one made any unfriendly move, nor any move at all; all five sat in silent dismay.

Once outside, he turned and ran toward where he had left Koros; he had little doubt that despite his warning, some other attempt would be made to stop him, and he wanted to put as much distance between himself and the village as he could before the humans could reorganize sufficiently to launch their attack.

His eyes were no longer accustomed to the darkness after his conversation in the lit tavern, and he stumbled on the rough roadway; annoyed, he called his warbeast's name.

There was an answering growl and the beast appeared in the darkness before him, its golden eyes gleaming in the moonlight. He sheathed his sword and reached out; Koros obediently stalked up to him. He grabbed the harness and swung himself into the saddle, then gave the signal for a trot—not the warbeast's fastest pace by any means, but Garth thought it would be sufficient and did not care to risk more in the darkness.

He directed the beast toward the west road, and then paused; how could he be sure it was the true west road, and that the humans had not used another illusion to confuse him? The moon's position was correct, and the red glow of the volcano lay in the right part of the sky, but he already knew that their illusions were good enough to encompass such details. He carefully reviewed his movements after leaving the inn, and determined that they had not in fact turned anything around—unless they had once again twisted his memories. He doubted that they had had time to do anything of the sort, though of course they could have distorted his time sense as well.

He could not in fact be *certain,* but after consideration it seemed that it was unlikely the road was illusory, and he had no way of proving whether it was or not. Accordingly, he would assume that no illusions were being perpetrated, and if it later developed that they were, he would come back here and demonstrate to the Seer and the village elders the folly of angering Garth, Prince of Ordunin.

He signalled for a trot again, and rode swiftly out of the village, away from the crossroads and the dimly-lit inn.

CHAPTER FIVE

The farmer had told him that it was three leagues from Weideth to Dûsarra; that was over an hour's ride, but a glance at the sky and some calculation indicated that he could still make it by midnight, with luck. It depended in large part upon how tired Koros was. So far, the creature showed no signs of fatigue at all.

They were leaving the village, passing the last few houses that straggled out along the road, when Garth glimpsed movement from the corner of his eye; he ducked, instinctively, and the shadowy batlike form that swooped at him swept silently by, its glittering black talons inches from his face.

The girl's bow was still clutched in one hand; he flung it aside, wishing he had taken her arrows as well, and dove from the warbeast's back, drawing his sword as he landed rolling on the rocky highway. Ahead and above, the bat-thing wheeled and came at him again.

He got a good look at it as it attacked; it was not a true bat at all. Its wingspread was a good ten feet, and though its wings were stretched leathery hide like a bat's, its body and head were those of a bird of prey, round black eyes and hooked black beak making up the face, outstretched talons gleaming. He ducked under its lunge again and brought his sword up to meet it.

The sword passed through it unhindered, leaving no mark, meeting no resistance.

The tension left Garth's body; he grinned and stood upright. The thing was another illusion, of course, not even a particularly clever one. Did they expect him to cower away from the thing without fighting?

Apparently they did, or they wouldn't have sent it. He turned back toward Koros, preparing to remount, ignoring the bat-thing that wheeled and dove.

Its claws ripped his helmet from him and raked bloody furrows across the back of his head.

He swung around again, sword ready, growling in pain and anger; his sudden turn sent spatters of blood flying from his wounds. They were real, no doubt about it, and painful, but not deep. The elders of Weideth had more magic than mere illusion at their disposal.

The thing was coming in for another pass; he dodged, and swung at it with his sword. As before, the blade passed through the monster as if it were a mere shadow. Garth growled.

On the next pass he dodged again, and lashed out not with his sword, but with his free hand, clutching at the thing's leg. His hand closed on nothing but air, and the claws raked his wrist.

This began to be serious; although not too bright, the thing was persistent and would eventually tire him out and claw him to pieces. It seemed to possess a curious one-way tangibility like nothing Garth had ever encountered. He had thought it might have some protection against cold steel when the sword had no effect, but his hand had been equally incapable of touching it. Hand and sword had passed through its body without touching it, yet its claws had made themselves felt twice.

Its claws had been felt—but only the claws! Even when Garth had left himself completely undefended in the mistaken belief he was dealing with an illusion, it had not used its great evil beak, nor struck him with its wings—wings that made no sound and created no wind.

As it turned for another assault, Garth studied its talons; they glinted in the moonlight unlike any claws he had ever seen, a glassy black sheen rather than the sparkling highlights of polished bone or nail. They were not smoothly curved, nor scaled and jointed, but twisted and jagged. They looked very much like some sort of glass or crystal rather than part of a living creature.

It swept down upon him again, those strange black talons outstretched, and Garth's sword came up to meet it, not sweeping through its intangible belly this time, but striking at the talons themselves.

He was rewarded with a tinkling crash as his blade struck and reduced one great spiked claw to a shower of glittering splinters.

The creature's mouth opened, as though to cry in pain, but no sound emerged; it swept up and away from him and circled briefly.

He took a moment to stoop and pick up a shard of the shattered claw; now that he held it in his hand, he could readily identify it. It was obsidian—black volcanic glass. It was quite tangible and ordinary.

Overhead the thing seemed to recover itself, and dove at him again.

This time he made no effort to dodge, but simply held up his blade horizontally before his face and kept it steady with both hands as the full force of the creature's claws smashed into it. The obsidian talons shattered spectacularly, sending glassy needles spraying in every direction; a few slivers stitched tiny cuts across his hands or spattered from his breastplate. His face was protected by the blade, but his eyes closed instinctively.

When he opened them again the creature was gone, the only trace of its existence the splinters of volcanic glass that lay scattered about, glistening in the moonlight.

He brushed himself off, sheathed his sword, retrieved his helmet, and looked about. No new threat was apparent, Koros was unharmed, and his own injuries were minor. He mounted the warbeast, then turned, and bellowed back toward Weideth.

"Seer, if you can hear me, be warned! If you send anything else against me, destruction will indeed be unleashed, as I will wipe your village from the earth! Hear me, and be warned!"

There was a faint echo of his shout from the hills on either side, but no other reply. He turned westward once more and rode on.

CHAPTER SIX

Something over an hour later he emerged from between two hills to find himself with a clear view of Dûsarra, crowning the long, smooth slope that rose in front of him. Moonlight glimmered from the city's domes and towers, a soft silver that seemed to give no light at all; comparing the silhouetted buildings with the smoky red sky behind them, Garth realized

that they were all dead black in color, and that therefore even the brightest moonlight could not illumine
them. The city was walled, though Garth thought it
unlikely any wars were ever fought in such rugged
land; the wall, too, appeared to be built of the same
black stone. In the poor light Garth could not see
where the wall ended and the ground below began;
the slope before him appeared to be a smooth sheet of
darkness that blended into the city without break.
Peering closely, Garth realized that the hillside was,
in fact, an ancient lava flow; it was a single vast slab
of stone, where nothing grew. The road he followed
ended at its foot, leaving the traveler to follow whatever route he chose across that rocky expanse.

He urged his mount forward onto the stone; Koros
obeyed without protest. They had come to the end of
the fresh cinders a league or so back, where the road
had curved toward the north; whichever volcano had
thrown them up, it was apparently not the one that
towered above Dûsarra, lighting the sky before them
a murky red.

As they made their way up the slope, something
caught Garth's eye; there was something about the city
wall that didn't look right. He stared harder, and saw it
again; there was a glimmer of light directly in front
of them, apparently in the middle of the wall. Could
someone be camped in front of the gate? It was possible, but the light somehow didn't look like a campfire,
nor did it look to be on the slope outside the walls. A
window in the wall, perhaps, with a lighted guard-
room beyond? That might be, except that it must be
an inordinately large window to be so visible at this
distance; although difficult to judge exactly at night,
Garth was sure there was still another mile or so of
this rocky slope to be climbed.

A few moments later he realized what it was; the
city gates were open, and the square just inside was lit
all around with torches.

It was very nearly midnight, yet Dûsarra's gates
were wide open, as if it were noon of market day.
Garth wondered what kind of strange city he was approaching; could this be some sort of religious festival?

Were they so trusting of strangers that they left the gates open at all times? If that was it, then why were the walls maintained, and why was the market lit? No, that could not be the reason, for he could make out vague shapes moving about; there were people there, just exactly as if the city's inhabitants were going about their ordinary business in the dead of night. He began to hope that it was, in fact, some kind of holiday or religious event; that at least would be understandable.

It suddenly struck him that his stealthy nighttime approach wasn't going to make much difference after all. Well, he thought, at least by torchlight it would be less obvious that he was an overman than it would be at noon. But then again, a city that lived by night might well sleep by day, and he might have done better to approach by daylight.

No, that was absurd; there had to be some sane reason for this nocturnal activity. He could not imagine what it could be, but there must be one. He'd know soon enough; he gave up wondering and rode on.

Dûsarra, he decided as he rode through the gate, was a very strange city, at least by his standards; but then, he had not actually travelled that much. Outside his own land he had seen only Skelleth, Weideth, and Mormoreth, and from a distance Ur-Dormulk; Mormoreth was a dead city, Skelleth might as well be, Weideth was only a village, and Ur-Dormulk he had not gone within a mile of. Perhaps Dûsarra was normal, and the others strange. He halted his mount, and looked about the square he found himself in.

It was a fairly conventional marketplace; merchants' stalls lined every side, each with torches illuminating it, one or two torches per stall. The market was busy; men and women strolled about or rushed, haggled over prices, gossiped with friends, and generally did whatever people ordinarily did in a city market. Only the stars overhead and the flickering torchlight made the scene seem unnatural.

Garth noticed with interest that the natives dressed differently from the people of Skelleth; where the men of Skelleth wore tunic and trousers and the women wore blouse and skirt, here both sexes wore long, shapeless robes. The poverty-stricken people of Skelleth could afford only the drabbest of dyes, but here Garth saw many attired in blood-red as well as the more usual browns, grays, white and black. The majority seemed to be wearing a dark blue shade; the current fashion, no doubt, or perhaps representative of some social class. Many had hoods pulled up over their heads.

Well, he should be able to blend in reasonably well; although for most of the journey he had worn openly his breastplate, helmet, and mail, with his sword on his belt—a welcome change from the scratching hilt of his stiletto, which was packed away in his bundle of supplies—he had had the foresight to throw his rough brown cloak on before approaching the city. The trader's hat he had worn in Skelleth was not appropriate here; none of the natives wore any headgear but the loose hood. His cloak naturally included a hood, though he had never had occasion to wear it. He pulled it up, then paused; he would already stand out as remarkably tall, and should do nothing to exaggerate his height. He removed his helmet, then pulled the hood into place before stuffing the headpiece into the pack behind him.

As yet, he had seen no sign that anyone had noticed his presence, which was all to the good; they were all too busy with their own concerns. It was odd that there was no guard on the gate, though.

He dismounted and ambled casually forward, stooping to disguise his height, hoping that in the uneven torchlight no one would notice that he wasn't human. They would, of course, notice Koros; there was no disguising a warbeast. But there was also no cause to object strenuously to a warbeast, most particularly since these people probably had no idea what one was.

Of course, he wouldn't want to take the beast along when he went temple-robbing; he would have to find an inn with a good stable. Besides needing a place to leave Koros, he was hungry and thirsty, and a tavern

would undoubtedly be a good place to pick up information about the temples, as well. It seemed reasonable that there would be an inn facing on the square,
convenient to the gate but, studying the shadowy
stone facades behind the merchants' stalls, he could
see no signboards indicating one, nor other evidence
of one's existence. With a mental shrug, he stepped
up to the nearest stall, where a silk dealer debated the
value of a bolt of his best bleached fabric with a
would-be buyer.

He waited politely until the two arrived at a mutu-
ally satisfactory price; then, while the customer carefully counted out his hoarded coins, he inquired of the
merchant, "Is there a good inn to be found near here?
I have travelled far."

The merchant, eagerly watching the small pile of
silver grow, said, "There's the Inn of the Seven Stars."

"Could you direct me there, then?"

Pointing without looking up, he said, "Take the first
street on the left."

"My thanks." There had certainly been no danger
there of being spotted as an overman; neither man
had looked at him at all. He returned to where Koros
stood, just inside the gate, and told the warbeast to
follow him; finding the break in the ring of booths and
buildings that marked a street, first one on the left, he
led the warbeast through the crowd into the darkness
of what proved little more than an alleyway. No one
took undue notice of him or his beast; he decided that
Dûsarra must be more cosmopolitan than he had
thought, if its people were so blasé about such creatures in their midst.

The alley was unlit and almost uninhabited; after
the relative glare of the market it took his eyes a few
seconds to adjust. Like their countrymen in the market, the few people who strolled the byway paid Garth
and Koros no heed. Here all wore their hoods up and
pulled well forward, unlike the market where the
bare-headed predominated.

He made his way carefully through the gloom; the
shadows of the buildings on either side kept the moonlight from lighting the way adequately, but the narrow

street was clear of obstructions. At least this inn stood on a cleaner street than the King's Inn, Garth thought.

He rounded a slight curve, and found the way brighter; light poured from around a second turn, which brought the street back to its original direction. He turned the second corner, and had found the inn; the light poured from its broad front window, and he could hear voices within. The door stood open, not surprising on a warm summer night, and above it hung a sign; the light from the window let him make out seven stars arranged in an oval, white paint on blue. A wide arch just beyond led, he hoped, to an attached stable. He crossed the field of light, and found a boy asleep in the archway. The distinctive odors of horse and ox reached his slit nostrils, convincing him that his hopes were correct. He prodded the boy gently with a booted toe.

The lad woke up immediately and sprang to his feet, but said nothing.

"I need stabling for my mount."

"One mark the night, sir, and feed is extra."

"I have no local currency; will this do?" He produced his smallest gold coin, and dropped it in the boy's hand. The lad looked at it, then carried it over to the light that spilled from the tavern door.

He studied it for a long minute, then asked, "What is it?"

"A northern gold piece."

"Gold?" The boy looked at it again, then tested it with his teeth.

"Of course it's gold."

"Yes, sir; but we see little gold here. Most pay in silver. My apologies for the delay; the third stall is yours, my lord." He bowed.

Garth ignored the stable-boy's obsequiousness and led Koros to the indicated stall, which proved spacious enough and well lined with straw, though not particularly clean. A bucket of passably clear water hung from one side, and in view of its recent feeding Garth saw no need to provide the warbeast with any other sustenance. He removed pack and saddle and placed

them to one side, then told Koros to stay and headed
for the tavern door. He had no worries that anyone
might disturb his supplies; anybody fool enough to try
would be ripped to pieces immediately. A warbeast
was a very useful thing to have.

Although from the street the tavern had seemed
brightly lit, once inside Garth found it otherwise; the
light came from a row of lanterns hung across the
window and from two low-burning hearthfires, one at
either end of the main room, and from nowhere else,
so that most of the room remained dim and shadowed. The chimneys did not seem to draw well, either; a haze of smoke seemed to hang over everything.

A dozen assorted locals adorned the various tables
that were scattered about, and there was not a lone
innkeeper, as Garth had expected, but two serving-
maids and a boy, all adolescent, distinguishable from
their patrons by virtue of gray aprons worn over their
robes. Probably the innkeeper's offspring, he decided,
and their father must be in the kitchen or tending to
rooms upstairs.

He beckoned to the nearer girl; she scurried over,
leaving the spit she had been turning, which held a
shapeless lump of meat a foot or so above one of the
fires. "Yes, sir?" she said.

"Bring me ale and meat; and have you any fruit? I
could use something sweet." Garth spoke in a voice
well above his natural range and stood stooping to disguise his inhuman height, his hood pulled well forward.

"Yes, sir." She hurried off, and he seated himself at
a convenient table.

As he waited for his food and drink he studied his
surroundings; he wanted someone to talk to, someone
who would tell him about the city and the temples.
What he saw were a dozen robed, hooded figures huddled over their tables, speaking little to each other, let
alone to a stranger who would not allow his face to be
seen. The universal Dûsarran garb made him wonder
momentarily if the Forgotten King hailed from this
strange city, but on consideration he decided it was
unlikely. The King wore yellow, a color he had not
seen displayed anywhere in this country, and went in

rags despite his claim of royalty, while here, dark colors predominated and most wore clothing in far better shape than his own travel-worn cloak. Further, the King was pale-skinned, while the Dûsarrans, from what he could see, were of a middling shade, lighter than his own hide but browner than the men of Skelleth; and finally, the Dûsarran robes tended to be loose and flowing, while the King kept his garments wrapped tightly about him.

But of course, Garth suddenly realized, not everyone in the room wore the standard robe and hood; the two serving-maids and their brother, if such he was, wore shorter, low-necked robes with no hoods, dark blue in color. All three were barefoot, with long brown hair tied back in single braids down their backs. The similarity in hair color further convinced Garth that they were siblings, as the shade and texture were almost identical.

These three might be more willing to converse than their customers; filling an eager ear would surely be more pleasant to such young folk than carting mugs and plates about. He paid them more attention than he had.

The boy was the youngest, probably well short of his full height, and still totally innocent of any beard; Garth was no judge of human ages, but the lad was plainly far from maturity. As such, he would probably be limited in his knowledge; among overmen, at least, religion and philosophy were not the concerns of children, so Garth guessed that the boy would know nothing of the temples.

Of the two girls, there seemed little to choose, from the overman's point of view; they were of about the same size, and presumably therefore near the same age. They were as tall as many adult human women; Garth wondered again at the quirk of nature that made men and women so different in size, unlike overman and overwomen. Women seemed such small, fragile things, and oddly proportioned, at that.

One girl seemed slightly the more active of the two; Garth decided she must be the younger. It was her older sister he had spoken to when he arrived, and it would presumably be the older who would bring his food. In that case, he would simply speak to her when his meal was ready.

Even as he decided this, the girl emerged from a door at the rear carrying a heaping plate and full mug, which she balanced easily as she crossed the room to set them on the table before him.

"My thanks." He kept his face hidden and his voice high as he looked at his meal; beside the expected slices of red meat were three chunks of some pasty yellowish substance, and a curious red fruit, like none he was familiar with, adorned one edge. "What are these?" he asked, indicating these strangers.

"Roast potato, sir. And our last good apple; we have no other fruit in store at present."

Both names were meaningless to the overman; he could not even be sure of their spelling, through the girl's thick Dûsarran accent. At least Nekutta spoke the same language as Eramma and the other northern lands, even if they spoke it strangely. Still, the "apple" was plainly a local fruit; the potato was another matter.

"What is potato?"

"Ah? Oh, you're joking!"

"No; I have travelled far."

"It's . . . it's a root, a vegetable. Eat it, and see." The girl was flustered; Garth was not sure if that was desirable or not. He did have her talking.

"Here, sit down; I will try this root of yours, but I have some questions about your city. Perhaps you can answer them."

"But . . ."

"I am a paying customer, am I not? You can spare a few minutes." He tapped the table with a gold coin, then suddenly realized that it was a mistake to draw attention to his inhuman hands; he dropped the coin, and drew his hand back out of sight. The girl apparently hadn't noticed anything out of the ordinary; she stared at the coin for a moment, then snatched it up and dropped it down the neckline of her robe. Garth was amused. He had never before seen a human keep anything there, but it seemed a logical place for a woman to put a pocket. The coin had been a full-sized gold piece, not one of the little bits such as he had given the stable-boy, and he remarked, "That will cover the meal as well, will it not?"

"Oh, yes!" The girl dropped herself into the chair opposite him, smiling.

"Good. Tell me of your city; I am a wanderer from far to the east."

"What is there to say?"

"Ah . . ." Garth had not expected that response. He was not experienced in dealing with humans. "Why is the marketplace so busy in the middle of the night? And the gate wide open?"

"It always is."

That demolished the religious festival theory once and for all. "But why? In most cities business is a matter for daylight, and the night is given to sleep."

"But this is Dûsarra!" Her tone implied, even to the untrained ear of an overman, that he was being purposely dense. He picked up a chunk of potato on his knife and ate it, while considering this; the stuff seemed edible, but not particularly tasty.

"And what is so special about Dûsarra?"

"You do not know?"

"No."

"The very name tells you."

Garth had paid little attention to the name, assuming it nothing but a noise that represented this particular place; he considered it a bit more carefully, and still saw nothing significant in it. The ending was a standard designation for a gathering place, and the root, *Dûs,* was completely unknown to him.

"I do not understand."

" 'Dûsarra' means 'the place of the Dark Gods.' Here we worship the gods shunned by the outside world; mostly Tema, the goddess of night. Perhaps, stranger, you have made a mistake in coming here if you did not know that."

"Perhaps I have." He sat silently for a moment, thinking.

He should have expected something like this from the Forgotten King. He knew very little about human

religions, beyond the fact that no two seemed to agree
about anything, but he had heard of the Dark Gods;
they were supposed to demand human sacrifices, and
to be wholly evil in nature. It had been rumored that
the Baron of Skelleth was a secret devotee of theirs,
and that had been considered sufficient grounds for
immediate execution if proven; it remained only a
vague rumor. It was said that, unlike most gods, they
still interfered directly in mortal affairs, and would
grant their followers special powers and abilities in exchange for gruesome payments of blood, death, and
torture. Evil wizards were said to have sold themselves—their souls, to use the human term that overmen did not use—to the Dark Gods.

And the entire city of Dûsarra worshipped these
deities? It seemed incredible. How could a thinking
being worship evil?

"Tell me, then, about these gods." At least the conversation had taken a turn toward the temples without
obviously being steered there.

"There are seven of them, the seven Lords of Dûs,
the counterparts to the seven Lords of Eir worshipped
elsewhere. I know very little about most of them; I am
a follower of Tema, like the rest of my family."

"How did you come to be such?"

"I was brought up in the faith, of course."

"How did the city come to worship these gods?"

"I don't know; it always has. My father told me
once that it was part of a cosmic balance that these
misunderstood and maligned gods should have one
city of their own."

"Are they not evil?"

"Tema is not!" Her face was suddenly animated,
and Garth was taken aback by her ferocity. "Tema is
beautiful! The night is wonderful, cool and calm; I
would never be a day worshipper! How can people
live with all that glaring light? And all the sweaty
heat? And all the beasts roam by day, and insects.
The sun is so bright you cannot look at it, and it
drowns out all the beauty of the flames. There are no
stars in the daytime! I . . . ." She subsided suddenly.
"Forgive me."

"No, forgive me; I did not mean to offend you. In other lands I have visited, the Dark Gods are thought to be the gods of evil."

She shrugged. "They are obviously ignorant heathens. There are no evil gods, really; evil is just misunderstandings between people, or between people and the gods. That's what the priests say."

"I see. You worship the night-goddess. What of the other six?"

"They have their followers, too, but I do not heed them. I sometimes think that some of them *are* evil, despite what the priests say. Aghad, for example; his followers make my skin crawl, and his priests frighten me. I have seen them gathering at his temple. And of course, no one worships The God Whose Name Is Not Spoken, though he has a temple."

Garth began to have a rather unsettled feeling; he had heard of The God Whose Name Is Not Spoken. That was the god of death, known throughout the world; it was said that to speak his true name was to die instantly. And they worshipped him here?

No, the girl had just said that they did not, but that there was a temple dedicated to him. Was it one of the seven he would have to rob?

It must be; everyone seemed to agree that there were only seven temples in Dûsarra. Although he would not admit to being in any way superstitious, and although his own people insisted that either there were no gods or they did not meddle in the affairs of mortals, he did not care to rob the temple of Death.

On the other hand, his practical sense told him, if there were no worshippers, it would be unguarded and the easiest of the lot.

"Tell me who the seven gods are."

"You mean the seven who have temples?"

"Are there others?"

"Oh, yes; there's Tema's daughter Mei, the lady of the moon, and any number of others."

"Just tell me the seven."

"Bheleu, P'hul, Sai, Aghad, Andhur Regvos, and Tema."

"That's only six, if I heard you rightly."

"Well and there's the Unnamed God. You know."

"Oh, of course." It was apparently considered bad luck to mention the death-god too often even by circumlocution. "I know him, and P'hul, and you have told me Tema is the goddess of the night; who are the others?"

. "Bheleu is god of destruction and war, I think. Andhur Regvos is the god of darkness."

"Why has he got two names?"

"I don't know."

"Oh. Go on; what about the other two?"

"I don't know; Aghad and Sai are secret. Their temples admit no outsiders. They both . . . well, that's just a rumor. Never mind."

"And all the city lives by night, to accord with their religion?"

"Oh, no! Not all! Only the worshippers of night and darkness. But we're most of the city. I don't know anyone who lives by day, but of course that's partly because I'm asleep all day."

"I am interested in this; could I visit the temples?"

"I don't know about the others, but I can take you to the temple of Tema."

"Good. But first," he said, realizing that he had been talking while his food grew cold and that he was ravenously hungry, "I will eat."

He did so, and found the food and drink good; the girl laughed gaily when he tried to eat the apple core and all.

CHAPTER SEVEN

The temple of Tema was a massive, imposing structure; most of its area was covered by a looming black dome, which Garth thought was probably the one he had first seen from ten leagues' distance, and the entrance was through the base of a tower that stood a good hundred feet in height. The entire building was constructed of huge blocks of black stone, finely polished, and with elaborate carvings on either side of the wide, open doorway. The door was reached by climbing a flight of thirteen black stone steps, flanked by balustrades carved into a maze of intertwined black serpents. Garth did not particularly care for the place; although undeniably impressive, he did not like the impression it gave of looming over one, black in the moonlight, and the way its size served to diminish its inhabitants. The robed and hooded figures entering the dark portal looked like little children, out of proportion with their surroundings.

He also didn't like the darkness within; not the slightest glimmer of light showed through the door. That was appropriate for the temple of the goddess of night, but he still didn't like it.

The tavern girl was beside him as he mounted the steps; it occurred to him suddenly that he didn't know her name. Of course, she didn't know his name, either. Ahead of them three other worshippers, robed in midnight blue, vanished into the darkness of the doorway.

A moment later, he and the girl also stepped into the gloom of the interior. Garth paused for a moment, to let his eyes adjust, and realized he could detect no trace of the three who had entered just ahead of them;

67

no sound of rustling clothing, no footsteps, no odor. His psychic discomfort increased.

The girl had not hesitated, as he had, and was across the room, an antechamber about forty feet square; he heard her whisper, "Come on!" He came, and rejoined her, standing a pace or two from the inner wall. He had expected a draped doorway, or some other opening into the temple proper, but could make out no sign of one; there seemed to be merely a blank stone wall. Then, with startling abruptness, a portion of the stone wall swung inward; the heavy scent of incense drifted out to him. He made out a figure in the opening, darkly clad, but with pale skin and white hair that gleamed in the faint moonlight that reached it. The darkness within that opening seemed no more absolute than in the antechamber; that was some comfort, anyway. The girl stepped through the opening, and he followed, to find himself in the main temple.

The odor of incense was almost overpowering; its smoke swirled in great clouds, almost invisible in the darkness. Moonlight filtered in from somewhere, though he could see no windows; the walls were blank and dark behind him, and he could not see the far side. The room he found himself in was obviously huge; all about him were constant indefinable whisperings and rustlings, which were distorted by distance and echoes and which seemed to drift in the smoke. He could not make out either the far wall or the roof; his eyes had not yet had time to adjust.

A change in the movement of the air prompted him to turn, and discover that the opening he had entered through had vanished; the wall seemed solid once more. The white-haired apparition had also disappeared. He turned to face the interior again, and was relieved to see, dimly, the figure of the tavern-girl, still only a few paces in front of him.

She motioned for him to follow, and led the way across the chamber; he obeyed, carefully maintaining his stooped posture, and noticed that where she moved silently, his boot heels tapped loudly on the stone floor.

They went perhaps a hundred feet, then stopped; the girl turned slightly, and knelt in a curious submissive position, head lowered, hands in front of her. Garth imitated her, and waited for his eyes to adapt themselves.

He was kneeling at the back of a crowd of humans, all in a similar devotional posture; the chamber, he saw, filled the entire interior of the great dome, easily two hundred feet across and sixty or seventy feet high at the center. The moonlight came from hundreds, perhaps thousands of tiny holes that pierced the dome, and which he realized after a moment's study were intended to resemble stars, arranged in the constellations that could be seen in the middle of a winter night.

The great circular floor was cluttered with people, both kneeling and prostrate, but none were speaking, not even in a whisper; the constant sounds that echoed and reechoed from the dome were the inevitable rustlings of the worshippers' clothing, no more. Or at least, nothing more he was sure of; some of the sounds seemed too strange to be so readily explained.

All these people, whether prostrate or upright, faced in the same direction; as his eyes continued to adjust, he gradually made out the object of their adoration.

The figure of a human female was carved from the same black stone as wall and dome; it was thirty feet or so in height, and a masterpiece of sculpture. She stood against the wall, upright, but not stiffly erect; her arms were upraised, spreading her stony cloak above the worshipping throng. The cloak itself blended into the wall and dome indistinguishably, and Garth saw, looking around, that its folds were continued indefinitely, so that the entire chamber was contained within it, "stars" and all. The figure itself was depicted as clad in a loose robe such as all Dûsarrans seemed to wear, but arranged so that the graceful curves of the woman's body could be seen. The face was oval, smooth and serene, and surrounded by a halo of drifting hair that blended into the dome in the same manner as the cloak. The overall impression, to the overman, was one of grace and soothing calm; he was not equipped to appreciate the goddess' sensual nature and although the symbolism of the goddess spreading her cloak of night across her followers was plain to him, he did not fully comprehend the comforting motherliness that the worshippers of Tema found in that image. Still, he understood, in an intellectual way, that humans would have little trouble in putting their faith in such a deity. No wonder the girl had been upset when he called the goddess evil.

He was so involved in his study of the magnificent idol that it was several minutes before he even noticed the altar that stood at her feet.

It was a great chunk of meteoric iron, its sides still burned and twisted from its fall, but with the top sheared off and polished to a gleaming metallic shine perceptible even in the darkness of the temple. There was no mistaking that this was the altar that Garth had come to rob, and there upon it was what he must steal; he could make out only a vague round shape, a foot or so in diameter.

There was a spot of light on its surface, he noticed; one of the pinholes in the dome was directly in line with the moon, and a beam of its light was now falling directly upon that thing upon the altar. He wondered whether it was intentional.

Then, so suddenly that he almost lost his balance in his startlement, the room was filled with chanting; the incense swirled more thickly than ever, billowing forth from a dozen niches spaced around the wall. Priests appeared behind the altar, completely hidden in black robes that exaggerated the usual looseness to near-parody; one reached forward, and what Garth suddenly realized was a cloth cover vanished from the thing on the altar.

It immediately blazed up into scintillating light, so bright in the darkness as to seem almost blinding; it was a great crystal, a sphere with a million facets, which trapped the thin beam of moonlight and reflected and refracted it into a glittering display of pure white light. Garth thought for a moment that it was a diamond, but dismissed that as absurd; no diamond could be so large, and he doubted that even diamond could catch the light like that. This was some sort of gem or crystal that was totally unfamiliar to him.

It was also a gem he would have to steal, if he were to perform his errand in Dûsarra.

He knelt, listening to the priests chant, and wondered how he was ever going to manage it.

CHAPTER EIGHT

There were words to the chant, and the ceremony undoubtedly had some specific significance, but Garth made out none of it; he was too lost in his own thoughts to listen, and the echoing dome distorted the singsong enough to make it difficult to discern its meaning. It sounded to the overman like nothing more than a randomly shifting drone.

He paid little attention as the dark-robed priests lifted the great crystal and moved it ceremoniously through elaborate patterns in the air, alternately sprinkling the crowd with sparkles of reflected moonlight and plunging them into darkness; he was planning out his actions. There were questions he would have asked the tavern-girl, but she was lost in the chanting, her lips moving silently, her face enraptured. He saw instantly, when a stray glint of moonlight lit her features, that she would be of no use to him for awhile.

Since this was the temple of night, it seemed a safe assumption that all prayers and worship were nocturnal; by day the place should be almost deserted, though probably there would be a few priests about. It was already well after midnight; he had merely to wait until dawn, grab the crystal, and depart. If possible he would wait until no priests were about, but if necessary he could force his way through them. There was no sign that they carried weapons of any sort; a drawn sword should awe them into letting him pass, most particularly since most humans had an almost superstitious fear of overmen, who were, after all, a good bit larger and stronger than humans, and by human standards hideous monsters.

It would be advisable to find some quiet hiding place where he could wait until daybreak; if he merely stayed where he was he might draw unwanted attention. He considered leaving and then returning at sunrise, but rejected it immediately. He had no idea how to open that swinging wall, or even whether it could be opened from the outside at all. Even if it could be, it might be kept locked by day.

The ritual ended with a simple chant that the worshippers repeated along with the priests; every other word was the name of the goddess, and it was just six words, but Garth could not make out the other three. It was recited three times; then the priest lifted the crystal one last time, placed it on the altar, and lifted its cloth cover back over it. Its final gleam lit the priest's eyes, despite his overhanging cowl, and Garth started with surprise; the priest's eyes were as red as his own! For an instant he thought that perhaps the robed figure was another overman, but dismissed it; he was too small, by far, and like the person who had admitted him to the chamber, his hair was gleaming white, while all overmen had coal-black hair. Besides, that quick glimpse had shown him eyes with pupil, iris, and white, while overmen had only pupil and iris. No, the priest was just a freak of some sort.

The ceremony was over, and the tavern-girl rose and motioned for him to follow her out; he shook his head. She frowned at him, and then shrugged and left. Almost all the worshippers, kneeling or prostrate, were getting to their feet and heading toward the entrance, but Garth remained where he was, to await the dawn.

It was a long, weary wait; he had not realized how

tired he was, but the effects of a long day's ride were catching up to him well before the night was over.

When the crowd had departed he was left alone in the middle of the stone floor, but the cowled priests, who moved with quiet rustlings but no words along the wall behind the altar, paid him no heed. Moments after the last of Tema's devoted had departed, new ones began to trickle in; by the time a half hour had passed the chamber was becoming crowded once again with people kneeling with hands clasped before them, or flat on their bellies, all facing the magnificent black stone idol.

The scattered bits of moonlight that found their way through the holes in the dome shifted as the moon crawled across the heavens outside, and an hour or so after the tavern-girl's departure a spot of light appeared on the cloth-covered sphere atop the altar. A priest withdrew the covering, and the chanting began anew.

This time it was not his planning that kept Garth from hearing the words; it was his efforts to stay awake. His knees hurt from kneeling so long without moving on hard stone, his eyes ached from the strain of seeing through the unchanging dark, and his whole body was weary from his long ride. He knew that to close his eyes would be to fall asleep. He had arisen early, before dawn, which meant that when the new day arrived he would have gone better than twenty-four hours without sleep; that was no remarkable feat, ordinarily, but after a day spent riding and now passing long, dull hours crouching in the dark, it began to seem impossible.

The second ceremony ended, the crowd dispersed, and newcomers trickled in; still he knelt there, and still no one paid any attention to him. The priests shuffled about at the goddess' feet; all seemed to have long, pure-white hair, and at least two had the same strange red eyes. All were pale-skinned, unlike the other Dûsarrans Garth had seen; even those whose faces remained completely hidden showed their hands on occasion, and those hands were uniformly white and apparently hairless. There were few other similarities amongst them; some were tall, some short, some fat, some thin. There seemed to be at least one priestess among them, judging by what little could be distinguished through the flowing robes. Garth had once seen a white wolf, a beast with snow-white fur and blood-red eyes; a Kirpan scholar had referred to it as "albino." These priests must be albino humans. He had not known such existed. And why should all the priests be such? It seemed a peculiar requirement, if such it was; why were albinos especially suited to serve the goddess of the night?

Wondering about such trivia managed to keep him awake through a third and final ceremony; this time, when the final simple chant ended and the gem was covered, the crowd moved more slowly, and for the first time Garth heard worshippers speaking amongst themselves. Likewise, the priests ended their apparently aimless wanderings; all but three of the half dozen or more he had seen vanished, though Garth could not see where they had gone. The remaining trio stood motionless behind the altar, the center one with his hands resting one on either side of the shrouded crystal.

Garth estimated it to be two hours before dawn still. Since this new behavior seemed to demonstrate that the temple's services were through for the night, he got to his feet; his knees stung, as circulation returned to the areas where it had been cut off. He gazed up at the idol, as if in adoration, so that no one would question his failing to depart.

His eyes had long since become adjusted to the faint illumination, but now he found himself unable to distinguish details of carving that had been clear before; he blinked, but it made no difference. The scattered moonlight was not evenly distributed; had it merely shifted? No, it was growing uniformly darker. He had a moment of irrational fear that he was going blind before he realized what was happening.

The moon was setting.

That, of course, was why there were to be no more ceremonies, and why everyone was departing; with the moon down, the temple would be far too dark for use.

People would run into one another, face the wrong way, and generally be unable to behave appropriately; even night-worshippers recognized that. He wondered what they did on moonless nights; were there no services at all? The starlight was plainly inadequate. Or what of overcast nights? Would torchlight from the streets or the glow of the volcanoes reflected off the clouds be enough? There would be no beam of moonlight falling on the great crystal.

Well, interesting as they might be, such considerations were irrelevant, since this night had been clear and moonlit. The spreading darkness would actually work to his benefit, since no one would be able to see him steal the gem; he studied the altar, measuring the distance between it and himself, so as to reach it quickly in the dark.

The three priests still stood behind it; the last worshippers had drifted out, and Garth realized they were looking at him, noticing this last straggler. That was not what he wanted. He turned and headed for the door, but stopped a foot from it, and turned to look again, hoping that anyone who saw him would not think that unusual.

Apparently the priests didn't, if they were able to see at all in the deepening gloom; Garth doubted they could see him any more, as he could no longer see them. Although he did not know for sure, it seemed unlikely that those squinty little human eyes could be as good as an overman's—though of course the priests' eyes were not quite normal.

A gong sounded somewhere, and the stone door swung slowly shut; whoever worked it thought Garth had left. He stepped away from it and lost himself in the darkness.

There were rustlings and whisperings in the blackness, which was now almost total; the moon was down. Although the dome made it very hard to locate sounds, Garth judged that the three priests were moving away from the altar. In a moment the sounds were cut off, as if a curtain had dropped across a doorway; straining, Garth could hear faint footsteps departing. The priests were gone.

Moving with all the stealth he could contrive, Garth inched across the broad stone expanse that lay between him and the altar; he could not see more than a few inches in front of him, and the quiet shuffling of his boots seemed magnified into a low roar by the echoes.

After what seemed hours, his outstretched hand touched something; he studied it with his fingertips, and decided it was a fold in the idol's cloak; he had missed the altar and hit the wall, off to the left. Cautiously, he felt his way along the fold until it swooped up out of reach, then moved on along the wall until he came to the idol's slippered feet, which he knew to be immediately behind the altar. He turned until he faced directly away from the wall, and peered into the darkness; he thought he could see the dim outline of the altar. He took a step forward and felt in front of him, reaching down to the height he estimated the altar to be; his hand brushed against a polished surface. Using both hands he groped about the altar-top and found the cloth-covered stone. He picked it up, cover and all, and tucked it under his cloak. Now he had only to get out of the temple undetected.

He knew that the concealed door to the antechamber was directly opposite the altar. He considered feeling his way along the wall until he found it, but rejected that idea; he might walk right into priests reentering the chamber, or at the very least be heard through whatever doorways they had departed by. Instead, he aimed himself by dead reckoning and set out across the floor.

Again, it seemed to take hours to cross; but at last an outstretched hand touched stone. He came up within inches of the wall, but could see only blackness; he felt along it with his hand, seeking a latch or seam or hinge. His left hand was occupied in holding the pilfered altar-stone under his cloak; it took a long time to cover an area with only his unencumbered right. He worked his way along, first three paces to the right, then twice that distance to the left, then back to the right once more; a feeling of desperation crept into him as his fingers found nothing but yard after yard of smooth stone.

Suddenly there was a sound behind him; he whirled, his right hand dropping automatically under his cloak to the hilt of his sword, but could see nothing in the darkness.

"If you return the stone you may go in peace, thief." He recognized the voice as one of the priests'. He made no reply.

"You cannot open the door; only the priests of Tema know its secret."

Garth wondered how many were there, and how they had gotten so close to him without being heard; he judged the voice—for so far only one had spoken —to be ten, perhaps fifteen, not more than twenty feet away.

"Return the gem."

He needed time to devise an escape. "And if I do not?" he asked.

"Then you will die here."

Garth adjusted his grip, hugging the crystal closer to him, and drew his sword. "I have a counter-proposal. You will open the door for me, or you will die, not I."

There could be no doubt that the priest or priests had heard and recognized the scrape of steel on leather as the blade left its sheath; there was a pause before the voice spoke again.

"It is possible that you may kill one or two of us before you yourself perish; if so, we will die in the sure knowledge that we have served our goddess and will be admitted to her realm for all eternity. You, on the other hand, will die damned forever for your sacrilege. I ask again, return the stone; it is not too late. Return it, and we will yet let you depart peacefully, even though you have drawn a weapon in our sanctuary."

Garth made no answer for a long moment, and the priest said nothing, apparently granting the thief time to consider the hopelessness of his position. The over-man, however, was not considering options or the lack thereof, but rather was noticing that he could distin-

guish, very faintly, the outline of a lone figure a dozen
feet in front of him. This was not the result of any adjustment; his eyes had long been at their extreme of
sensivity. No, there was new light filtering in, the first
dim gray of approaching dawn. That reminded him
how long it had been since he last slept, and he suddenly felt weary even as he considered how the growing light would work to his advantage. The priests
were undoubtedly accustomed to living almost entirely in darkness; they would not do well outside their
temple in daylight, if he could once get out into the
streets.

He wondered if the priest could see him at all; the
light was not evenly distributed. Further, was he
aware that he, himself, was visible? And it was now
apparent that the priest was alone. Probably the lone
man had been making a final inspection round of
some sort, and tried to bluff out the intruder; unfortunately for him, his bluff was now ruined.

Knowing that he faced a single opponent, Garth
finally struck upon a scheme.

"If I hand you the crystal, will you then open the
door and let me go, unpursued?"

"Yes."

"Will you swear it, by your goddess?"

"I swear it, by Tema."

"Very well." With a great show of reluctance,
Garth held out the gem with his left hand, purposely
extending his arm not directly toward the priest but a
little to one side, as if he still could not see where the
man was. His sword remained ready in his right hand.

The priest stepped forward, and carefully lifted the
stone, using both hands. He stood for a moment, and
Garth demanded, "Now open the door."

"Let me return the stone to the altar first."

"No! You said you would open the door when I returned the stone." He lifted his sword as if to slash
blindly in front of him; although the light was actually
growing steadily, and already permitted him to distinguish such details as the cracks in the floor and the
folds of the priest's robe, he hoped to continue his
ruse of blindness a few moments longer. He had no

specific reason for it; he was merely snatching every advantage he could, as his training in war and statecraft had taught him.

"If you insist." The priest tucked the crystal under one arm and crossed to the wall; his free hand brushed across the black stone surface and caught something Garth could not make out. With a considerable effort, the priest pulled; the section of wall swung open, and gray light poured in. Garth had forgotten that the great portal faced east, but such was the case; and although the sun was still below the horizon, the sky above it was already warmly pink. The spacious antechamber was much less ominous in the cold morning light than it had been by moonlight, merely a large, bare room, with half one wall opening onto a stair to the street.

Garth smiled with satisfaction. Moving with superhuman speed, he leapt across the few feet separating him from the priest; in scarcely a second from the opening of the door, his sword was at the man's throat.

"Now, O priest, you will give me back the stone. I have handed it to you, and you have opened the door; now I will take it again and go, unpursued."

"No!"

"Yes."

"You cannot take it!"

"You will die if you do not give it to me."

"My brothers will find you."

"What of your oath? You swore I would not be pursued."

"No! I swore you would leave unpursued, not that there would be no pursuit after your departure. If you take the altar-stone, the followers of Tema will seek you out, wherever you go."

"Perhaps. I will risk it. Now give me the stone, and I will go."

"No!"

"Listen, fool, if you give me the stone I will leave you alive, and you may lead the pursuit; if you force me to kill you, there will be no one who knows who took the stone. It would be to my advantage to slaughter you out of hand, but that is not my wish. Give me the stone and live."

"You could kill me anyway."

"Why should I wait? Give me the stone!"

"No! Help! Brothers! Thief, murderer!" The priest began shouting at the top of his lungs. Disgusted, Garth grabbed for the crystal, and got a tenuous hold with the long fingers of his left hand; his superior reach had caught the human by surprise, and the priest's own grip slipped for an instant. That was all the time Garth needed; he snatched his hand back, the stone clutched as tightly as he could manage. With a scream that echoed and reechoed from the dome, the priest lunged for it, and automatically, without thinking, without meaning to, Garth reacted as a warrior reacts; he ran the man through, impaling him on his broadsword. Blood spattered the wall behind the priest, and Garth exclaimed in disgust, a wordless noise in his throat.

There was no doubt that the man was dead, or as good as dead; Garth's reflexes were as reliable as ever, and if he had not put his blade straight through the heart it had been a very near miss indeed. He had the stone, though. Now he had only to get away with it; the other priests must have heard the shouting, especially that final scream.

He yanked his sword out of the priest's body; a good foot of the blade had protruded through the back of the robe, and it took a second pull before it came completely free, allowing the unfortunate man to fall to the floor. His hood fell aside, and for the first time Garth saw his face; a thin, pale face, red eyes wide and glazed in death, mouth gaping and filling with sluggishly flowing blood. Long white hair was flung across his features, tangling with a skimpy white beard; he had been a young man, perhaps only a novice rather than a full priest. Garth was not at all pleased. He had hoped to avoid killing anyone on this errand. He wiped his sword on the hem of the man's robe and stepped across the corpse into the antechamber, carefully avoiding the spreading pool of blood, then paused for a moment to sheathe his sword.

There was a cry from behind him; he glanced back and saw nothing but darkness. Nonetheless, he sprinted for the steps.

More shouts sounded, and something whistled through the air by his ear; disdaining dignity he dove forward, curling into a ball around the stolen altar-stone and rolling down the thirteen steps to the street, where he sprang up and ran, paying little heed at first to direction but merely dodging at random from alley to street to alley. His hood flew back, revealing his inhuman visage, but none of the startled passersby attempted to stop him.

At last, well after the shouting was lost in the distance, he slowed; he paused in an unoccupied alleyway to restore his obscuring cowl and height-disguising crouch, and hobbled out, doing his best to appear a harmless old man. The altar-stone was under his cloak, hidden by his crouch.

It took him half an hour to find himself on a street he recognized; from there he made his way to the market place, and thence to the Inn of the Seven Stars. He dared not enter the tavern, as the followers of Tema might find him there; instead he went to Koros' stall in the adjacent stable. There he decided to take a look at his booty, and pulled the great crystal from under his cloak.

It sparkled eerily in the morning light; he gazed at it in fascination. It was very beautiful, an intense, cold beauty. He found himself studying its depths raptly, searching for something he could feel there; he had a sensation of being observed, and of unearthly power, as if the night-goddess herself were watching him from within the gem. He was unaware of anything but the gem, and the deep cold gleaming light within; he lost his sense of time, and felt as if he had been looking into the crystalline glow for all eternity, trying to meet the gaze of Tema. A cool stillness, like the air of a clear night, absorbed him, and he knelt utterly motionless.

With the abruptness of a lightning bolt he felt a warm touch on his face, like a flame on ice; he turned away from it involuntarily, and the spell was broken as the gem ceased to be the center of his direct gaze.

He blinked, and realized he was kneeling foolishly in the straw of the stall holding the stone while Koros nuzzled him curiously, wondering why he did not move.

He had survived hypnotic spells before, and had a healthy respect for them; he covered the great crystal with straw, being very careful not to look directly at it. The straw would also hide it adequately; no one would be able to come close enough to find it without first disposing of the warbeast. Garth pitied anyone who might attempt such a feat.

His booty secured, he paused for a moment to decide his next action; he seated himself comfortably on a pile of straw, his mount standing placidly over him. Long before he could reach any decision his fatigue caught up with him, and he slept.

CHAPTER NINE

He awoke slowly, his mind fuzzy; there were voices somewhere nearby. It took him several seconds before he recognized his surroundings as Koros' stall in the inn's stable; more seconds passed before he remembered that he had fallen asleep there unintentionally. His neck ached; he had slept with his head propped awkwardly against the side of the stall. He rubbed it absently and listened to the voices.

There were two of them, both young human males; they were arguing about something, apparently the ownership of some item. A small item, it seemed, since the one who possessed it apparently carried it on his person.

Garth sat up and looked around; it was daylight, and judging by the shadows either very early or very late. He thought for a moment, calculating the orientation of the stable, and decided that it was late afternoon. He had slept most of the day away, which was probably just as well. He had needed the rest.

He recalled the events of the night before, and checked to be sure his loot was still secure; it was. He had thought that the crystal was clear, but looking at it in the sunlight—being very careful not to let it trap his attention once again—he saw that it was milky white. Not that it made any difference, he thought; he had no use for the thing. He covered it over with straw again.

The argument outside was winding down; some sort of compromise had apparently been reached.

It was none of his concern. He clambered to his feet, promising himself that never again would he sleep wearing mail; every link seemed to have left a permanent impression on his back, despite the quilting underneath and the breastplate on top. Reminded of the breastplate's presence, he removed it; mail alone should certainly be sufficient for anything he was likely to encounter in the city. He was still wearing his sword as well, he realized when he almost tripped over it.

Koros growled a greeting, and the voices outside suddenly stopped. Then one asked, "What was that?"

The other replied, "I don't know. Dugger said there was some kind of foreign monster in number three, but I figured he was lying as usual."

There was a pause. Garth patted the warbeast's nose, and reached down to his pack for the wire brush he used for cleaning the monster's ears, which had a habit of picking up burrs and other such unpleasant little items. The first voice spoke again.

"Should we check?"

"I don't know."

"I'm going to look. Come on."

"Go look yourself."

"Oh, come on."

"Well, all right. If you want." There was the sound of footsteps approaching; light footsteps. Definitely young humans, Garth thought, as he stood with brush in hand.

A moment later two adolescent faces peered over

the stall door, and almost immediately vanished again. Garth grinned to himself. Then, slowly, first one face and then the other inched back into sight.

"Greetings," Garth said.

"Uh . . . greetings," said the taller of the two boys.

"I hope my beast didn't upset you."

"No." Then, after some hesitation, the lad went on, "You're an overman, aren't you?"

"Yes." There was no point in denying the obvious, since his cloak and hood were lying in disarray on the straw, leaving his noseless, leathery face and black mail in plain sight.

"Oh."

The other boy asked, "What's that?" pointing timidly at Koros.

"A warbeast."

"Oh."

"How'd you get in here? I've been here all day."

Garth shrugged. "I got in."

The boy decided further questions were not in order; instead, he explained, "But I'm supposed to watch the stable and make sure everyone pays their bills."

"You needn't worry; I will pay. I paid the other boy for the first day."

"Dugger? Oh." There was silence for a moment; the two had apparently exhausted their questions for the moment. Garth began cleaning the warbeast's ears with the brush; there were no burrs or thorns visible, but the creature seemed to enjoy it anyway.

When the silence seemed to be becoming uncomfortable, he asked, "What's the news today? I have been busy since dawn."

"Oh! Then you haven't heard! Someone murdered a priest in Tema's temple, and half the city is hunting for him."

"Who did it?"

"No one knows. Mernalla says she took a stranger to the temple last night, an old man with a funny accent, so they're looking for him, but the priest was killed with a single sword-thrust, so it probably wasn't anyone old. It must have been a warrior."

"Why would anyone kill a priest?"

"I don't know; I think there's some kind of secret about it." Garth noticed from the corner of his eye that the boy who hadn't spoken as much was looking at him strangely, paying altogether too much attention to the sword on his belt. The youth suddenly fell back out of sight, and a moment later, apparently in response to a tug, the other followed.

Inevitable, Garth thought to himself as he put the brush away. Still, there was no proof of any sort against him. No one had seen him clearly. It was interesting that the temple priests had not revealed the loss of the altar-stone.

Perhaps it would be wise to remove himself from the premises, at least for the present; perhaps he should move Koros, too. He was unfamiliar with the city, though, and hiding places might be hard to come by. This stable was convenient, and as yet there was no real evidence against him; with luck he would not be bothered. He reminded himself to do a proper job of cleaning his sword at the first opportunity.

He also reminded himself that he had six more temples to rob. Furthermore, since as a stranger he would automatically be under suspicion, the sooner he finished his task and departed the better. Therefore, he should get on with it.

First, however, he would get himself a meal; he had not eaten since the preceding midnight, more or less, and the sun was now well down the western sky.

He debated whether or not he should wear his cloak; the boys had not reacted negatively to the presence of an overman, but that said nothing about the re-action of adults. He picked up the garment, and saw to his disgust that there were bloodstains on it; he had not seen them in the dim morning light, as they blended with the brown fabric. There was the evidence to convict him of murder and sacrilege. The cloak would have to be promptly disposed of; he rolled it up and tucked it under his arm, making sure the stains were not in any way visible. He would have to do without it; he hoped that overmen were not utterly abhorred in Dûsarra. To the best of his recollection, Nekutta had not fought in the Racial Wars, but of course history had never been his favorite subject of conversation. And even if it had, no word of anything significant had reached the Northern Waste for three centuries; anything could have happened in that time. Still, so far as he knew, no overman had been seen in this part of the world since the wars; the humans would probably be too surprised to do anything much about him.

Besides, he had no choice. He had only brought the one cloak, since he had planned on a trading journey to Skelleth, not a long adventure. With a word of praise to Koros, he opened the stall door and stepped out into the stableyard.

The sun was even lower than he had realized, and the western sky a smoke-streaked expanse of crimson. He could hear the clatter and conversation in the Inn of the Seven Stars, and faintly, in the distance, the sounds of the marketplace; through the archway that was the only connection between the stable and the outside world he glimpsed occasional passersby, hurrying or strolling, striding, ambling, or strutting about their business.

He had seen little of the stable the night before, for want of proper illumination; he looked about him, hoping to see some convenient place to dispose of the incriminating cloak.

The yard was a long, narrow strip of bare dirt, with half a dozen large box stalls on either side, built of rough unpainted wood and roofed with red tile. One end was the archway to the street; the other end was a blank gray stone wall. Against the stone wall was a trough, itself carved from the same gray rock, presumably intended for watering whatever beasts of burden used the stable.

Garth strolled along the yard, peering into the stalls; most were empty, but three contained horses, the creatures that the overmen of the Northern Waste had long considered merely a legend. Garth had encountered such animals once before, far to the east; he had not expected to see them here.

He considered burying the cloak in the straw that lined the stalls, and rejected it; it was too likely to be found, drawing suspicion on the patrons of the inn, and possibly resulting in the conviction and death of whatever innocent happened to be renting the stall he chose.

He reached the end of the row of stalls without striking on any better solution, and saw that the stone trough was empty and apparently had been for quite some time; a spider had spun its web across one corner.

It occurred to him that probably no one had even noticed that the trough was here for years; people became accustomed to their surroundings and forgot the parts that did not concern them. He dropped the bundled cloak into the trough.

There was still a fair chance that some person—perhaps one of the stable-boys—would find it; but the trough was deep, and the cloak was material that would burn, but not too brightly. The flames would not show, and with luck no one would notice another wisp of smoke in this smoke-shrouded city. He had tinder, flint, and steel in a pouch on his belt, as always; it was a moment's work to set the garment afire.

Whatever ashes might remain would not be particularly noticeable in the accumulation of dust and debris in the bottom of the trough, and the bloodstains would certainly not be recognizable; the matter was dealt with. He rose, and started toward the arch.

Before he was halfway down the yard he heard voices approaching; before he was more than a pace or two past Koros' stall four figures appeared, not merely passing by on the street but coming through the arch toward him. He stopped.

Two of the four were the two boys; a third was the girl who had taken him to Tema's temple, and the fourth was a large man, clad in the usual Dûsarran robe, black in this instance, but belted about the waist and with a long, straight sword and sheath hanging from that belt.

"Greetings." Garth spoke politely.

"Greetings, stranger." The foursome stopped, a few feet into the yard. Garth nodded, then started walking again, as if to pass them by and depart.

"Wait, stranger." The man's hand fell to the hilt of

his sword. Garth stopped again. The man kept his gaze on the overman as he asked his companions, "Is he the one?"

Both boys replied, "Yes." The girl said nothing.

"Mernalla?"

"I don't know. I don't think so."

"Could it have been he?"

"No . . . no, it couldn't. The man was shorter, with a higher voice, and he wore a dirty brown robe."

"You said he was tall."

"Fòr a man, yes."

Garth interrupted, "Might I ask, sir, why you are interested in me?"

"We're looking for a murderer."

"What has that to do with me?"

"You are an armed stranger; naturally, that makes you suspect."

"I suppose it does. When was this murder done? I only arrived in Dûsarra last night."

"A priest was slain early this morning."

"A priest? Could it not have been an internal matter?"

"The priests of Tema do not kill their own."

"Then perhaps some rival cult is responsible?"

The man started to reply, then stopped himself. The girl looked at him as he considered the suggestion, while the two boys continued to stare at Garth. At last, after a long pause, he said, "You have a good point. It could have been them. It could well have been."

Garth was pleased to see that the man was accepting his decoy so readily. "After all," he said, "what cause could a stranger have to commit such a sacrilege? I am in Dûsarra to obtain some goods for my employer; what have I to do with temples, or with murders?"

"Nothing, I am sure." The man smiled. "My apologies for detaining you." He stepped aside, making room for Garth to pass.

One of the boys demanded belligerently, "What have you got that sword for, if you're a trader?"

"What?" Garth looked at his waist in feigned surprise. "Oh. Just habit, I assure you; an adventurer such as myself is accustomed to travelling armed."

The man swatted the boy on the shoulder and said, "Come now, there's no law against wearing a sword, else I'd be a criminal myself. From what I hear, travelling the Yprian Coast without a good blade is akin to suicide." He smiled at Garth again.

Garth smiled back, unenthusiastically, and moved on past the foursome. He turned into the adjacent tavern and found himself an unoccupied table. The swordsman's final comment was bothering him. Why should the fellow assume that Garth had come by way of the Yprian Coast? Why was no one particularly surprised at the presence of an overman in Dûsarra?

Could it be that other overmen came to this city? Could there be an established trade route through the Yprian Coast?

A middle-aged man took his order for a meal and a drink.

If any overmen had come here from the Northern Waste, he should have heard of it; he was, after all, high in the councils at Ordunin, to which all his people swore allegiance. Perhaps there were renegades, along the western shores of the Waste?

His ale arrived, and the innkeeper assured him that his food would soon follow.

Another possibility finally struck him; could there be overmen living *outside* the Waste? On the Yprian Coast itself, perhaps? That explanation worked quite well; should such overmen exist, Dûsarra would be a natural place for them to trade with Nekutta and the other southern lands. The map showed the coastal plain lying just the other side of this volcanic mountain range; although the road across the mountains would most likely be rougher travelling than the routes east into Eramma, the Yprians, if they existed, would probably not dare to venture into Eramma. The overmen of the Northern Waste had not dared to do so for three centuries; the bitter memories of the Racial Wars had kept them out as effectively as any physical barrier.

Likewise, the northerners had never ventured to the

west, across the Gulf of Ypri; their histories taught that the western lands were empty and desolate. Undoubtedly, the Yprians were taught that the Northern Waste was an uninhabited wasteland, as it actually had been until three hundred and fifty years ago.

This was a matter that would bear investigation when he returned home; he considered abandoning his quest and leaving Dûsarra immediately. He could drop off his one piece of booty with the Forgotten King in Skelleth on the way . . .

No, he couldn't. He could not return to Ordunin yet; he was still bound by his oath. Nor could he re-enter Skelleth without first going to Ordunin; the Baron would not tolerate that. He could perhaps sneak into the village, but to skulk about thus, and to bring only one of the items he had been sent for . . .

No, his pride would not allow that. He would complete his task here in Dûsarra first.

The innkeeper was at his elbow, setting a plate heaped with steaming mutton and those vegetables—potatoes?—before him. He pulled a gold coin from the pouch on his belt and said, "Is there a room available?"

"Oh, yes, my lord. I'll fetch the key." He took the proffered coin and vanished again.

There were six temples remaining; if he recalled the girl's words correctly, one of them was as nocturnal as Tema's, and inasmuch as it would be dark by the time he finished his meal, that would be his next target. The worshippers of darkness, of course; the god with two names. Andhur something. That was the one.

Time enough to find it later; he turned his attention to the food. The mutton was excellent.

CHAPTER TEN

The temple of darkness was a huge black pyramid, topped by a small dome that replaced the apex, and surrounded by a wide, empty plaza paved with basalt. Upon receiving directions from a passing Dûsarran, he had had no trouble at all in finding it; it stood near the center of the city, and several broad streets ended at the stone plaza.

Unlike the temple of Tema, this structure had no imposing tower, no vast open doorway; it was stark and simple, completely unornamented, and the only entry Garth could see was a single small door in the center of one side of the broad base. There were no steps; it opened directly onto the plaza.

The whole area seemed deserted; only a very few pedestrians made their way around the perimeter of the pavement, moving from one street to the next. None approached the temple. Perhaps, Garth thought, it was because the twilight still lingered; the western sky was still rosy, though overhead the sky was dark indigo, and in the east it was almost black and sprinkled with stars.

He still couldn't recall the god's second name; he had merely inquired after the temple of darkness, which had been sufficient.

Even if the god's devotees thought it too early, Garth was impatient; he crossed to the door, and found it open. Inside he could see nothing but darkness; that was to be expected. Cautiously, he stepped inside.

He was in a small antechamber, scarcely ten feet across; enough light trickled in from the door behind him to show him that. Another door was in the center of the opposite wall; there was no other opening in the

91

bare stone. With a shrug, he crossed the room and tried the inner door.

It was unlocked, but held with a simple latch; he pressed the latch button, but before he could pull on the handle a sound behind him startled him into releasing it.

The door to the outside had slammed shut when he squeezed the latch, which perhaps wasn't as simple as he had thought; apparently there were mechanisms to make sure no light was permitted beyond this chamber. He was now surrounded by total blackness, a darkness so complete that his eyes could not adjust no matter how long he waited. He could not see his hand in front of his face, he discovered. By feel, he found the handle of the inner door once more, and swung the portal open.

The darkness beyond was just as total; cautiously, he stepped through.

With arms outstretched before him, he took a second step; his fingers struck stone. He turned right; another step, and again he hit stone. Turning full about, he tried the one remaining direction, and again encountered a wall.

He stopped. Had he walked into a closet?

There was a rustle of garments; he could not identify the exact direction from which the sound came. He listened more closely, and made out the faint sound of breathing. Someone was in this tiny room with him.

"Is someone there?" he asked.

"Who are you?" The voice was soft and hissing.

"I am but a curious stranger. What is this place?"

"This is the central shrine of Andhur Regvos, Lord of Darkness and Master of the Blind. Why have you come here?"

"I was curious, good sir."

"Is it the custom in your land to enter holy places unbidden?"

"I was unaware of your temple's nature; I meant no harm."

"Very well; then you may depart in peace."

"Sir, are you a priest of this temple?"

"I am."

"Could you, perhaps, permit me to stay? I am as yet uncommitted to the worship of any god, and I would learn more of your cult, for I may want to pursue your creed."

The priest said nothing for a long moment, and Garth wished he could see the man's face. Finally, the priest replied, "I know no reason this should not be; though I doubt very much if you will choose to follow the path of Regvos, I have no desire to turn away a seeker of truth, even one as casual as yourself. Give me your hand."

Garth held out his hand, and almost immediately felt a bony grip upon it; he wondered if the priest had some magical means of seeing in the dark. He said nothing as he was led through a door he would have sworn was not there a moment ago when he felt the wall. Beyond, he judged that he and the priest were passing through a narrow corridor; it turned and twisted unmercifully, doubling back on itself, turning at unexpected angles, and generally giving the impression of being designed to confuse. Garth held out his free hand to avoid collisions with walls and pillars, and discovered by so doing that they were passing by several branching corridors; they were winding their way through a maze, there could be little doubt. Garth became disoriented, despite his best efforts, and was astonished when a final turn left them standing in a room he judged to be quite sizable, from the echoes and the feel of the air, where he would have expected the blank outer wall of the temple to be.

The priest released something, and Garth felt a heavy velvet curtain fall upon him; he stepped forward and it slid behind him, closing off the winding passages from the chamber he now stood in.

"Have you a tinderbox, or other agent of light?"

The priest's voice distracted Garth from his attempt to estimate the size of the chamber; he admitted, "Yes, I do."

"Such are not permitted here; surrender it, please."

Reluctantly, Garth took the pouch containing flint, steel, and tinder from his belt and handed it over.

"Thank you. Now, I must return to my duties; I leave you to contemplate the darkness. Another will be with you, in time." The priest's hands were gone; Garth heard three footsteps, and then, without so much as a rustle of garments, the priest was gone. Garth could hear nothing of him; no breathing, no heartbeat, no movement.

Unsettled, he took a few tentative steps forward; gauging the echoes of his boots on the stone floor, he judged the room he was in to be very large indeed, though not as immense as that under the dome of Tema's shrine. The air was chilly; he could feel that even through his armor and padding.

This was, then, most likely the temple sanctuary. Altar and idol would be in this chamber, somewhere —if they existed. It occurred to him that there was no need of an idol to the god of darkness when this chamber was full of the presence of the god himself. Even an altar might be thought unnecessary; how would he explain *that* eventuality to the Forgotten King?

Before he started worrying about that, he told himself, he should be sure it was the case. Arms outstretched, he took another few steps. Nothing there.

A voice suddenly spoke, not a dozen feet away.

"Greetings, stranger. Welcome to the shrine of Andhur Regvos. I am told you seek instruction; the best instruction is the darkness itself."

"What?" Garth realized his response was scarcely diplomatic, but it escaped him before he could control it.

"The best proof of our faith is felt in the darkness; do you not feel it? In this absolute darkness, do you not feel the sensation of supernatural presence? Does not a subtle fear, a certain respect, find its way into your heart?"

"I . . . I am not sure."

"That very uncertainty is a sign of the awe that our lord inspires; you, an unbeliever, feel only the lightest touch of his power. You have known only Andhur, the darkness that passes; before entering this shrine, you have most likely never even known what full darkness was like, for in the outside world the light creeps in everywhere, continuing the eternal battle. Here, though, is the fortress of Andhur, where the darkness does *not* pass, but endures forever. The darkness goes on, though you and others like you may leave and return once again to the light."

"You speak of Andhur; I thought your god's name was Andhur Regvos?"

"The two names identify the two aspects of the deity; Andhur, the lesser of the two, is that darkness which may be penetrated by light, the darkness that is external. Regvos is internal darkness, that darkness of body and soul which does not pass; you would call it blindness. As darkness comes in many forms—night, shadow, and shade—so does blindness. We, the priests of Andhur Regvos, are seekers after the totality of blindness, as we have, in this temple, achieved the totality of darkness."

Garth was becoming confused; this bizarre philosophy was distracting him from his purpose. He suppressed the urge to say he did not understand, for fear of triggering a long explanation. Instead, he said, "And what of your rituals?"

"Our ceremonies are of no concern to outsiders."

"Have you an idol, as do most shrines?"

"No; what need we with some stone image when the palpable presence of our divinity is all around us?"

"An altar, then, where the rites are performed?"

"Yes, we have an altar, only a dozen paces away from you. Fortunately, our god keeps it safe from your defiling gaze. I see that you have not the makings of a worshipper of darkness; you are too concerned with mundanities."

"Perhaps you are right. Pardon me, then." Garth strode on recklessly in the same direction he had headed before, which he believed to be directly toward the center of the chamber; he hoped to locate the altar and remove whatever it held before the priests could do anything to stop him. After all, would not the darkness hinder them, too? True, they lived in it much or all of the time and were fully familiar with the temple, as he was not; still, finding and stopping a thief in utter blackness would not be easy.

He had gone only eight paces, rather than the dozen the priest had suggested, when his leg struck a low obstruction. He felt about, and decided it was indeed the altar, about three feet high, ten feet long, and perhaps five in width. In its center his groping hands found an object, vaguely spherical and covered with cloth, perhaps a foot in diameter. Another stone, no doubt, like the one he had taken from the temple of Tema. Curious.

"Hold! What are you doing?"

"I merely wished to touch the altar." He picked up the stone; having no cloak to hide it under, he tucked it under his left arm. It wouldn't matter that it was visible until he was out of the temple, and in the open streets he would rely on his superior speed to escape.

He had what he came for, and in the darkness no one would even know it was gone until the ceremonies began. He returned the eight paces to where he had stood before, and said, "My apologies if I startled you."

There were rustlings behind him; a new voice spoke. "The stone is gone! He has the stone!"

Garth growled, wishing he knew an appropriate curse; his people, being atheistic, used none.

Suddenly there were rustlings on all sides; there were priests all around him. Had they been there all along?

"Return the stone to its place, defiler." The voice was that of his instructor, but lower, more authoritative in tone.

Garth ignored it; if he spoke it would only help them to locate him. He crept toward the entrance.

A dozen hands clutched at him; fingers curled around his wrist.

With a bellow, Garth leapt back and drew his sword, keeping his left arm firmly around his prize.

"Away!" he shouted.

"No, desecrator; you must return the stone."

"I have no wish to harm you, but I will if I must."

"Yes, thief, we heard you draw your sword; but can

you use your blade in the dark? There are many of us and but one of you. We can find you, for we have lived all our lives in darkness, but how can you find us? Here, of all the world, the blind rule and the sighted serve."

Garth slashed out blindly with his sword, but hit nothing. Again, unseen hands clutched at him; he tore free, and slashed again. He wished he had not so willingly surrendered the flint and steel that had been his only means of making light; if he could see, he would have the advantage.

At least, he so assumed; so far he had detected no weapons. Certainly none had been used against him, and how could the priests risk them in the dark? It would be far too likely that they would hit their companions instead of their opponent. And if the priests were blind, as the voice had implied, light would give him a truly immeasurable advantage.

"Give up, defiler. You cannot get away from us; even should you somehow slay us all, you will never escape. The only exit is through the maze, and without a guide you will never find the true path."

Garth made no answer, but swung the sword again, and again struck nothing. Fingertips brushed his arm, and he moved instinctively away. He was no longer sure of his location relative to altar and entrance; escaping the priests' attempts to capture him had distracted him and moved him he knew not where.

"Do you know what will happen, defiler, if you do not surrender? You will tire eventually; you will fall, and sleep, and when you do we will capture and bind you."

Garth slashed again, and thought he nicked something; perhaps a sleeve. Not flesh, unfortunately.

"Then, when you are securely bound, you will make a sacrifice. Not to Andhur, the darkness that passes, but to everlasting Regvos; you will become one of us."

Instead of a sweeping slash, Garth tried a lunging jab; he was lucky, and a yelp of pain answered him. He doubted he had inflicted a serious wound; there was as much of surprise as pain in that cry. He had probably pinked someone's arm.

"Blasphemer! Do you know how the sacrifice is performed, in cases such as yours? A rope, a thick rope knotted twice, is placed around your head, with the knots resting upon your closed eyelids."

Garth attempted another jab, this time aiming for where he judged the voice to be coming from; the speaker paused as steel whistled near him, but the blade did not connect. When next the voice spoke it had moved well to one side, although Garth had heard no footsteps or rustling garments.

"Then we will begin the Great Ritual, and with each chant the rope will be twisted a half-turn tighter, until the knots crush . . ."

A particularly fast, vicious lunge tore cloth audibly, and the voice cut off abruptly; Garth heard two quick steps away from him. He was heartened; he was beginning to think that nothing could faze the man.

The voice did not speak again; instead, he felt fingers groping. He whirled abruptly and slashed close in and was gratified to feel the blade cut into flesh and scrape on bone; he had caught a wrist before it could be withdrawn. There was not so much as a whimper of pain, though; Garth marvelled at the fortitude that implied.

Even in the dark, the sword gave him quite an advantage; all about him were his enemies, so he could strike freely. That would not get him out of the temple, necessarily, but it might drive away his tormentors, at least temporarily. He charged, swinging wildly.

The sword whistled and cut through cloth, but struck nothing more substantial. He charged again, in a different direction, and struck nothing at all. He stopped and listened.

He could hear nothing; had the priests retreated? He knew they were exceptionally good at being silent, but he was fairly sure that none stood within reach. He wished he could feel about him, but his left hand was occupied with the stone and he dared not lower the sword in his right. He stood for a moment, trying to decide on his next move.

He had not planned on this fight; he had not expected these annoying priests to notice the loss of the altar-stone so promptly.

A hand closed on his right forearm; he yanked free and slashed. The blade bit into something; there was a gasp, and when he raised the weapon back to the guard position something wet ran down over the quillons onto his hand. He felt a grim satisfaction at that; a blow that drew so much blood so quickly might well be mortal. He almost wished that the priest would taunt him again; the silence was making him nervous, and surely the others must have some comment to make about the man he had struck?

There were retreating footsteps, two sets moving together, as if carrying something between them; he heard something drag. There had been no sound of a body falling, however; his victim was still upright, merely being helped away.

In hopes of surprising and further discouraging his antagonists, he leapt forward without warning and laid about him with the bloody sword; there were short, sharp cries, but he did not feel the blade connect with anything. He recalled that he was dealing with humans, much shorter than himself; were they ducking under his blows? He went down on one knee and made a long, horizontal sweep with his blade, scarcely two feet from the floor; it ended abruptly when his steel struck something much harder than flesh or bone, and he almost lost his grip as the blade rebounded, ringing, from what he realized must be the stone altar.

Two hands grasped at his shoulder; he twisted away and struck without thinking, swinging the sword in a downward arc. It struck the altar again, rather than his assailant, scraping across stone, and for the first time since entering the temple Garth's eyes responded; there was a blue-white flash, almost painful after such a long time in absolute darkness, and Garth stood motionless for an instant, dazed, wondering what he had just seen.

At last, he realized what had happened; his sword had struck sparks. The altar, whatever stone it was made of, had served as flint to his weapon's steel.

A hand closed on his right ankle; he guessed that the priest who had grabbed his shoulder had ducked, and was now aiming lower. Remembering the direction the grip on his shoulder had had, Garth guessed where on the floor his attacker would have fallen and chopped downward; the blade bit into cloth and flesh, and a high-pitched scream echoed through the chamber. Garth stepped away, without attempting to finish the human off; he had another idea.

The altar, he realized, could provide the light he needed, if he could find something to use as tinder. He mentally reviewed everything he had with him. A purse, containing a dozen gold coins; a dagger in his belt; the belt itself; a leather pouch that held dried beef, dried fruit, an awl, and other useful items—such as the map the Forgotten King had given him, showing the route to Dûsarra. It was old, dry parchment; it should burn readily.

Unfortunately, he had both his hands full at present.

It was also necessary not to let the priests know that he was up to something; he made a few feints and jabs with his sword, not seriously expecting to hit anything, just to keep up appearances. Then, carefully, he bent down and placed the stone firmly between his knees; he dared not put it down anywhere for fear a priest would snatch it away. His now-free left hand plunged into the pouch and pulled out the map; he placed it in his right hand, held tightly against the hilt of his sword by his outer thumb and two fingers, then returned the stone to its place under his left arm.

He made a trial pass at the altar with the sword, and with a long, diagonal blow scraped up a shower of sparks. This time he was ready, and saw them plainly; the altar was rough stone, his sword was smeared with blood that was black in the faint light. He watched where the sparks fell and placed the map accordingly, still neatly rolled.

It occurred to him that the map would not burn for

very long once lit, but he had nothing else readily combustible; he would have to make do.

As he withdrew after placing the map, a hand pressed against his back; he whirled and slashed, and was rewarded with a yell and the hiss of steel cutting cloth. Thinking quickly, he dropped the altar-stone, and simultaneously clamped a foot atop it and reached out with his left hand.

He caught something; he held a handful of cloth, and yanked. There was loud ripping, and a long piece of fabric came away in his grip.

"What are you doing, blasphemer?"

He ignored the voice as he drew his dagger with his left hand and awkwardly twisted the cloth around the blade, securing it as best he could one-handed; with his right hand he took a few aimless swings with his sword, to make the priests maintain their distance. The dagger-torch thus produced wouldn't burn well, he knew; it wanted grease or fat or oil on the cloth.

He placed it on the altar beside the map, feeling carefully to be sure the roll of parchment was still there.

Again the voice asked, "What are you doing?" Garth thought he detected a worried tone; undoubtedly the priests could hear everything he did, making it plain that he was up to something.

"Why do you draw your dagger, thief? Is not your sword sufficient to deal with unarmed priests? Is that cloth a bandage? Have we wounded you so severely?"

Garth was relieved that his scheme had not been deciphered. He pulled his largest piece of dried meat from his pouch and smeared it along the blade of his sword, letting it soak up what remained of the blood; for the first time in his life he was grateful that his provisions were of less than premier quality, for there was a significant amount of fat in the meat, and he hoped the blood would serve to soften it up somewhat.

There were rustlings all around him; the priests were also up to something. Something was being dragged toward him.

He smeared the bloody meat against the cloth

wrapped on the blade of his dagger, then flung it aside.

He had prepared as well as he could; he struck at the altar again with his sword.

The angle was wrong; only a very few sparks glimmered briefly. He swung again, and a more encouraging shower of blue-white pinpoints spattered across the altar and parchment, but they vanished without igniting anything.

"Do you seek to enrage us further by smashing our altar? Fool! You cannot damage it, no matter how strong your arm; no man can!"

Garth was amused that they thought him a man; he resisted the temptation to correct their mistake, as it would hinder his identification once he was gone. He struck at the altar again, and sparks flew; again, and again, his blade grating on stone. He was ruining the edge, he knew.

He paused to catch his breath, and the darkness swallowed him up again, seeming more complete than ever after the brief respite the sparks had provided; but was it complete? From the corner of his eye he caught a faint flicker; he bent near the altar.

Yes! A dull orange glow tinged the edge of the rolled map; a spark had caught!

Holding his breath, ignoring the rustling movements behind him and the dragging which was scarcely ten feet away, he gently fanned the ruddy glow; his efforts were rewarded with a tiny tongue of flame that leapt up suddenly. Exulting silently, he carefully lifted the burning parchment and held it high, turning to take his first good look at his surroundings.

As he turned, a heavy net was flung across him; that, of course, was what the priests had been dragging. He managed to hang onto his sword and the burning map, but his foot slipped from atop the altarstone. Fortunately, it, too, was tangled in the net, where the priests could not get at it readily even if they were to locate it.

He struggled to remain upright, and succeeded; the priests, thinking him human, had underestimated his strength.

For a moment, he was too busy studying his newly visible environment to pay the net much heed. He was in the middle of a large room, perhaps a hundred feet across, totally devoid of furniture save for the altar itself, which was a single block of rough stone. The walls were bare, unfinished stone; here and there were hung heavy draperies, presumably concealing doorways. The dim light of his small flame was not sufficient to make out color or detail.

The heat of the flame began to reach his fingers, and he recalled himself to his immediate situation; he set to methodically cutting his way out of the net with his sword, which was fairly easy. In only a moment, he had cut a hole large enough to let the net slide down across his body onto the floor.

The priests formed a ring around the net, tugging at it, trying to force their captive down; they were unaware that their actions actually made Garth's escape much easier, providing the tension necessary to cut the strands, and pulling the severed net down off him.

Once mostly free, he wasted no time in snatching up his prepared dagger and setting the greased cloth ablaze; it produced a dim, smoky, malodorous flame, but it burned. He dropped the flaming remnant of his map and again looked about.

This time he studied the priests; all wore black, or at least colors dark enough to be indistinguishable in the available light. They were babbling excitedly, aware that their captive had somehow eluded the net and set something on fire; the odor was unmistakably that of something burning. Garth regretted that, as it removed much of the element of surprise.

There were about two dozen of them; they covered a wide range of sizes and shapes and, judged by their faces, varied in age from scarcely adult to positively ancient. Their garments were uniformly dirty and ragged, and their faces filthy; but after all, who would care in the eternal darkness of the temple? Or even outside, who expected the blind to be concerned with appearances? That thought drew Garth's attention to their eyes, which he immediately regretted; some were not bad, being merely permanently closed or open and staring sightlessly, but others were glazed, whited over with cataracts, flooded with blood and scar tissue, or simply gone, leaving bloody sockets.

He noticed that one had a long, jagged tear in his robe, revealing a cut across his chest; it seemed singularly clean and bloodless until Garth lifted his makeshift torch for a better look. When the dim light shone full on the man's chest the cut suddenly began oozing blood thickly, and the priest hissed in pain.

Another had a makeshift bandage tight around his wrist; as the light hit it blood seeped through, staining it a dark red.

A man, an old man, lay on the floor not far from him; a trail of blood showed that this was the priest who had grabbed Garth's shoulder and ankle, only to be wounded at the base of the altar. Whatever dark magic had stanched the wounds of his companions until light hit them had apparently been overtaxed by the severity of his injuries, as his blood seemed to have flowed freely enough. The old man was still breathing, faintly, and Garth wondered if he would live.

Looking across the floor beneath the net Garth saw another trail of blood, where two priests had dragged away the first one he had seriously wounded. His eyes followed the trail to where it vanished under one of the curtains; that, he supposed, would be sleeping quarters, or some similar place where they could tend their wounded.

"So, thief, you lied to us, and brought in some way to make fire. We dare not attack you, thus, when you have your sword and we are unarmed; but still, you cannot find your way out. The maze will stop you."

For the first time Garth could see who spoke; it was a tall, elderly man, his hair gray with age. One sleeve was slashed where Garth's sword had cut it. He had no eyes, but merely empty sockets, long since healed from whatever injury had destroyed his sight.

It seemed unlikely to Garth that the maze could actually be all that impossible; with a wary eye on the priests, he put down his sword for a moment, transferred the dagger-torch to his right hand, picked up the cloth-covered stone with his left, tucked it back in its former position under his arm, put the torch back in his left hand—which could still hold it, although it was not free to make large motions—and picked up the sword. This operation took a minute or more before he was comfortable again, but the priests kept their distance; they knew they were no match for him except in the darkness.

Thus organized, with sword in his right hand, torch in his left, and stone under his left arm, he crossed the dirty stone floor to the drapery through which he had entered; he identified it by its position relative to the altar.

The curtain was wine-colored velvet, he saw when the torch came near enough to make colors distinguishable; it was stained and dusty. It was also, he thought, a good place for an ambush; he slashed at it with his sword, rather than marching through.

There was a piercing scream, and a body fell forward, dragging the drapery down beneath it; he had cut the man's throat. A long, serpentine-bladed dagger rattled on the flagstones as a new, darker stain spread across the ruined velvet.

The bulky stone under his arm kept him from thrusting the torch forward to illuminate what lay beyond the now-open doorway, so he proceeded with deliberate caution, in short steps, looking both ways and always aware of the double-dozen enemies behind him.

There were no further attacks; he stepped through the doorway into the maze.

No fewer than five corridors branched away from where he stood; he studied them all, and then, without hesitation, marched up the one second from the left. He could not hope to remember the twisting route he had followed coming in, let alone reverse it, but he had no need to; in four of the corridors dust lay thick on the floor. Only one route was actually used.

This same method served him well at every intersection, and there were a good many of them; no doubt it would be a great mystery for the surviving dark-worshippers to ponder.

At last, when he was beginning to wonder if he had somehow managed a wrong turn after all, the corridor he followed ended, not in a blank wall, but in a heavy iron door, bolted on his side. He sheathed his sword; surely, no enemy would be able to reach him here! He slid the bolt, and the door swung inward silently with only a gentle tug, revealing the closet-like compartment he had entered from the antechamber.

"Who's there?" The black-robed figure whirled to face him, though the man's eyes were blank and sightless; it was the priest who had led him through the maze, he was sure. "Why did you not signal?"

Annoyed, Garth drew his sword again, and held it to the man's throat. "Silence," he commanded. The priest obeyed admirably. Garth pulled him back into the maze, then stepped past him into the closet space and let the iron door swing shut; it apparently had springs to keep it closed. The side he now saw was not iron at all, but stone; a thin panel of cut stone had been rivetted to the metal framework.

He was pleased the man had not put up a fight; he had killed at least one of the priests here, perhaps two or three, and wanted no more bloodshed.

He had no difficulty in opening the door to the antechamber; however, when it swung open, the gust of wind caught his already-dimming torch, which flickered and almost died. He stood where he was for a moment, hoping it would recover; instead, it faded to a dull glow. Most of the cloth was ash.

It mattered little; he was almost out. He crossed the room, and pulled at the door to the outside.

It refused to yield. He bent to look at the handle, as the last flicker of his torch waned and died. He felt for a latch, but found none.

A possibility occurred to him; he groped his way back across the room and closed the door to the maze entrance, making certain it latched securely.

That done, he returned to the exterior door; this time it opened easily and he stepped out into the plaza, to stand blinking in the bright moonlight.

CHAPTER ELEVEN

There was no sign of pursuit; perhaps the priests of Andhur Regvos thought him lost somewhere in their labyrinth.

The plaza was still mostly empty. A few humans wandered about, ignoring him, though he was sure he must be a rather strange sight; an overman emerging from the temple with a bloody sword in one hand and a scorched and blackened dagger in the other, and a great black stone—the cover had twisted out of position, and he could see that the altar-stone was of some material resembling obsidian—under one arm.

Of course, he was still mostly in the temple's shadow; or perhaps the Dûsarrans assumed him a participant in some secret ritual best left uninvestigated.

It would not do, he knew, to walk the streets of the city like this; he shrank back into the doorway, and seated himself on the paving, letting his three burdens fall.

He took the cloth cover from the stone, and carefully wiped his weapons clean before sheathing them; now the only problem was to conceal the stone itself.

Or was that, in fact, a problem? After all, he realized, no one had ever seen the thing. To the uninitiated, it would appear merely a large chunk of obsidian, a substance that he had seen sold freely in the marketplace the night before.

He knew it was still somewhat risky, but could think of no way to conceal his booty; so, once his blades were cleaned and sheathed and he had removed what soot and blood he could from his hands and mail shirt, he tucked the stone casually under his arm and strolled away unmolested.

It was still relatively early; he had to some extent lost track of time while in the temple but, judging by the position of the moon, he estimated it to be well before midnight. He would have to decide whether or not to tackle another of the remaining altars immediately, or whether it would be better to delay. The decision, however, could wait until he had disposed of his prize.

He found his way back to the Inn of the Seven Stars and headed for the stable, to deposit this new stone with his earlier prize. There was a boy sitting in the arch; Garth recognized him as the boy he had paid for Koros' keep when he first arrived. If he had understood the conversation of the other two boys correctly, his name was Dugger.

It occurred to Garth that the lad could be a loose end; he would identify the warbeast-riding overman with the brown-cloaked old man who had expressed a suspicious interest in Tema's temple. That was not something Garth wanted known.

He stepped into the arch; the boy clambered to his feet and said, "Greetings, sir. How may I serve you?"

A rather more polite greeting than he had given the night before, Garth thought; gold had a truly salutary effect on human manners. "In two ways, boy. Firstly, you will see that my mount is fed tomorrow night; it is to be given as much fresh, raw meat as you can carry, or a live goat or two if you prefer, and a bucket of water. Secondly, you will make no mention of me to anyone unless asked, and if you *are* asked, you will deny seeing me in any guise other than my present one. Is that clear?" As he spoke this last phrase a large gold coin appeared in his hand, held up so that it sparkled in the moonlight.

The boy nodded eagerly. "Oh, yes, sir!"

"Good. Excuse me; I would tend my beast." The coin dropped into the boy's hand, whence it promptly vanished to some hidden pocket, and Garth passed into the stableyard.

Koros growled a greeting as its master opened the stall door; Garth ignored it while he dug out two sacks from his bundled supplies. He stuffed the obsidianlike stone down into one, then dug up the now-clear white crystal he had hidden beneath the straw and packed it on top, with straw around the edges to keep the sharp facets from cutting the rough fabric. That done he tied the sack shut and stashed it under his other supplies. The other sack he folded into a small bundle and stuffed under his belt; it would, he hoped, carry whatever he found in the next temple.

Five temples remained. There was no point in wasting time, he decided; he would immediately pursue his quest and loot a third shrine. Things had not gone well in the first two; he had killed at least two people so far, possibly as many as four. That was not good. He would try to be more careful henceforth. If he kept on killing people at that rate . . .

He did not like killing people. A major reason he had been reluctant to serve the Forgotten King was that his first errand had resulted in a dozen deaths, perhaps more. However, whenever he found himself in a combat situation, his reflexes took over; he acted first and regretted it later. He was not proud of that, but recognized it as a part of his nature; all he could do was try to avoid combat situations.

Five temples remained, including the temple of Death; he would leave that for last. What were the other four? P'hul, the goddess of decay, was one. There was one that the tavern-girl had said frightened her; Agha? No, Aghad. That was it. He recalled hearing the name spoken back in Skelleth, as an oath; that sounded promising.

He considered visiting the tavern again, but decided against it; he was not hungry, nor even particularly thirsty, and could just as easily get directions on the street.

That in mind, he left the stable, nodding to the stable-boy who winked in reply, and headed for the marketplace.

As it had been the night before, it was bustling, crowded and torchlit. He strolled about a bit first, watching the reactions of the Dûsarran populace to an overman in their midst.

There were none; they accepted him as a matter of

course. There must indeed be established communi-
cations between Dûsarra and a population of overmen
somewhere.

Casually, he struck up a conversation with a merchant, pretending an interest in his display of stone
carvings; when he learned that the carvings represented the Dûsarran gods, his feigned interest became
quite genuine.

"Who is this, then?" he asked, indicating a six-inch
carving of truly astonishing ugliness; it had a fanged,
twisted, sneering face, with exaggerated masculine
characteristics, and was done in a rough, primitive
style.

"Aghad, of course."

"And this?" He indicated a skull-faced, helmetted
statuette that held a miniature sword almost the length
of its body.

"Bheleu, god of destruction. One of your kind, so it
is said."

"What?" Garth looked more closely, and saw that
the face was not a skull; the statuette had ragged,
straight hair, two thumbs on either hand, and eyes
rather than sockets. In short, it was a carving of an
overman.

How very odd, Garth thought, that humans should
worship a god in the form of an overman. After all,
overmen had nothing to do with the gods, being athe-
ists; and weren't gods supposed to have existed
throughout time, while overmen had only come into
being a thousand years earlier? He looked over the
whole display. He recognized the slender, graceful
Tema, though these little idols did not have cloaks
that spread out above them; a god with two eyeless
faces he readily guessed to be Andhur Regvos. There
were more of those two, in various sizes and with
some variation of detail, than any others; there were
a dozen or so of the fanged horror depicting Aghad,
and perhaps half that number of the overmanlike
Bheleu. There were two other recurring forms, both
female; one held dagger and whip and wore a cruel
smile, while the other was robed and cowled. He took
a closer look at one of these; under the cowl the

artisan had carved the face of a mummy, wrinkled skin stretched over bone. It had a nose, however, so it was not intended to be an overwoman; Garth guessed it must be P'hul.

That was only six, however.

"I only see six of the gods here."

"Naturally." The merchant looked surprised. Garth realized his mistake; the seventh god was Death, and even were there a market, it would probably not be considered safe to try representing him.

He tried to cover his foolishness. "Of course. Who is this?" He indicated the woman with whip and dagger.

"Sai."

Garth looked blank.

"The goddess of pain and suffering."

"Oh, yes." He contemplated the display again. "And each has a temple here in Dûsarra?"

"The name says as much."

"Where are the temples? I might want to visit them."

The merchant looked at him strangely. "Very few foreigners visit the temples."

"I was just curious."

"Oh. Well, the temple of Tema is back that way," he said, indicating the direction, "and most of the others are on the Street of the Temples, over that way." He pointed toward the northeastern part of the city.

"My thanks." Garth took a final look at the array of idols, then turned away, heading northeast.

The Street of the Temples was not hard to find; it was a broad, straight avenue, paved with stone and obviously intended for ceremonial processions. Most of its length was lined not with temples, but with houses and palaces; it was obviously one of the more desirable neighborhoods. There were a few shops, all closed for the night; this part of the city belonged to the day-people, not the night-worshippers.

One end of the street was the gate to a palace, the largest and most elegant Garth had yet seen; that, presumably, belonged to the city's overlord. The other end, which was much further from where he had happened onto the avenue, appeared to be nothing but the blank stone face of the volcano on whose slopes the city was built; the street was cut into the stone for a few yards, keeping it at a negotiable slope, and then abruptly stopped.

Along the considerable distance between palace and mountainside, Garth saw four temples; they were readily distinguished from the adjoining residences because each was built entirely of black stone and surmounted by a dome of some sort, while the palaces and other buildings were flat-roofed and built of various materials. The temples were arranged two to each side, spaced along the street, dividing it into five equal lengths.

Garth had arrived on the street directly across from the temple second from the overlord's palace; it made little difference to him which he visited next, so he chose the nearest and strode across the pavement.

The temple was mostly hidden by a high wall, built of the ubiquitous black stone; only the dome, a relatively modest one, could be seen. The wall had no windows, no eaves overhanging, nor any other architectural features suggesting it was part of the temple proper; Garth assumed it enclosed a yard, and that the temple lay within the yard.

The only visible entrance was a pair of gates, perhaps ten feet high and eight feet wide, made of some metal that gleamed an eerie silver in the moonlight; they were not simple flat surfaces, but shaped into ornate curves and ridges. With a start, Garth realized that the ridges formed recognizable runes, two to each gate, spelling out *AGHAD*.

As he approached the gates he noticed another surprising feature; the wall was built of carefully cut stones, all exactly the same size, and every stone block had carved upon it those same four runes: *AGHAD*. The name of the god was repeated a thousand times over on the wall of the temple.

Well, Garth thought, at least he need not wonder which temple it was. He reached out to try the gates, but before his hand touched the gleaming surface it parted and swung open before him, revealing the courtyard beyond.

He did not much care for such trickery; he looked carefully in all directions before cautiously stepping through, but could see no sign of how the gates had been opened. He tried to peer through the crack at the hinges, only to discover there was none; each valve hung from a single intricate hinge that extended for its full height.

The courtyard beyond seemed innocent enough; a broad expanse paved with loose gravel, with a fountain playing in its center. A long colonnade surrounded it on three sides; behind the far colonnade there stood the temple itself, an elegant building of black stone, with many windows and much ornamentation.

On every column, on all three sides, was a bracket holding a blazing torch, a welcome change from the darkness of the first two temples.

It should have been beautiful, with the soft hiss of the fountain, the dancing firelight, the columns and arcades. It wasn't. There was something dim and menacing about it, and its proportions seemed somehow wrong, as if the architect had calculated the perfect dimensions and then maliciously distorted them.

Garth stepped past the gates and noticed for the first time that there were curious faint brown stains on the silvery metal. He had no time to study them, however, for as soon as he was clear the gates swung shut behind him, as mysteriously as they had opened.

He was debating whether to try and reopen them or simply to proceed, when a long, lingering scream sounded from somewhere inside the temple; Garth tensed, his hand on his sword hilt. The scream cut off abruptly, to be replaced by soft, mocking laughter that echoed eerily along the colonnades.

His curiosity was piqued, and the matter of the self-closing gates was forgotten. He started forward.

"Greetings, overman." The voice was deep and somber. It came from somewhere behind him, he thought; he whirled, sword drawn, but saw nothing except the closed gates. He noticed that they were now barred. He had not heard the bar falling in place;

he reprimanded himself for not being sufficiently alert.

"Welcome to the temple of Aghad." The voice now sounded somewhere to his right; he turned, more slowly, wishing that these Dûsarrans weren't all so fond of trickery. He still saw no one.

"We do not receive many visitors here." Again, the voice had shifted; he decided to ignore its movements, since they were obviously some sort of trick. "Aghad is not a popular god, I fear. The masses prefer harmless, impotent little Tema." The voice laughed, softly.

Garth announced petulantly, "I don't like speaking to someone I cannot see."

"It is not intended that you should like it."

"Why not?"

"Dear infant, you are ignorant, aren't you?"

"In some areas, yes. Religion and its mystical trappings are not popular in my homeland."

"Oh, dear, not popular! Aghad is not popular anywhere, fool. Aghad is fear, hatred, loathing, all the things men—and though you will not accept it, overmen—feel for the unknown, for the different, for what they cannot understand."

"I can understand why such a deity holds little appeal."

"Oh, yes, I'm sure! Why have you come here, then?"

"I wish to visit all the seven temples."

"You lie with half-truths."

"What would you have me say, then?"

"You come to steal, scum. The altar-stones of Tema and Regvos are hidden at your warbeast's feet, at the Inn of the Seven Stars."

Garth did not answer, but merely tightened his grip on his sword.

The voice laughed again.

"Oh, witling, put down your silly knife. We serve Aghad here, and Aghad alone, not Tema nor Regvos, nor Sai, P'hul, or Bheleu. Aghad is hate, thief, hate, envy, and every emotion that turns fellow against fellow. We who serve Aghad have no reason to aid or sympathize with our brother priests of the other temples. Sack all Dûsarra if you will, burn the city to the ground! We will not stop you."

"Do you not care for your own temple? You have said I came here to steal."

"Idiot, self-hatred is most basic of all; if one does not hate himself, how is he to despise others so like him? You may take what lies on our altar, for it is no unique thing, but a common substance, replaced at each ceremony. We do, however, demand payment."

Garth did not lower his blade. "What payment?"

"You must make a proper sacrifice to Aghad."

"What sort of sacrifice?"

"Ordinarily a supplicant must betray a friend, deceive a lover, or in some other way spread dissent; but in view of your foreign origin, filth, something else is in order. A service to our god: Slay us six priests or more, one from each of the other temples. You slew the one at the door of Tema's temple, and a priest and priestess both of Regvos, though a third you let live. You have made a good beginning. Now, you must slay four more, from each of the four remaining temples, or the devotees of Aghad will make certain you do not leave the city alive."

Garth made no attempt to conceal his astonishment. "Are you serious?"

"We are."

"Why?"

"Because our agents in each cult will blame your actions upon another, and discord will spread. You have already begun our task for us, you know."

The reference to his conversation with the swordsman in the stableyard did not escape his notice. It was obvious that the cult of Aghad had some truly superb means of gathering information, whether it was by magical methods or merely an efficient system of spies and informers. He still found it almost incredible that these people *wanted* him to kill their countrymen.

"You serve a strange master, priests of Aghad."

"No stranger than yours, Garth of Ordunin, late of Skelleth."

Garth hid his surprise; after all, whatever their methods, there was no reason to believe they were limited to this one city. The cult of Aghad could easily extend throughout all the human kingdoms, for all Garth knew.

"What if I decline to pay your price?"

"You are free to do as you please, dolt; we merely present you with the following options, for you to choose from as you will. You may take what you find upon our altar, and fulfill our demand, and go in peace. You may take what you find upon our altar, refuse to do as we ask, and die before you leave Dûsarra. Or, lastly, you may decline our offer entirely and live, but with the knowledge that your cowardice has offended our god and our cult."

"None of these options is particularly appealing."

"That does not concern us. Now, if you would see our altar, slave, pass the fountain, and before you will be the door to the sanctuary."

Garth considered for a moment. He had no wish to kill anyone; however, it might prove necessary, as it had in the first two temples, in which case he might as well take whatever there was here. He had no intention of wantonly slaying priests just to please these abominable Aghadites, though. If it did not become necessary to dispose of the required four priests, he would simply rely on his own strength and wit to elude the Aghadites and escape the city.

He moved cautiously past the fountain toward the temple itself, only to halt abruptly. Lying on the gravel behind the fountain was a human corpse, face down, an empty tin cup near its hand.

"What is this?"

"Note the odor of the fountain, wizard-spawn."

He was beginning to resent the constant supply of insults the hidden priest provided. He obeyed, though, and sniffed the crystal-clear spray. The scent of bitter almonds stung his nostrils; had he had a nose, he would have wrinkled it in disgust.

"Very pretty."

"The poor fool came seeking a cool drink; we could not refuse so simple a request, could we?" The priest burst out laughing, a roaring laughter tinged with hysteria. Garth began to suspect the man was mad. It would seem reasonable; would a sane man serve such a god? Unsettled, he walked on, keeping his sword ready in his hand.

The colonnade was perhaps ten feet across, a distance sufficient to put the wall of the temple in darkness; the columns which held the torches blocked out the light, since the flames were all on the courtyard side. Garth hesitated to step into that shadow, particularly since he could not see the door the priest had said was there. Then part of the shadow opened inward, and light the color of blood poured out.

Garth stepped forward through the double doors into a room hung with tapestries and lit by flames behind sheets of dark red glass set in the walls between the hangings. The room was not overlarge, and Garth wondered if it were, in fact, the sanctuary, or merely an antechamber; it was scarcely twenty feet square. He saw no altar, but there were no doors other than that by which he had entered, either.

He moved to the center of the chamber, and the doors promptly closed behind him. He was getting used to this sort of thing.

The ruddy light made it hard to distinguish details; he could not say what any of the tapestries depicted. He stood, waiting, to see what would happen next.

A curious thrashing noise came from somewhere above and ahead of him, and a muffled voice, too high for a man or overman, made a wordless noise. Harsh laughter rang out, growing louder and higher; the thrashing ceased, or perhaps was merely drowned out by the laughing, and the tapestry directly before him suddenly slid upward into the ceiling, revealing a large alcove. A more normal light shone from this opening; hundreds of candles were arranged in tiers on its three walls, every one burning brightly, illuminating an elaborate golden altar. The top of the altar was a panel of red-enamelled wood, almost completely covered by a flood of coins, gold and red.

As he approached and cautiously reached for the coins, Garth wondered what the red ones were made of; he had never seen a metal so brightly crimson in hue, and stone coins were rare, being too brittle for everyday use.

He scooped up a handful and realized they were all ordinary gold; the red was fresh arterial blood, blood that ran down his wrist and dripped from his fingers. Revolted, he flung down the coins and turned away.

The tapestry plunged back into place, trapping him in the alcove, but not before he had seen the outer wall of the room to be blank, with no trace of the door he had entered by except a space of bare stone between hangings.

The laughter rang out louder than ever.

CHAPTER TWELVE

He stood frozen with surprise for an instant; a soft sound behind him brought him whirling around to face the altar again, only to discover that it was gone. In its place was a crouching panther; Garth raised his sword, ready to meet its attack, and stepped back against the tapestry, so that the big cat would have further to leap and therefore less momentum when it hit.

No attack came. Instead, a heavy velvet curtain fell between him and the beast, leaving him enclosed in a space scarcely three feet wide. A few of the myriad candles were included in his compartment, so that at least he could see.

He pushed at the velvet barrier; it did not yield. Something held it taut. It was apparently secured to very solid retainers all around. He leaned his full weight against it with no result.

He shrugged, and turned to the tapestry that separated him from the main part of the room. It was anchored just as firmly. He looked about.

His enclosure was perhaps eight feet long; he stood in the center. At either end a dozen candles stood on black iron brackets bolted to the walls. Below him, the floor was a single slab of stone, a dark gray stone, probably slate. Looking up, he saw that the ceiling was covered with gold leaf, worked into elaborate swirls and floral designs. At one end, partly obscured by shadows, hung what appeared to be a cord; its lower end was above his line of sight, which explained how he had failed to notice its presence before.

He took a step and reached for it, hoping it was the draw-cord for one of the hangings; it raised a serpent's head and hissed angrily at his approaching hand.

Things were happening too fast; he bisected the serpent-rope with a sweep of his sword, and then slashed at the velvet curtain.

The blade penetrated with no difficulty, and Garth peered through the rent in the fabric; the panther was gone, if in fact it had ever truly been there, and the altar restored, the gold exactly as he had left it, the blood beginning to dry. He wondered how much of this was illusion, how much magic, and how much simple mechanical tricks.

"Very good, Garth." The laughter had stopped, and now the familiar taunting voice spoke. "You have slain a harmless rock-snake and destroyed a thousand-year-old Yeshitic hanging. Take your gold and begone. Ignore the blood; it came from an Orûnian virgin, just turned sixteen, but she was none of your kind. You need not regret her death." The priest tittered obscenely, and Garth's growing anger crystallized into hatred. At the back of his mind he knew that the priest wanted this, that he, like his foul god, thrived on hatred, but that only served to strengthen the emotion. Growling, he stepped through the ruined curtain, sheathing his sword as he did so, then pulled the sack from his belt and scooped the golden coins into it, ignoring the clotted blood.

"Oh, fine, underling; we might hire you as a parlor-maid, should you have the courage to apply. Now go and slay us four priests, if you can; or priestesses, if that is more to your taste, though Bheleu and the Final God are served only by men. Go, and bother us no further, scum."

There was a click behind him; he turned, to see that the tapestry had vanished again, and that the double door stood open once more. A sudden gust of wind brushed him, coming from nowhere that he could detect, and the candles flickered and died, leaving only the crimson glow of the torchlit panels.

He took a step toward the exit, then paused. In a final act of defiance, he drew his sword, set aside the sack of gold, gripped the hilt in both hands, then turned and chopped at the altar, sending the enamelled top flying to either side, hewn in half. Another blow, and the golden filigree splintered and crumpled. He sheathed his weapon, spat at the broken remains of the altar, then picked up his booty and strode out the doorway. No laughter followed him.

The tapestry fell into place behind him, and the doors slammed shut. He marched through the colonnade and across the courtyard, noting that the corpse was gone from beside the fountain; then he stopped, as his gaze fell on the silvery gates.

The body of an old, old man, withered and emaciated, was nailed to the gates, the feet on one valve, the outstretched arms on the other; horrified, Garth saw that the narrow chest was still rising and falling, slowly and irregularly. The man's face was twisted in agony, his eyes tightly shut. Garth shivered in revulsion as he saw that strips of the man's skin had been cut loose from his flanks and nailed to the gates as well.

Sickened, Garth bellowed, "You filth! Why is this man here?"

There was silence for a moment as his cry echoed and was lost among the columns; then, very softly, that hideously familiar voice spoke, in a smiling, insinuating, smirking tone.

"You seem to enjoy wielding that sword of yours, child; use it to open the gate."

Garth stood motionless for a long moment. Then he

dropped the sack of coins and strode to the gate; with all the care he could manage, he began pulling out the nails that held the old man. It was a delicate, difficult job; they had been driven in firmly and required all his strength to pry loose, while the slightest twist or tug might wrench the torn flesh and cause the victim new agony. Garth was very glad that the man was unconscious before the first nail came free.

Fortunately, the metal of the gates was soft, and did not hold the nails as well as wood would have; the superhuman strength of Garth's fingers was sufficient, with some slight aid from his dagger in prying at the larger spikes that held the feet.

At last, Garth had the man free, and lowered him gently to the gravel; the gates opened to only a slight tug. He picked up his sack and stepped through to be sure the way was clear; he intended to carry the old man back to the Inn of the Seven Stars and see that he received the best possible care, but it would not do to be seen carrying him about the Street of the Temples.

The street was empty; he turned, to see the gates swinging shut. Desperately, he reached out, flinging himself forward to try and stop them, seeing the old man lying on the gravel through the narrowing gap, but he was not fast enough; the portal slammed shut, forcing him out into the avenue.

With a bellow of rage, Garth flung himself at the gates again; they did not yield. The shock of his impact bruised his shoulder, despite the padding and mail that protected it.

He whipped out his sword and hacked at the metal; the weapon had served him well but suffered in consequence, and this was too much. It broke, leaving him clutching a hilt and a half-foot of blade, and sending slivers of steel in a dozen directions. The gates remained firm, though the top of the *GH* rune was scratched and battered out of shape.

Once again, he heard laughter; something was flung over the wall, to fall heavily on the pavement at his feet. It was the old man's corpse, hacked messily in

two, as it would have been had he used his sword to
open the gate as the priest of Aghad suggested.

Speechless, Garth stood staring at the bloody remains for a long moment, then turned and left, as that
final hysterical laugh trailed after him.

CHAPTER THIRTEEN

The moon was still well above the horizon; Garth
estimated he had three hours or more until dawn. Although ordinarily he might have called it a night and
returned to the Inn of the Seven Stars, the events in
the temple of Aghad had enraged him, and he was too
full of fury and adrenaline to go quietly back to the
inn. Instead, he swung the sack of gold over his shoulder and marched down the avenue toward the overlord's palace, and toward the temple that stood
nearest it. He was aware, with part of his mind, that
he was being slightly reckless, since he no longer had
a sword and was encumbered by the Aghadite gold;
he was, however, too mad to care. He would have
preferred to devote himself to destroying the temple of
Aghad, and hunting out and killing the owner of that
taunting voice, but knew that he wouldn't have a
chance of succeeding; the priests would undoubtedly
be expecting an attack. Instead he would take out his
anger on whoever might be guarding this other temple. Even armed only with a dagger and a broken hilt,
he knew he could handle any two humans. He regretted that he had left his battle-axe in Koros' stall
with his other supplies, as an inappropriate item to be
carrying about the city streets.

This next temple, he saw, was the most bizarre he
had yet approached; where the others had been built
of black basalt or marble or similar stones, this one

was constructed of gleaming obsidian, arranged with sharp, broken edges projecting wherever possible. It was a high, narrow building, surmounted by a pointed dome, and fronted with a small forecourt. The court was perhaps twenty feet square, with obsidian walls eight or nine feet high around it, and a pair of large openwork steel gates at the front.

Garth wondered where, even in this volcanic country, they had found so much obsidian. Further, how had they constructed a building from it? Obsidian was not suited for construction purposes. It must be a facade, he decided, covering up a more ordinary structure.

The gates did not spell out the name of the deity here, nor was it carved in the walls. Instead, the gates were made of twisted, jagged spikes welded together into portals resembling a wall of thorns. There were no handles, and from each of the large spikes projected dozens of needlelike smaller spikes. Where there was no room for these, the metal had sawtoothed edges.

Even in his anger, these gates gave Garth pause; there was nowhere that he could touch them without risking injury. The points appeared razor-sharp. Appropriate, he thought, for the god of sharpness, should there be one. He wondered what sort of insane cult would build such a thing.

He ran the broken stump of his sword through one of the gaps in the glittering tangle of sharpened steel, and pulled; to his surprise, the gate opened readily. He had expected it to be locked for the night.

He stepped through, and noticed for the first time that the courtyard was paved, or perhaps lined, with obsidian, arranged with all possible points and sharp edges projecting upwards, and left thoroughly uneven. Walking on it was difficult, and even through the thick soles of his boots he could feel the knife-edged volcanic glass cutting into his feet.

He made his way gingerly across the broken expanse to the door of the temple building; it, like the gates, was a web of steel spikes. He shoved at it with the broken sword; a long needle-pointed projection caught his finger and gashed it painfully, but the door swung open. It, like the gate, was unlocked. As it began to move, Garth suddenly realized that the night was not silent; somewhere, several voices were wailing, as if in great pain or abject despair. As the door opened wider, he knew it was coming from inside this temple; it swept out over him.

Light also assaulted him, a sharp white light totally unlike the yellow of torchlight or the red of a fire. This glare was tinged with blue, like the flash of lightning. He ignored it. He was in no mood for caution. When the door stopped swinging, he stepped through.

He was at the bottom of a set of uneven steps, steep even for an overman, and all crooked; he clambered up them into the temple proper.

It was a single vast room, twenty feet wide, a hundred long, and at least fifty feet high, not counting the interior of the dome. The walls were jagged, rough stone, and seemed to lean inward; Garth was not sure if this were some illusion, or whether the room actually narrowed toward the top. The floor was broken, uneven flagstones, but far more negotiable than the obsidian courtyard. The light came from dozens of flares that blazed on one wall, burning with a vivid, painfully bright light and casting sharp-edged black shadows of the score or so of worshippers who knelt before the altar. The shadows did not move; the flares had none of the comforting flicker of more ordinary flames.

The altar itself was a single chunk of granite; behind it stood three black-robed priests, faces hidden by hoods, and on it lay a naked young woman—perhaps only a girl. Garth was a poor judge of human age or maturity.

The central priest held a long narrow-bladed dirk clutched in his fist; the man to his right held a coiled whip, and the third priest held a loop of ordinary rope.

The wailing came from the worshippers; the priests and the girl on the altar were making no sound that Garth could detect.

Behind the priests, carved on the end wall of the temple, Garth glimpsed the image of a smiling naked woman, hands outstretched toward the altar; the shadows of the priests made it hard to distinguish details. Although the image he had seen in the marketplace had been robed and held weapons, he recognized the face and evil smile of the idol; this was Sai, goddess of pain and suffering.

No one was paying any attention to him. He put down his sack of bloodstained Aghadite gold and strode forward across the shattered floor. As he drew nearer, he saw that the priest's dirk had blood upon its tip, and that the naked girl's body was laced with narrow, shallow cuts. He wondered whether the ceremony was to have ended with her death as a human sacrifice, or whether she would merely have been tortured and released; it was clear from her face that she was not a willing participant. He grinned at the prospect of frustrating these sadists. It would be almost as satisfying as killing Aghadites. Still, he hoped he could avoid killing any, not only because he disliked causing unnecessary deaths, but because he did not want the Aghadites to have the satisfaction.

He was even with the back of the small crowd of worshippers, now; he bellowed as the priest lowered the dagger for another cut. He did not want the girl injured further. After all, she was what he had found upon the altar, and therefore what he was to take back to the Forgotten King. He wondered what the old man would make of her.

Startled, the priest stopped his motion; the crowd's wailing wavered.

"Drop that knife or die, priest!" He kicked aside a kneeling figure that blocked his path and stepped up to the altar; his broken sword was still in his hand and, although scarcely the weapon it once was, it could still cut. It should, he thought, be adequate for dealing with this bunch.

The priest backed away, but the dirk remained in his hand.

Garth drew his own dagger, which was now longer than his sword, and also longer than the priest's blade, having been made for an overman rather than a mere human. He saw that the sacrificial victim was tied to the altar and cut away the ropes.

Immediately she rolled off the altar, sprang up, and started toward the door; Garth caught her before she had gone more than a single step, dropping the stump of his sword but keeping the dagger ready in case a priest or worshipper should attack. His hand gripped her arm, none too gently, as he said, "Wait. You go with me." She winced, and nodded.

The wailing had ceased altogether; the worshippers knelt in shocked silence. The man who held the dirk, presumably the high priest, cried out, "Blasphemer! The girl is our sacrifice!"

Garth grinned broadly. "No longer, priest." It occurred to him that, had he come at a different time, he might have found something entirely different on the altar, something more to the Forgotten King's liking, and added, "I was sent to fetch what lay upon this stone."

He was actually quite pleased he had arrived when he did; the girl was obviously an unwilling victim.

"You have made a mistake! She is nothing but a sacrifice!"

"What else was upon your altar?"

"Who sent you? Some wizard?"

"I come from the temple of Aghad." Garth was perfectly willing to stir up discord as long as it was directed properly, and in fact he spoke the literal truth.

"What do they want with our ceremonial weapons?"

"No one said anything about any weapons."

"There is no need for subterfuge; you came for the whip and dagger. What . . ." The priest's question was cut off abruptly as Garth, releasing the girl, leapt over the altar and grabbed the man by the throat.

"Priest, you talk too much. Give me the dagger." Garth marvelled at the man's stupidity; it had been remarkably cooperative of him to reveal so quickly what was ordinarily kept on the altar.

The priest made a desperate and futile stab at Garth's side with the dirk; it was turned by the overman's mail. Garth's own dagger was not turned. He ran it through the priest's wrist, and the fingers sprang open. The dirk clattered to the floor.

The priest who held the whip suddenly came to life; like everyone else in the temple, he had been watching motionlessly, too confused and surprised to do anything about this intrusion, but now he lunged forward and came up holding the dropped dagger.

He stabbed at Garth; the thrust was parried, and the man retreated. Meanwhile, the high priest struggled in Garth's unbreakable grip. His hands clutched at Garth's arm, impeding his movement as his fellow made another thrust, and the dirk missed Garth by mere inches. Annoyed, Garth flung the high priest aside; he struck the wall at the feet of his idol, fell limply to the floor, and lay still. With one disposed of, Garth turned to face the other, who had assumed a proper knife-fighting stance despite his hampering robe.

The third priest leapt upon Garth from behind and swung a loop of rope around his neck.

To the priests, this seemed to give them an advantage; to the overman, it was a petty annoyance. Keeping his dagger in his left hand, he reached up with his right, and closed it on the would-be strangler's throat. As the man tried to pull his rope taut, Garth's grip tightened, digging in with both the thumbs on his right hand.

He misjudged the strength of the man's neck; there was a loud crack, and the priest tumbled from his back, eyes already glazing over. As he fell, his head struck the edge of the granite altar with another, similar crack of breaking bone. There could be no doubt that he was dead.

The remaining priest froze; he was facing the wall of flares, so that the lower half of his face was visible despite his overhanging cowl, and as Garth watched his mouth fell open and the blood drained from his jaw. The dagger and whip dropped from shaking fingers.

"Girl! Get them!" Garth's voice was sharp, and the girl hastened to obey; she had been watching the fight, and any thought of failing to cooperate with her saviour—or new captor; she was as yet unsure which Garth actually was—had vanished. She hurried around the end of the altar, ignoring the effect of the rough floor on her bare feet, and snatched up the weapons. The lone conscious priest stepped back out of her way without protest.

"Go wait on the steps. And," he added in a bellow, "any who hinders her will die!" Again the girl obeyed immediately, and the worshippers made no move to stop her. Garth followed her at a more leisurely pace, pausing to pick up his sword hilt from in front of the altar.

At the top of the steps he sheathed his dagger and picked up the sack of coins he had deposited there upon entering; he paused, considering, and glanced at the girl's feet. They were bleeding, and the obsidian courtyard was far worse than the shattered flagstones of the temple. He handed her the sack, telling her to hold it; she accepted it and nearly dropped it, astonished at its weight. He then put his arm around her middle and picked her up, dagger, whip, gold and all. After some adjustment he found a position that was fairly comfortable for both of them, though he suspected his mail was scratching her bare skin more than she cared to admit, and strode down the steps out of sight of the worshippers of Sai, who had silently watched the entire proceeding without making a move in his direction.

CHAPTER FOURTEEN

The door and gates were still open, which was gratifying; he was heartily tired of portals that closed themselves. With the added weight of the girl on his shoulder, the jagged obsidian cut even deeper into the soles of his boots. When he finally stepped out onto the pavement of the Street of the Temples, he could feel that one puncture had gone clear through and, although his foot was not bleeding, the boot was plainly ruined. He sighed. The whole escapade in the temple of Sai had been a satisfactory way of working off his rage, leaving him reasonably calm, but it was sure to have unpleasant repercussions and results, of which ruined boots were only the first and least.

Adventuring seemed to be hard on feet and footwear; his first errand for the Forgotten King had destroyed a good pair of boots and various makeshift replacements and given him an assortment of burns, cuts, and blisters.

He found the street he had followed before and turned off the Street of the Temples, heading for the Inn of the Seven Stars. When he was out of sight of the avenue and presumably reasonably safe from immediate pursuit, he sheathed the stump of his sword and lifted the girl down off his shoulder. There was no reason to wear himself out carrying her; she should be able to walk well enough. Besides, it would be difficult to converse while carrying her, and he had several questions.

She seemed glad enough to be on her feet again; she brushed herself off slightly, making small yelps of pain whenever her hands accidentally disturbed the blood clotting on the dozens of cuts that crisscrossed her belly and breasts. She looked with dismay at the wounds, and at the reddish smudges left by Garth's hands, which were still damp with the blood of the various victims of the cult of Aghad. Garth guessed that the cuts must be very painful, though she did not whimper or complain, but stood, waiting for him to speak.

"Follow me; we are going to my inn."

She nodded, but hesitated.

"What's the matter?" he asked.

"My lord, I am naked." This was obvious, of course, but Garth had given it no thought.

"Is that bad?"

"It . . . it is not proper. I cannot walk the streets naked."

Garth sighed. "You will have to; I have no spare garments with me."

"But everyone will stare!"

Although not out of any concern for her modesty, he found that argument was the most effective she could have used; Garth did not want to draw attention to himself. Although he had thought he was safe from recognition by the followers of Tema or Andhur Regvos, the Aghadites knew that he was responsible for the desecrations of both those temples as well as their own, and he had made a public display of himself just now in the temple of Sai. If he maintained a casual manner and walked the streets openly, he doubted that most Dûsarrans would pay any attention to him; they hadn't done so previously. However, if an unclothed female was sufficiently unusual to attract stares, he could not afford to be seen with one. Someone might well point him out to Aghadites or followers of Sai who might otherwise have missed him.

Accordingly, he removed his belt, peeled off his suit of mail, and began untying the gambeson underneath. He stopped abruptly when he noticed the girl backing away apprehensively.

"What's wrong with you? I'm just going to give you this to wear; I have nothing else available."

"Oh!" The girl calmed visibly; Garth stripped off the quilted garment and handed it to her, standing uncomfortably in little but his soft leather breeches and natural coat of thin black fur. She accepted it, but then stood motionless, watching Garth don his armor once more.

He looked at her, wondering why she was just standing there.

She burst out, "You're furry!"

"You're not," he replied. "Put on the gambeson; this night air is cool."

"Oh!" she exclaimed again. Flushing slightly, she managed to pull the oversized padded shirt over her head; Garth noticed that she winced in pain as she worked it down over her body, and realized that it must be rubbing against the cuts inflicted by the sacrificial dagger. It must be horribly painful and irritating, yet she gave only a single quiet squeak, then began struggling with the ties at either side intended to keep the garment tight on the wearer's body. The lower hem, which came to slightly below Garth's waist, reached her knees; it not only covered her nakedness, but completely hid the cuts, which was doubtless all to the good if it didn't hurt her too much.

When she had the gambeson arranged as best she could manage, she asked, "Are all overmen furry?"

Garth, still struggling to get the mail settled comfortably, took his time about answering and limited his reply to, "Yes."

When he had the iron links arranged so that they did not scratch or chafe intolerably, he turned his attention to the girl. It was fortunate, he thought, that he had had his armor and accoutrements dyed or painted black, to decrease visibility. The gambeson's quilting did not show in the dim light, where it might have in a lighter-hued fabric. From a distance one might well mistake it for more ordinary attire—if not for the fact that it only reached the girl's knees. Still, it was better than nothing. He picked up the dagger and whip, stuffed them in the sack with the gold, and swung it over his shoulder.

"Good. Come on."

The girl obeyed, as he led the way back toward the Inn of the Seven Stars. He kept to the shadows and back alleys as much as possible and looped around the marketplace, giving it a wide berth. These tactics were fairly successful; the few passersby they encountered gave them no more than a passing glance.

This journey was hard on Garth's nerves; he kept expecting to hear someone shouting out the presence of the wanted thief and committer of sacrilege. Eventually, however, the pair reached the inn without being accosted, and crept through the archway into the stable. Dugger the stable-boy was still on duty; Garth motioned for him to be silent, and he assented with a grin and a nod.

Koros was curled up asleep but still occupied most of his stall, which had been designed with smaller animals in mind. Garth stepped in and settled comfortably on the straw on the other side, beside his supplies and the concealed loot from his first two thefts; with only a slight hesitation the girl obeyed his gesture and sat down beside him. He found a sponge in his pack, wetted it with water from one of his canteens—he would have to fill them soon—and said, "Get that thing off so I can clean your wounds."

She obeyed, untying the gambeson and pulling it over her head; despite the delicacy she displayed in this, Garth saw that several of the cuts beneath had been rubbed raw by the garment and were bleeding anew. He began washing away the blood and dirt as gently as he could but she still twitched away occasionally when the contact of water or the pressure of his hand stung her.

As he attended to this task he asked, "Now, girl, who are you?"

"My name is Frima." The girl's voice was high, but not unpleasant; she spoke timidly.

"Are you Dûsarran?"

"Yes, of course!"

"How did you come to be a sacrifice to Sai? Are you one of her devotees?"

"Oh, no! I worship Tema. The priests of Sai kidnapped me from my father's shop last night."

"How is it that the ceremony was being held at that hour? I had heard that only the cults of Tema and Andhur Regvos lived by night."

"That's right; that's why the sacrifices to Sai are—ow!—always at night."

"I do not understand."

"The cult of Sai is secret; its members do not—ooh! —do not admit their allegiance. Therefore, they hold all their ceremonies at night, when—oogh!—when the darkness provides cover, and when they will not be missed from their daytime occupations."

"Are the other cults equally secretive?"

"The day-dwelling cults are, yes. Ouch. That's part of why the night-dwellers avoid them; would you want to associate with someone who worships pain—ow! Damn them!—or disease? It is said that many of the day-dwellers worship no gods at all, but that's not much better, and there is no way of knowing which are which."

Garth finished his cleaning, and rummaged in his pack for the pouch of healing herbs he carried. "Your city has a very complicated way of life. Are kidnappings such as yours common?" He located the herbs, and worked some into the sponge.

"Oh, yes; people disappear all the time."

"Your overlord allows this?" He began rubbing the herbs gently along each cut; the girl cooperated by remaining as still as she could while she answered.

"There is nothing he can do. The bodies are never found, and there is no way of knowing which cult is responsible."

"Then why does he not destroy all those cults that practice human sacrifice?"

"Oh, that must never happen! The gods themselves have chosen Dûsarra; the Dark Gods *must* have temples here, or there would be a great disaster! Besides, nobody knows which cults have human sacrifices and which don't."

"It would seem obvious," Garth said as he finished spreading on the healing compound, "that the cult of The God Whose Name Is Not Spoken must practice human sacrifice; cannot the overlord at least destroy that one? I have noticed that even in Dûsarra most people want nothing to do with that god."

"There is no cult to destroy; no one worships the Final God but a single old priest. The god himself calls sacrifices to his temple, and no one who has entered the shrine has ever been seen again, except the priest. No one knows what is inside; no traces are ever found. No clothing, no bodies. Whenever a Dûsarran wishes to die, for whatever reason, he merely goes to the god's temple, and when the god is not satisfied with the number of suicides, he turns men mad, so they go to the temple without knowing what they are doing. The overlord would not dare to harm the priest or the temple, for then he himself might be called."

Garth made no further comment on the subject; instead, he said, "I am afraid I cannot properly bandage your wounds; they are too many, and I have not the necessary cloth. I hope they will not trouble you." He sat back to consider his situation, and the information Frima had just given him.

Frima, hesitantly, asked a question of her own. "Who are you? Why did you rescue me?"

"I am Garth of Ordunin, and I came to Dûsarra to steal whatever I found on the seven altars. You were on the altar of Sai, so I am stealing you, and will take you back to Skelleth with me."

"Are you going to ravish me?"

Garth looked at her in surprise. The question explained her behavior when he had stripped off his gambeson for her use, but the ignorance it implied was startling. "I couldn't if I wanted to. We are different species, as different as Koros, here, and an alley cat. Overmen take no interest in anything but overwomen."

"Oh." He was unable to see her blush in the darkness, and would not have understood its significance if he had.

"I am taking you to Skelleth because you were on the altar of Sai; I have no other interest in you." He wondered if her sexual expectations were justified by her appearance; she seemed fairly clean and healthy, with little excess fat but no bones showing, but beyond that he had no more idea of whether she was attractive than a bull would have. Overwomen were as noseless, flat-chested and furry as himself; they relied on scent for stimulation, not appearance, and Frima held no more interest for him than any other animal. He supposed men would like her, although her chest seemed rather overdone even for a human.

She was silent for a few seconds, and then burst out, "I don't want to go to Skelleth! Besides, if you're from Ordunin, why are you taking me somewhere else? And where is Ordunin, anyway? And Skelleth?"

"Ordunin is in the Northern Waste. Skelleth is in Eramma. I have undertaken this task for someone who dwells in Skelleth. I care very little whether you want to go or not, and I suggest you not argue. It was not specified that I bring you back *alive*." Garth was not seriously annoyed, but merely wanted quiet to think in and spoke harshly to silence the girl. His ploy succeeded; Frima shut up and shrank back into the straw.

He had not intended to kill any of the followers of Sai, though he was repulsed by the use of torture and human sacrifice; he hoped the high priest, scum that he was, survived. He regretted snapping the other priest's neck, not so much out of respect for the life lost as because it would undoubtedly please the cult of Aghad. It had been inevitable, though; he had been attacked, and had responded appropriately. Besides, the man's death had cowed the others very nicely.

He had plundered four of the seven altars; three remained, two of them on the Street of the Temples. The robberies of the temples of Tema and Andhur Regvos had not gone particularly well, but would produce no definite identifications; on the other hand, several devotees of Sai and Aghad now knew him on sight, and the Aghadites knew his name as well. Frima claimed that both cults were secret societies, and presumably would not therefore spread their information about, but on the other hand might well try to dispose of him themselves.

This whole affair was getting very complicated.

He had intended to use his room in the inn in the normal manner and sleep in a comfortable bed; he had not done so previously only because he had collapsed from fatigue before he made it that far. However, now that he was definitely a hunted fugitive, even if not readily identifiable to all his pursuers, he decided that that would be a mistake. He would remain here in this stable. It was uncomfortable and uncivilized, but it was where Koros was, and where his loot and his weapons were. No one would be able to sneak up on him while he was guarded by the warbeast. Furthermore, although a siege might be effective, no frontal assault here would be able to defeat both him and his beast; it would be impossible to pour men into the stall in large enough numbers. He knew, with neither false modesty nor overconfidence, that he was capable of handling at least three human warriors at once, and that Koros could deal with twice that number. In a room at the inn, half a dozen men might slip in and kill him; in the stable, with the warbeast beside him, those same men wouldn't have a chance.

Not only that, but by keeping Frima here he avoided any inconvenient questions as to what a human female was doing with an overman—quite aside from her attire.

That reminded him of her current state of undress; he recalled that somewhere in his bundle of supplies he had a spare tunic, intended for social occasions, that would doubtless serve her better than his gambeson. Even should she fail to appreciate it, at the very least he would have padding for his mail once more; it was digging ferociously into his back where he leaned against the wall of the stall.

He reached for his bundle of supplies, and discovered that he could no longer see it; the moon was down, having sunk beneath the horizon while he mused, and the dawn was still an hour or two away. He reached for his flint and steel, only to be reminded by their absence that he had surrendered them to the priests of Andhur Regvos.

Well, the inn would have lanterns, or torches, or some form of portable illumination. "Wait here," he ordered the girl, as he stepped out of the stall.

There was very slightly more light in the stableyard than in the stall, a peculiar reddish light. He looked up, wondering why starlight should be such a color, and discovered that no stars were visible. Clouds had blown up out of the east, and most of the sky was overcast; the reddish glow was the reflected fires of the active volcanoes and the city's torchlit market. The strip of clear sky to the west narrowed as he watched, a vanishing black gap between the stable wall and the encroaching red-gray clouds.

He shrugged. A little rain never hurt anyone. He strode out the arch to the tavern adjoining.

The taproom was not crowded; half a dozen dark-robed customers sat scattered about among the tables. There was no sign of the two serving maids or their brother, but only a middle-aged woman of unhealthy appearance, carrying away empty mugs and replacing them with full ones.

"Ho, there."

She glanced his way, but did not pause until she had dealt with her current batch of ale; that properly distributed, she wound her way through the chairs, shoving them under appropriate tables as she went, until she stood in front of the overman.

"And how may I aid you, sir?"

"Have you a lantern? I would tend to my mount, but the light is inadequate."

"A lantern? Not for sale."

"Could I borrow one, then? I can pay."

She shrugged. "As you please." She departed, winding her way across the room again to vanish through a door at the back. A moment later she emerged again, a shuttered lantern in her hand. Garth took it, thanked her, dropped a coin in her palm and left; he failed to notice the steady gaze of one of the patrons studying him, and was out of sight through the stable's arch when the same man also departed, walking quickly in the direction of the temple of Tema.

CHAPTER FIFTEEN

Frima didn't think much of the tunic. It was scarely longer than the gambeson, and she insisted there was a cold draft on her shins despite the fact that Garth could not feel a breath of air. Further, it was embroidered in red and gold, as was appropriate for a Prince of Ordunin on formal occasions, and she seemed to consider such adornment a sign of decadence. She pointed out that no Dûsarran wore any garment with more than a single color to it, and although the midnight-blue of the tunic was perfectly acceptable, she found the bright trimmings utterly appalling.

Garth let her complain, so long as she wore the

thing and returned his padding. He pointed out that he preferred to have her look like a foreigner; she replied that she hadn't known foreigners were so tasteless.

Despite her complaints, Frima donned the tunic. Garth, meanwhile, returned his gambeson to its proper place beneath his mail, tossed aside the hilt of his sword and its now-useless scabbard, and tied his battle-axe to his back. He wished he had thought to bring a second cloak. It was something he would do on any future adventures; that, and a spare pair of boots. He felt very exposed wandering the streets wearing armor openly, as if he were inviting attack; it seemed though that he had no choice. He also thought that carrying the axe was inviting trouble, but it was undoubtedly safer than going unarmed.

Besides, he relied on the fact that the humans would not expect a fugitive to walk openly in their midst.

He had no real plans at this point; he still had three temples to rob, but he was tired and hungry and had a captive to take care of. It occurred to him that he should have gotten food while in the tavern getting the lantern. He stood, and leaned over the door of the stall, peering through the arch at the street.

A pedestrian passed by, and a second later an ox-cart followed. There was a hint of dawn in the eastern sky, visible only as a slightly paler shade of gray in the cloud-cover, but present nonetheless. Dugger the stable-boy was gone, and presumably one of his daytime compatriots would show up at any minute; Garth had no desire to waste more money bribing them to silence as he had Dugger. He decided he did not care to venture forth just now, and instead found his meager remaining supply of provisions, left over from his journey.

Frima looked dubiously at the strips of dried meat and the handful of berries he offered her, but took them and ate them; he ate his fill likewise, and washed the unappetizing fare down with the metallic-tasting water from his one remaining canteen, leaving enough for his prisoner to do the same. He was surprised when she made no complaint; it was just as well, though, as she would probably be eating more of the same throughout the long ride back to Skelleth.

His hunger assuaged, he sat back and contemplated whether he would do better to tackle the remaining shrines by daylight or at night; after some thought, he decided he simply didn't have enough information, and asked Frima her opinion.

"Would it be safer to rob the altars of P'hul and Bheleu by night or day, girl?"

Frima, who had said nothing since she stopped complaining about her new garb, answered, "I don't know."

"The worshippers live by day, but their ceremonies are held at night, correct?"

"Yes."

"What of the priests? When do they sleep?"

"I don't know. Perhaps they have no need to sleep at all."

"Everyone, human or overman, needs to sleep."

It seemed plain the girl was to be of no use in deciding. It appeared to him that the priests must sleep during the day, and that therefore that would be the optimum time to make his attempt, but if he were seen abroad in daylight he would be inviting retaliation from the cult of Sai.

Of course, at night he was risking the revenge of Tema and Andhur Regvos.

It was no use; he was unable to decide on such a basis. He considered instead what he would do if he did *not* choose to rob another temple immediately.

Obviously, he would sleep.

Did he want to sleep?

Well, yes, now that the subject came up, he realized he was quite weary and could use a nap. He would take one, and when he woke up he would go rob the next temple.

The matter finally decided, he announced, "We will sleep now." Without waiting to see what Frima thought of this, he stretched himself out as best he could on the straw and fell soundly asleep.

Frima did not immediately follow his example, but instead sat and reviewed the events of the night just ending and the one before it. She had been tending her father's shop while he attended the regular moon-light ceremony at the temple when three large men had entered, claiming a pot they had bought there had a faulty seam; she had known that they were lying, for her father was undoubtedly the best tinker in Dûsarra, but had looked at the pot anyway, and found herself gagged, then grabbed, then bound, and carried off in a sack over one man's shoulder. She had spent the following day in a small, cramped cell somewhere, but had been too frightened to sleep for a long time, even though it was obviously after dawn; when at last she had dozed off, it was to be rudely awakened by the same three men, who removed not merely her bonds but her clothes as well, before dragging her, struggling all the way, to the altar of Sai.

She had known, from the instant that the gag was pressed into her mouth, that she was being kidnapped by one of the day-dweller cults; it was a familiar concept, a traditional childhood fear, suddenly become much too real. She had had no real hope of escape; nobody ever escaped from the temples. Instead she had tried to behave properly, as befit a true follower of the night-goddess and the daughter of the city's best tinker. And then, when the ceremony was well under way and she was paying attention to nothing but the pain from the cutting of the priest's knife, this great red-eyed, bloody-handed monster had appeared and freed her.

She was familiar with overmen; every so often one would come to the shop, to buy a belt-buckle or have a harness repaired, never to buy the pots and kettles that were her father's pride. They spoke rudely and carried swords, and had faces like Death himself—or at least like Bheleu, as represented in the little idols she had seen in the marketplace. She did not like overmen; they were big and dangerous and mysterious, and it was said that they laughed at the gods yet were not struck down, which implied some sorcerous might, although she had never heard of an overman magician.

But then an overman had rescued her, and she sud-

denly owed her life to an inhuman monster. This creature casually snapped a man's neck with one hand and
spoke of killing her as if she were no more than one
of the dogs that prowled the alleys, but then fed and
clothed her and bathed her wounds. He even declined
to rape her; she didn't seriously believe his statement
that he couldn't. She was, in fact, still virgin; the high
priest of Sai was to have ravished her as part of the
sacrificial ceremony, a part that had not yet been
reached when she was rescued. Her three captors had
not dared to usurp the priest's privilege.

Further, Garth spoke to her in a perfectly civil manner, more so than any overman she had met before,
and did not strike her, but merely threatened. Then
when he spoke, he claimed to be from some semi-
mythical wasteland and said that he planned to take
her to someplace in the forbidden land of Eramma,
whether she wanted to go or not. It was all very confusing. Overmen came from the Yprian Coast, and
rode oxen or great horses, not huge black panthers.

She found the whole affair imcomprehensible and
was unsure of her feelings toward Garth. He had kidnapped her, but saved her from death; he had threatened her life, but now lay sleeping peacefully a few
feet away, trusting her with his own life. What was to
prevent her from escaping, or even killing him with his
own weapons? She stood.

A low growl reached her, and she sat down again
very quickly. She had thought that the huge black
beast was asleep, but it was watching her now, its
golden eyes gleaming in the pale morning light that
filtered dimly in. She stared back.

It blinked, then casually lowered its head and appeared to go to sleep once again.

She stared for a moment longer, then relaxed. There
was no point in arguing with the monster. Still thoroughly confused, she settled back, realized that she
was in fact exhausted, and fell asleep.

She slept uneasily, and when Garth had rested
enough to take the edge off his fatigue, he was awakened by her thrashing about. At first he did not
remember his situation very clearly and his hand in-

stinctively went to his axe, but he recalled himself in time to avoid smashing the girl's skull.

It was midmorning; he had slept four or five hours. Frima had not, having kept herself awake until after dawn, and he saw no reason to wake her. Unsettled though she might be, her troubled sleep was probably better for her than no rest at all. Garth suspected it was the discomfort of the dozens of unbandaged slashes that kept her from resting easily; he regretted that he had not been able to bandage them properly —assuming, of course, that she would have allowed it —but at least he had done what he could.

Although he could have used more rest himself, he decided against going back to sleep. Instead he got to his feet and brushed off the straw that stuck to his mail; then he slung his axe on his back, stuffed a sack under his belt and, with a calming word to Koros, left the stall.

Heretofore, all his crimes had been committed at night; he hoped that undertaking his next in broad daylight would make it that much more unexpected. It is to a fugitive's advantage to be unpredictable.

One of the two stable-boys he had spoken with the preceding day sat in the archway, whittling carelessly at a scrap of wood with an old table knife; he showed no sign that he was aware of Garth's presence. That was fine with Garth; for the first time, he gave serious consideration to finding some other way out of the stableyard.

The sun was faintly visible, well up in the eastern sky, but obscured by a layer of cloud. Elsewhere the clouds were thicker, and nowhere was the sky any color but gray. Any lingering glow from the volcanoes was submerged in the more powerful drabness of the daylight. It was not raining, but puddles on the packed dirt showed that it had been while Garth slept.

He looked about, studying anew the double row of stalls, the blank wall, the open arch. There was no exit at ground level except the arch. There was no truly compelling reason not to use it. The stable-boy was certainly no threat in and of himself.

Garth looked at the lad again, who was still intent

on his lackadaisical carving; it was the boy who had been the more belligerent of the two, who had demanded he explain why he carried a sword. It occurred to him that the boy might think it strange that he no longer carried the blade.

Garth decided he did not want the boy to see him. He did not want anyone to see him leaving the stable; he did not want to make his connection with this place any better known than it already was. Quite aside from logic, he was emotionally and intuitively displeased by the idea. His position had become so complicated that its logic was beyond him, and he resolved instead to rely on his instincts. Accordingly, he found himself another way of leaving the stable.

There was no alternative at ground level unless he wanted to knock out a wall; he had not the time to burrow his way out. That left one direction—up. He swung open the broad door of Koros' stall until it stood out perpendicular to its closed position; it projected out from beneath the roof of the stable. He tested its strength; although it was not as solid as he might have desired, it was adequate. Using the door as a stepping-stone, he vaulted upward so that his head, arms, and chest were above the level of the roof's edge; he caught himself, then crawled upward until his full weight rested on the wet red tiles.

He was very pleased to note that he had made the ascent with a minimum of clatter; the lack of his scabbarded sword was an advantage in that respect. He drew himself carefully upright, being sure not to put his full weight upon any part of the roof until he had tested it sufficiently, then surveyed his position.

The roof he was standing on was about ten feet wide and fifty long, sloping toward the stableyard; on the far side of the yard was another virtually identical to it, and the two were connected at either end by a narrow wall, which looked wide and strong enough to walk on if it became necessary—but not if it remained unnecessary. Beyond the other roof was the wall of the upper story or stories of the Inn of the Seven Stars; along the upper edge of the roof he stood on was a blank wall of gray stone, extending upward at least twenty feet. He wondered what it was; he had not noticed from the street what building occupied that position, and the featureless expanse gave no clue. There was no exit in that direction. The wall was too high to leap, and he was not a very good climber.

On the opposite side, the stone wall of the inn was spotted with windows, half a dozen of them, but all, he was happy to see, shuttered; there was no danger of being noticed by the occupants of those rooms, and having his presence on the roof questioned. That wall was lower; the windows were all in a single tier, and he judged the distance between the roof of the stable and the roof of the inn to be no more than a dozen feet, probably less. The inn's roof was constructed of the same tile as that on which he stood, but was much, much steeper, and there were at least two skylights visible between the chimneypots. There was no exit by that route, either. At the one end, beyond the wall, lay the open street. That left only one direction unexplored; he could not see what lay beyond the blank wall at the stable's inner end. Though the upper stories of other buildings were visible beyond, there was a definite gap immediately behind that wall.

He made his way carefully along the sloping surface, trying to avoid dislodging any of the battered tiles, until he stood within a pace of the edge. He peered over and found himself looking into a small enclosed yard, strewn with garbage and half-flooded by the morning's rain. An unpleasant odor drifted faintly to his slit nostrils.

The far side of the yard was filled by a simple two-story structure, apparently an ordinary house; on either hand walls five or six feet high separated it from similar patches of earth, though due to the angle of his vision he could not see much of either, despite the height of his perch. The left-hand yard was, as far as he could see, cleaner than the central one; of the right-hand yard he could not even see that much.

He paused to consider, and glanced back at the stableyard; from his elevated position he could see that the abandoned trough where he had burned his

cloak now held an inch or so of murky rainwater,
black with the ashes of his garment.

There was no reason to bother crossing over to the
right-hand yard; of the other two, both were accessible
from the roof he was on. The central yard spanned
the stable yard and perhaps half of each of the roofed-
over stables; the left-hand yard extended across the
remaining four or five feet.

The left-hand yard would be a longer drop, being
below the higher portion of the roof; therefore, he
made his way to the bottom corner, where the gray
stone of the wall extended out from beneath the red
tiles, lowered himself over the outer edge, and let himself drop.

He landed with a splash, and immediately felt water seeping into his right boot through the puncture
made by the obsidian in the forecourt of Sai's temple;
it was cold and sluggish, probably made up of filthy
mud as much as water. He wished he knew how to
curse, as humans did; he tried muttering the names of
a few gods but it provided no relief, and he growled
instead.

It was hard to judge accurately the depth of the water, because his boots sank into the mud beneath the
weight of his armored body; there was at least an
inch, though.

He slogged across the little court, his boots thrusting
aside decaying fruit peels and muck-coated old bones,
and climbed onto a stone doorstep that rose above the
water; he could feel the water draining slowly from his
ruined boot, leaving a slimy residue and a wet lining.

The door was centered in the wall. There were two
narrow windows on either side, all dark and curtained,
but with their shutters open. That implied that there
was someone somewhere within, but most likely not
in these rearmost rooms. He tried the latch. It yielded,
and he leaned on the door. It did not yield.

A wordless noise of annoyance burst from him. He
leaned harder, letting his left foot fall back into the
befouled water the better to brace himself.

The door still did not yield, and in a burst of anger
Garth lifted his axe over his head and swung it at the

recalcitrant barrier. Splinters flew. He struck again, and felt the blade slice through into the space beyond. The door was not unreasonably thick.

He pulled the axe free and let it dangle loosely in his right fist as he leaned to peer through the crack he had made.

The room beyond was dark, and he could see nothing. He stood back, and swung the axe again; the wood of the door gave, bursting inward, leaving two wide gaps. He slung the axe on his back once again and ripped out the broken wood between the two slits, giving him an opening wide enough to get his hand through. He reached in and, as he had expected, found that the door was barred; the bar lay only a few inches below the opening, and it was no great feat of dexterity to lift it free and let it drop to the floor inside.

It occurred to him that he was making a great deal of noise, yet so far no one had appeared to question him; luck was apparently with him. It did not occur to him that he might have made less noise going in through one of the windows. He worked the latch and pushed on the door again.

It still did not open. He pressed harder, and it bowed inward but remained closed. There were other bars; judging by the way the door bent, one near the top and one near the bottom.

His patience, which had been in very short supply since his embarrassing display of ineffectuality in the temple of Aghad, ran out, and with a roar he freed his axe again and swung it horizontally into the wood. Splinters sprayed, and a large chunk of one of the boards that made up the door snapped off and fell with a loud splash into the murky water. He struck again, with no thought or care as to the effects of his blow, and the blade wedged itself into the wood, scattering more shards. He ripped it free, bringing most of a plank with it, and let it hang from one hand again while the other reached through the greatly enlarged hole.

He could feel the upper bar, but his forearm was not long enough to allow him to dislodge it; he withdrew, then thrust the other hand in, and used the axe to knock the bar away. It fell with even more noise than the first. He felt for the third bar, and hooked it upward with the corner of his weapon; its fall could scarcely be heard. Then, still angry, and with his hand and axe still thrust within, he tried the latch again.

The door opened a few inches.

He withdrew his hand and slammed the door aside; its shaken frame gave way when it struck the wall behind it, and collapsed, twisting out of shape and leaving a disarrayed mass of tangled wood, rather than a door, hanging from the bent hinges.

Ignoring it, Garth stepped inside.

He was in a small kitchen; a stone sink stood against one wall, and tables and cabinets abounded. There was no sign of life, but it was reasonably clean, with no accumulation of dust; the house was not abandoned. Perhaps the owner was deaf; Garth could not imagine any other reason not to investigate such noise as he had just made, if the occupant were there at all and capable of movement.

Perhaps he or she had gone out and not bothered to close the shutters; perhaps he was bedridden. In any case, Garth was not particularly concerned; he had merely wanted some other route out of the stable. He crossed the kitchen, and strode through the open archway that led to a large front room. Unlike the kitchen, this room was the full width of the house, about twenty feet; it was slightly longer than that from front to back, and the low ceiling made it appear even broader. Garth found that he had to stoop. The kitchen had allowed him to stand upright so long as he avoided the beams that supported the upper floor, but this larger room had a plank ceiling.

There was a door in the wall behind him, which he guessed led to a storeroom of some sort beside the kitchen, and along the left-hand wall a stairway led to the upper level. Assorted chairs, rugs, and tables were scattered about; a broad hearth and massive fireplace occupied the right wall. The far side had two wide bow windows, with curtains drawn across them, and a heavy oaken door between.

He crossed to the door, drew the lockbolt, and opened it slightly, peering out; it appeared to be a residential neighborhood, with no shops or public buildings visible. He opened the door and stepped out.

The sun had broken through the clouds; the street was deserted. He closed the door behind him but left it unlocked, and headed to his right, the direction he judged would best bring him to the Street of the Temples.

CHAPTER SIXTEEN

He had been very fortunate in emerging on an empty street; he found few others as he made his way across Dûsarra, but somehow he reached his goal without being accosted. Several people had cast curious gazes in his direction and a mutter of conversation had frequently followed him, but no one had dared to stop him. Now, he strode openly along the Street of the Temples, hoping his luck would hold.

He was approaching a temple, the third from the overlord's palace; it loomed before him, a huge cube of black stone, dotted with dark windows and topped by a broad dome. Seven shallow steps led to its open portals; there were no gates, no courtyard, no indication which deity was worshipped here. He was only a few paces from the bottom step when someone behind him cried, "Hold, overman!"

He hastened his pace, hurrying up the steps; he heard running feet somewhere behind him as he stepped through the doorway into an antechamber.

The room was small, with a wooden floor that gave dangerously beneath his feet, and walls hung with moldering, faded tapestries. He wondered briefly if the place was abandoned; since the daylight cults

were secret, one might have died out without anyone
knowing it.

There was a door in the inner wall with a rusty iron
handle; Garth grabbed it, only to have it crumble in
his grasp. He raised a fist to pound on the door, in
hope that someone would admit him; to his astonishment, the door burst inward at his first blow, its hinges
screaming in protest. Dust flew up in clouds, and a
paroxysm of coughing overtook him, but he managed
to stumble through. As he did, he realized there were
no further sounds of pursuit behind him; instead, a
voice exclaimed in dismay, "We can't go in there!"

He stopped. If he were not pursued, there was no
need for haste. He wiped the dust from his stinging
eyes and looked about.

The door he had entered through stood beside him,
and it was immediately obvious why it had yielded so
quickly; it had been eaten away from within by ter-
mites and rot, so that his blow had merely finished
their work. The latch that had held it remained where
it was, rusted to the frame, and the wood had turned
to powder around it, so that the door's edge now had
a gaping hole in it.

He was in a room perhaps fifteen feet across and
twenty feet long; like the antechamber, and unlike
any of the other temples he had yet visited, it was
floored in wood, wood which sagged visibly at the center beneath the weight of a thick carpet. The walls,
too, were wooden, except for one end; that was stone
and obviously one of the temple's outer walls, since
three narrow windows pierced it, providing the chamber with light.

The room's ceiling was upholstered in silk, silk that
was discolored with half a hundred old and new
stains, that was black with rot in spots. Like the floor,
it sagged in the center. Cobwebs hung from every corner.

There were furnishings; two ornate tables adorned
the far wall, flanking a doorway, and an assortment of
faded, dusty chairs were strewn about.

Over everything hung the smell, the stench of rot,

mold, and decay; Garth suddenly felt quite certain he knew which temple he had entered.

He took a cautious step forward into the room; the floor creaked ominously, and new odors of corruption assailed his nostrils. He put a hand on a wood-panelled wall, only to snatch it away quickly when he felt the wood start to give; like the door, it was riddled by worms and rot. There could be no doubt that this was the shrine of P'hul, goddess of decay.

"Greetings, stranger." The soft voice came from somewhere to his right; the usual guttural Dûsarran accent was modified by a curious lisp. He turned, to see that a gray-robed figure had entered the room.

He started to speak, but stopped as the figure threw back its hood, revealing the reason for the lisp.

"Is something wrong?" The priestess' voice was so-licitous.

"No. I was just startled."

The woman's lower lip was a twisted mass of ooz-ing, festering flesh, and much of her face and neck was swollen and shapeless; one of her hands lacked a finger. Garth recognized the human disease of leprosy and shuddered slightly. His pursuers had had reasons other than religious respect for declining to enter this place.

The priestess smiled, the friendly expression made hideous by her affliction. "Of course. It is customary that the servants of P'hul bear her handiwork upon their flesh, but I suppose it might well startle those not accustomed to such sights. Why have you come? What brings a healthy overman to the temple of decay?" Garth noticed that she was aware of her lisp, and struggled particularly hard to be sure she pronounced the name of her goddess correctly. He felt a twinge of pity.

"I was merely curious."

"I am surprised. We see few strangers here. How may I help to satisfy your curiosity?"

"Tell me of your goddess, if you would." Garth was not particularly interested in learning about P'hul, but he wanted time to think, and guessed that the priest-ess, absorbed as she was with her beliefs, would be

quite willing to talk for hours about them with only
minimal encouragement. Where he would have raised
suspicion by questioning her on more mundane matters, he was sure that in the enthusiasm of the true be-
liever she would not find anything strange in his
willingness to listen to endless blather about her religion.

"If you wish, gladly! I am sure you know the basic
nature of P'hul; she is the cause and essence of all disease and decay throughout our world. She ages us all,
she makes us easy prey for death, so that the old will
make way for the young. She turns the leaves from
green to brown, pulls them from the trees, and makes
them rot, so that they will feed the earth. She eats
away fruit, that the seeds within may flourish. By
plague and disease, she removes the unfit and un-
worthy. The worms of the earth and the lowly insects
serve her, devouring all that she gives them, and in
turn they feed the birds of the sky and the beasts of
the field. She is the handmaiden of death."

As the priestess spoke, her words distorted by her
lisp, Garth thought back over recent events; it struck
him suddenly that he had been behaving recklessly,
almost idiotically, since leaving the temple of Aghad.
Marching openly into the temple of Sai had been foolish, even if it had allowed him to save an innocent
life. He had not planned well there; even his fight
with the priests had been mismanaged, as he should
have been able to overpower all three without killing
any.

"There are those who say that death is the great
evil of our world," the priestess went on, "and that if
P'hul serves him, then she must likewise be evil. That
is not so; death would exist regardless of P'hul. The
goddess readies us for his touch; is it not better to die
old and weary, than to be cut down while still healthy
and vigorous?"

His behavior this morning had been even more er-
ratic. There had been no reason to go leaping about
on the roof, smashing down the doors of unsuspecting
citizens, and so forth. He had merely been responding
to the repressed anger that still seethed within him,

using up as much energy as possible and finding excuses to destroy anything handy.

"Knowing that one must die after a set number of years, is it not better to know that death will come as the end of a decline, a surcease from decay, than to see it strike abruptly while one is still strong? Our lives are thus in balance, with the ascent from infancy countered by the descent into senescence. Aal, the Eir-Lord of growth, is P'hul's twin and counter; neither could exist without the other. Aal dominates our youth, P'hul our age."

Obviously, he was still resentful of the helplessness he had felt in the temple of Aghad.

"In order that there be growth, there must be decay; for there to be new, the old must make way, else the world would be buried beneath growing things."

It was plain that his effective exile from his homeland at the hands of the Baron of Skelleth, through that stupid oath he had so foolishly taken, still rankled.

"Yet still, even granting the necessity of decay, why should we worship the goddess?"

Buried still deeper, he knew, was anger at the Forgotten King, who treated him like a foolish child and manipulated him like a marionette, and at the Wise Women of Ordunin, the trusted oracle that had first sent him to Skelleth.

"Because we see the underlying beauty in her works; because we perceive that decay brings peace, and that contentment can be found therein. She provides an end to struggling against our inevitable fate, and a surcease from care."

All, of course, were symptoms of his anger at his own helplessness, his resentment of his insignificance in the cosmos; it was his inability to reshape the world as he chose that underlay his rage at all these manifestations of his lack of omnipotence.

"Every farmer prays to Aal; every parent of growing children worships him. He has no need of the service of such lowly creatures as ourselves amid this flood of adulation. Yet without his sister he would be nothing, and we choose to give her the recognition she deserves, as best we can, in response to her marks upon us."

Early in the priestess' lisping dissertation, she and Garth had both seated themselves upon the nearest chairs; the priestess had ignored the cloud of dust that rose from the cushions, and Garth had tried to do the same even as he hoped that the moldering seat would support his weight. Now the servant of P'hul leaned forward, her chair creaking beneath her, and asked, "Do you have any questions?"

"I . . ." Garth had not yet given any thought to the matter on hand, that being how he was to rob the altar; he stalled, asking a question he was only vaguely interested in. "I have heard that this is the Thirteenth Age of the world, the Age of Decay, and as such it is ruled by P'hul. Could you explain this? Do not all the gods prevail over their own concerns in every age?"

"Yes, of course they do. The ages of the world are little more than a theory worked out by the theologians, philosophers, and astrologers, yet they seem to apply in some ways. I do not understand how they are determined, but it is said that certain signs mark each era. Our own age has been one of declining population, fading wealth, and loss of knowledge, and thus is credited as the Age of P'hul, since these are the symptoms of a decay of mankind—and overmankind —as a whole, just as P'hul's diseases cause the decay of individuals. The theologians say that this is because during this age P'hul is at the height of her power, while those gods equal to or greater than herself are resting, or somehow weakened. Decay progresses faster than growth; but there is still growth, and when this age ends the balance between P'hul and Aal will be restored, and some other deity will temporarily rise above the cosmic balance.

"The astrologers say that the age is ending even now; that the Fourteenth Age may in fact have already begun, or if not it will soon arrive."

That caught Garth's attention; months earlier, the Forgotten King had told him that it was hopeless to try and halt the spread of death and decline while the Age of P'hul lasted. If it were in truth ending, perhaps there were better times ahead, an era in which great things could be accomplished.

"What will the Fourteenth Age be? What god will predominate?"

"I do not know. The Twelfth Age was the Age of Aghad, marked by great wars and great betrayals, and much of the world's history was lost in that period, which lasted much longer than the three centuries of P'hul's dominance, so that although scholars may know something of the Eleventh Age, I do not. Thus I cannot see any pattern. Perhaps it is time for one of the Eir, the Lords of Life, to flourish; although I serve a Lady of the Dûs, I would not regret such a change."

"Might not any god rule? I have heard of gods who were not of the Dûs, nor, I believe, of the Eir."

"Such gods, if they exist, are but lesser beings—except for Dagha, of course. There are the seven Dûs, the seven Eir, and the God of Time who created them all; these are the fifteen great gods, and you may be sure that one of these will represent the world's new age."

"This is the Thirteenth Age; the Fourteenth is soon to begin; but there are only fifteen of these higher gods. What will happen when each has ruled for an age?"

"Perhaps they will start over."

Garth sat back and considered that. The whole system sounded rather haphazard; ages of varying length, in no known order? Only fifteen possible rulers? Interesting as it might be, and despite the seeming appropriateness of describing the last three centuries as an age of decay and the period ending in the Racial Wars as an age of hatred, he decided the whole system was just another human exercise in meaningless theorizing. After all, men could not even prove the existence of a single one of their myriad deities; how, then, could any trust be put in a system based on those gods? Besides, if this was currently the Thirteenth Age, then long ago there must have been a First Age; what came before that? He shook his head.

"I am confused. Perhaps you could show me your temple while I digest this new knowledge."

"If you wish." The priestess rose; Garth followed her example, pleased that she was being so cooperative. Any tour of the temple must surely include its altar.

The gray-robed woman led him through a creaking, cobwebbed door into a dim wood-floored passage hung with ragged, decaying tapestries; he was surprised to see several doors opening to either side. This temple was much more elaborate than some.

"These are the study chambers of our scholars," his guide explained. She opened a door, apparently at random, revealing a small room, little more than a cell, lined with shelves that sagged beneath the weight of hundreds of books, scrolls, and papers, and illuminated by a single miniscule window. A narrow desk stood in the center, with a single rickety chair behind it; more papers were spread out upon it, held in place by a human skull that served as a paperweight.

"The skull is just a reminder of the mortality of mankind," the priestess explained.

"How is it that your . . . that you maintain such scholars? I have seen no sign of such learning elsewhere in Dûsarra."

"It is the way of our faith. The more we know of the world, the more we know of the gods who created it; and the more we know of the gods, the better we are able to serve our goddess. I have heard that there are many scholars among the followers of Aghad, though perhaps that is more from a wish to harm mankind than to serve the gods; and there is a splendid library in the temple of Tema. The priests of Regvos, of course, are unable to read. The priests of Bheleu have not the patience for study. Of the cults of Sai and the Final God I know nothing."

As she spoke the priestess led her guest away from the uninhabited scholar's cubicle, closing the door behind her. At the end of the passage, ignoring another corridor that ran perpendicularly to the first, she started up a narrow spiral staircase of rusty iron that swayed unsteadily beneath the weight of the two. Garth inquired where the bypassed corridor went.

"The dormitory," she replied.

"Have you some reason not to show me that?"

"I did not think it would interest you; our accommodations are simple. Besides, most of my fellow servants of P'hul are asleep at present, and I did not wish to disturb them. Are we not entitled to our rest and privacy, as much as ordinary people? Our diseases make us outcasts, but we are still human."

"Of course; I meant no offense. Your ceremonies are at night, then?"

"Oh, yes. The Lords of Dûs are, after all, the dark gods; all are nocturnal, whatever the habits of their worshippers." As she said this she emerged from the shaky spiral and waited for the overman to join her.

They stood in a fair-sized antechamber, its far wall dominated by a vast double door; either end was of wood, hung with rotting remnants of cloth so far gone in decay that Garth was unsure whether they had originally been banners, tapestries, or something else. The staircase was in a curved niche in the rear wall, which was of unadorned black basalt, pierced by three narrow lancet windows. The priestess crossed the room with an assured, easy stride, which Garth took note of. The woman might be diseased, but as yet the sickness had not seriously weakened her; she moved as well as most humans. Garth could not guess her age; she was well out of adolescence, beyond doubt, and had not yet acquired the white hair and stooped posture of extreme age, but beyond that he could not see any indication of her years. The ruination of her countenance erased any wrinkles that might otherwise have provided a clue.

She swung open the great doors and the pair stepped into the chamber beyond.

Garth found it necessary to hold his breath until the dust had subsided somewhat.

The chamber seemed vast, larger than it actually was; it extended up the full remaining height of the temple and included the entire inside of the dome. It was approximately square, about forty feet on a side, but its dimensions were distorted by smoke and dust swimming thick in the stagnant air. Dim colored light seeped through dirt-caked stained glass, painting murky patterns on the worn wooden floor and on the intricately carved railings that adorned three tiers of balconies. These extended completely around all sides. A brighter patch of untinted light flooded the center of the room, pouring from a ring of windows at the base of the dome; in the middle of this circle stood the altar, Garth saw hazily. The brilliant sunlight lit it in a blaze of splendor, but simultaneously obscured it behind a wall of equally well-lit cobwebs, incense smoke, and drifting dust.

The altar was a broad, square platform, raised two or three feet off the floor, built of carven wood, its sides upholstered in silk, its edges clad in corroded copper thick with verdigris; the top had strips of faded, moldering carpeting along each side, and a square of plain mahogany in the center.

There was nothing upon it except a thick layer of dust.

Garth stared at it resentfully.

"This, of course, is the temple sanctuary. It is here that we perform our rituals, affirming our devotion to the goddess, asking her to remember us and deal mercifully with us."

She paused, expecting Garth to comment; the room was beautiful, or had been once, and she seemed sure the overman would appreciate this. He, however, was not paying complete attention, and said nothing. Unsure whether this was rudeness, or whether he was too taken by the room to respond, she added, "Many of us like to come here often, aside from the ceremonies, and simply enjoy it."

Garth recovered himself. "Forgive me. I was distracted." He looked at the rest of the room: the web-strewn galleries, the cracked and dirtied colored windows, the smoke-softened column of sunlight. Despite the universal decay, the room was lovely, warm and inviting; perhaps the decay even helped, softening harsh colors, rounding sharp edges, blurring the flaws. It struck him that there was something very strange about such beauty in such a place. Should not the temple of decay be foul and malodorous? Should it not be slimy and rotting?

"It is not what I had expected," he said truthfully, when he saw that the priestess was still awaiting some comment.

"Oh?"

"No. I . . . I had thought there would be an idol."

"Perhaps there was, once; much of the original interior fell to dust long ago. As is inevitable for our faith, every part of the temple has been refurbished at least once; since we are required to use only perishable materials and to do what we can to promote their decay, eventually they fall away completely and must be replaced if the temple's usefulness is to continue. Save for the stone and some of the glass, I doubt any of the present structure is more than four or five centuries old."

"Four or five . . ." Garth was dumbfounded; his native city of Ordunin was less than three hundred and fifty years old, the most ancient surviving overman community. "How old is the temple?"

"Oh, it's only about two or three thousand years old, but of course it's not the original either; there has been a temple of P'hul ever since Dûsarra was founded."

"When was that?"

"Nobody really knows."

"Oh." It had not occurred to Garth that the city, or any city, could be more than two thousand years old. He struggled to accept such a concept.

"In any case, there has been no idol in my lifetime."

"Oh." Garth had hoped to somehow bring the conversation to the empty altar unobtrusively, but seemed to be meeting with no success—although these digressions were informative. He decided that a more direct approach was in order.

"I see your altar is empty, while the other temples in the city keep precious objects or ceremonial devices there."

"I know nothing of what the others do. We keep

nothing upon the altar. It serves merely as a center-piece for our rituals. Supplicants sometimes pray atop it; it is said such prayers are especially heeded."

"Has there ever been anything kept upon it, then?"

"Not that I know of, save for the dust; that, of course, is everywhere. Why do you ask?"

Garth saw no reason to deny the truth. "I was asked —by a philosopher of sorts—to see if I could obtain what stood upon your altar."

"Oh, I see." She smiled, the expression all the more horrible in the wash of green light that fell across her from a nearby window. "It must have been a surprise to see it empty."

"Yes, it was."

"You are welcome to take the dust, if you wish."

"Thank you; I appreciate this courtesy."

"It makes no difference to us; we sweep off the altar every few months anyway."

"Oh." Garth pulled the bag from his belt and looked at it dubiously; it was of a moderately coarse weave. It was quite likely it wouldn't hold dust very well.

But then, how much could that matter? It was, all in all, only dust. He knew nothing of magicks, but surely dust was dust. Feeling foolish, he scraped up a heap of dust from the altar, gray fluff of no distinction whatsoever, and stuffed it into the bag. That done, he knotted it shut and shoved it back under his belt.

"Thank you," he said again.

"Is that all you came for, then?"

"Yes."

"So I have spoken to no purpose?"

Garth did not like the tone of the priestess' voice. "I have found your words very interesting, woman. Do not feel that you have wasted your time."

"Have I not?"

"No. This visit has been most informative, truly."

"It may be more than that, of course." Her smile had returned.

"How mean you?"

"You have been in our temple for some time; per-haps the hand of the goddess is already upon you."

"What do you mean?"

"All those who serve P'hul here bear her signs; her priests are the senile, the diseased, those with leprosy and cancer and tuberculosis and all the other wasting sicknesses. The very air of this shrine is rich in disease. You have spoken at length with a leper, where most men flee from my slightest touch. It is very likely that you already carry some illness within you; if not my own, then one of the others."

Garth said nothing; he felt a brief instant of panic, but suppressed it immediately, reminding himself that, despite what this creature might believe, no overman had ever contracted leprosy. Nor were most other diseases worth his concern; very few human diseases could affect overmen, and those that could were either not contagious, or of the more virulent and fast-acting sort, not wasting sicknesses. Overmen had their own ills.

"Shall I escort you out, then? You have what you came for."

"I am in no hurry. I do not wish to offend your goddess by so quickly shunning her shrine."

"Truly? Perhaps I have wronged you in my thoughts."

Garth shrugged.

There was a sound behind them; both turned to see a bent, shuffling figure at the head of the stair, on the far side of the antechamber beyond the still-open doors.

It was a man, clad in the soft gray robes of a priest of P'hul; he was shrivelled with age and moved slowly, as if in pain. His hair was white and unkempt, straggling down about his face, tangling indistinguishably with his beard. He blinked at the overman and the priestess.

"Greetings, Tiris. This overman is a visitor to our temple." The priestess spoke loudly, slowly, enunciating every word as carefully as she could with her deformed lip. The old man shuffled nearer; she said softly to Garth, "His hearing is poor. Tiris is the oldest of our priests; he is said to have the special favor of the goddess, to see things that others do not."

Garth was not impressed. He had seen enough of humanity to suspect that men and women were far more gullible than his own people; age and a mysterious manner could be sufficient to create the reputation of a so-called wizard. He could not deny that true wizards existed and that magic was abroad in the world; he had been confronted with the real thing on several occasions. That did not mean that he was willing to bow before every crazed old man with a trick or two on hand. He said politely, "Greetings, Tiris."

The old man stopped and studied Garth thoroughly with squinting blue eyes. Suddenly, in a voice that did not shake, a voice that was far stronger than the man's withered form seemed capable of holding, he announced, "Greetings, Bheleu."

CHAPTER SEVENTEEN

For a moment no one moved; Garth and the priestess were too startled, and the old man had apparently exhausted himself. Then Garth said, "I am not Bheleu; I am called Garth of Ordunin."

Tiris shrugged and said, "As you please."

Garth was irritated, but tried not to show it. It seemed plain to him that the old man had confused him with the idols of Bheleu that were sold in the market; perhaps the senile old fool was not even aware that he was an overman, but assumed the idols depicted a unique being, in which case his bizarre error seemed almost reasonable. He considered pointing out that, quite aside from the absurdity of casually meeting a god in a temple not his own, he carried no sword and wore no helmet, but it would do no good, he decided.

The priestess was edging away from him. He found that amusing; a leper, the most shunned creature in all the world, avoiding an ordinary overman because an old man called him by a god's name.

"I assure you, I am no god."

"As you please. Whatever you are, you are beloved of our goddess; if you are not her brother lord, you are his representative. The Age of Bheleu begins to-night, you know; you have come just in time."

"In time? In time for what?"

"To receive P'hul's service. Her power wanes as her age ends, yet she owes her elder brother fealty; before she withdraws from our mortal realm she will do her duty and serve you, to aid the cause of the Lord of Destruction."

The priestess was now openly backing away from the overman. Garth muttered, "This is absurd. I have no connection with any god." He was uneasily reminded of the prophecies cited by the Seer of Weideth; people seemed determined to see him as a bringer of destruction.

"Perhaps you are not aware of your role. We all serve the gods, and you more than any other."

Garth was unsure whether the reputedly deaf old priest had heard his remark, or merely guessed his thoughts. Whichever it was, he was not pleased. He wanted to retort that he served no one, but could not do so, since he was in fact serving the Forgotten King. Strange as the old man was, he was no god.

Was he?

What was a god like? Could the mysterious old creature be some sort of divinity? It seemed unlikely.

"I serve no god," Garth said.

Tiris shrugged, but said nothing further; instead, he turned and shuffled away, along one side of the sanctuary.

Garth turned to his guide, who was now almost cowering against the wall. There could be no doubt that she, at least, believed completely in the old man's mystical powers of discernment.

Disgusted, he marched past her and made his way down the rusted spiral stair; he had what he came for.

He strode down the passage, ignoring the creaking of the floor. The door at the end still stood open; he passed through that, then through the one he had burst in with his fist. Across the outermost chamber and out onto the sun-drenched steps he went.

Only at the last minute did he recall that he had been pursued to the temple's entrance, and that his pursuers might well be waiting for him.

They weren't. Luck was with him.

It was early afternoon; the avenue was spattered with strolling citizens, enjoying the warm sun that had long since erased all trace of the morning's rain. Several noticed him emerging from the brooding darkness of P'hul's temple, but raised no outcry, preferring instead simply to give him the widest possible berth. Remembering the leper-priestess' face he understood their attitude, and was grateful for it. He would not be bothered for a few moments, at least, not so long as it was known where he had just been.

He was slightly hungry but not at all tired. There were but two temples remaining. He thrust aside thoughts of food and joined the northbound traffic, heading for his next target.

He glimpsed the temple of Aghad to the southeast, and recalled with pleasure that he had not harmed anyone in the temple of P'hul.

Ahead of him loomed the fourth temple on the street, and presumably the last, unless the city's final shrine was concealed somewhere further along; he saw at once that it was a ruin. He had not noticed it at night, when the black of the sky blended with the black temple, but it was unmistakable in the golden daylight. The great dome was a skeleton, a metal framework, bent and sagging, with only a few broken fragments of its original stone sheathing left, clinging forlornly to its lower limits. It sat atop a broad, low structure, mostly hidden by the surrounding buildings, but with wide cracks and gaping holes visible.

This was either the temple of destruction or the temple of death; in either case, a ruin was appropriate. Therefore he did not assume it to be abandoned.

He suspected it to be the temple of Bheleu; it

seemed more fitting. That would make the temple he had not yet located the temple of The God Whose Name Is Not Spoken, which was also reasonable. A god whose very name was secret would not have his shrine openly upon a major avenue.

As he approached more closely he saw that the temple had a courtyard in front, similar to those of Sai or Aghad; a pair of steel gates stood open, blasted from their frame and hanging, twisted metal remnants, from bent hinges. Garth wondered what force had ripped them apart; he knew why it was done, if this was indeed the temple of Bheleu, but he could not imagine what means had been employed.

Inside the gates the court was a rubble-strewn expanse of stone, tall grass growing unchecked between crooked flagstones. The temple itself was closed off by a pile of wood, stacked across a shattered doorframe. No trace of the original doors remained; only the rough planks and logs. They looked like nothing so much as firewood; Garth wondered what in the world they were doing there. He had never before seen firewood stored in someone's front door.

He paused before the gate, and suddenly realized he was becoming a center of attention. Several passersby had noticed him approaching and studying the temple, and were in turn studying him—though none dared approach more closely.

He decided that it would be advisable to wait until nightfall before entering the temple. For the present, he would get himself a meal.

He turned away from the blasted temple and headed back down the avenue. He thought he remembered seeing food shops somewhere near the overlord's palace.

His memory had not failed him; he found a butcher shop, a bakery, and a vintner. A slice of good beef, fried in the baker's best dough, and washed down with a sweet red wine did much to ease his hunger.

Thus fortified, he decided to return to the Inn of the Seven Stars until nightfall. It should be fairly easy to get into the temple of Bheleu under cover of darkness, particularly since it stood in a diurnal part of the city. There was always the possibility that he would once again be interrupting a ceremony of some sort, of course; he would have to be cautious in his approach. He hoped to get there shortly after sundown, when the night's festivities, if any, would not yet have begun.

Had it been later in the day he might have chosen to wait closer at hand; but it was little more than an hour past noon, and he was slightly apprehensive about leaving Frima untended all day. Furthermore, it was about time Koros was fed, and he didn't entirely trust Dugger to see to it.

Accordingly, as he left the vintner's shop he turned his steps southwestward; he had gone scarcely a block when he heard a commotion behind him. He started to turn, to see what was happening, when he heard a voice shouting, "Overman! Hold!"

Instantly he began running, dodging into a narrow alley; behind him he could hear disorganized pursuit.

It was no great feat for him to outrun even the fastest humans on a clear field, but he was unsure how he would fare amid the winding streets of Dûsarra; therefore he kept running and dodging long after he had ceased to hear his pursuers, leaving a trail of startled citizens. Overmen in and of themselves were no strange sight to the city's hooded inhabitants, but an overman running full-tilt through the streets, mail clinking and battle-axe slapping his back, was something else; they stared after him in astonishment.

At last he found himself in an uninhabited byway, with no sign that anyone was still after him; he stopped, caught his breath, and tried to figure out where he was.

He had not seen this street before. He was lost.

His flight, he knew, had led him primarily southward; therefore, since the sun was now past its zenith, he need only head toward it to make up for the westward progress he had missed. He moved on, following the sun, proceeding with stealth and caution, carefully peering around each corner before crossing intersections.

He had apparently found his way, somehow, into a

nocturnal quarter; there were no people about, and he passed at least one street-corner shrine holding a black onyx idol of Tema. He was slightly surprised that such a costly item was not stolen; either it had some protection he could not see, or even the day-dwelling Dûsarrans did not care to offend the city's most popular goddess.

The streets narrowed, and their twists and turns sometimes forced him off his intended course until he reached the next corner; he made a full circuit of one particularly crooked three-sided block without meaning to, and had to head further southward to find another street that ran to the west.

The continued emptiness of the streets lulled him, and his caution decreased as corner after corner revealed nothing but closed shops, shuttered windows, and drying mud. Thus, he almost walked openly into the marketplace when it appeared unexpectedly before him. Recovering, he backtracked into still-unoccupied alleys, and looped around to the north, giving the square a wide berth. This took him through areas not wholly asleep, and he found himself peering around corners and furtively scurrying from one alleyway to the next.

Finally, he emerged into the street where the house he had broken through stood; it was still apparently empty. Cautiously, he tried the door, and found it just as he had left it. He guessed that the owner had not yet returned home.

He made his way through the house into the yard, where the rainwater had subsided to a few small puddles and a broad expanse of mud; it was a simple matter for him to vault onto the wall separating this yard from the next, and from there to clamber onto the roof of the stable.

It was midafternoon; the sun's angle was about the same as it had been when he left, save that it stood now in the west instead of the east. He eased himself over the edge of the tiles, and dropped into the stable-yard.

The stall was as he had left it, save that Koros was awake and standing quietly; Frima still slept. Garth tucked the bag of dust into the larger sack that now held the two stones, the bloodstained gold, and the whip and dagger from the other temples, then sat, considering what to do until nightfall.

Nothing suggested itself; he closed his eyes for a brief nap, and was quickly asleep.

CHAPTER EIGHTEEN

He awoke to moonlight in his face; it washed the stableyard in silver, fading to gray the hard yellow dirt, and blurring the several shades of gray wood and gray stone to a single paler hue outlined in black shadows.

With a growl, he climbed to his feet; he had overslept. It was obviously two or three hours past sunset.

Something moved in the dimness of the stall. He peered into the gloom, and realized it was Frima shying away from him. His growl had frightened her.

With a start, he noticed where she was; she stood beside Koros, her tiny hand on the warbeast's great black head, petting it. She had apparently gotten on friendly terms with the monster. Her other hand held the wire brush Garth kept for grooming his mount, and the beast's eyelids drooped in an expression of feline contentment; obviously the two were getting along very well indeed. Garth felt slightly sorry he had interrupted such a pleasant scene.

"Excuse me," he said, "I overslept. I meant to wake at sundown."

"Oh! I didn't know; I would have wakened you if I had." Frima sounded genuinely contrite, although she had not been at fault, and Garth felt a twinge of annoyance. This girl thoroughly confused him with her abrupt emotional changes that seemed to have no perceptible logic to them. He forbore to comment further, and instead readied himself for his assault on the temple of Bheleu, straightening his mail—which was really quite uncomfortable to sleep in; once again he was stiff and sore—and checking his dagger and axe, wishing his sword were still intact.

He also wished his boots were still intact; he discovered that the mud in his right boot had dried to an abrasive grit. He removed it, and wiped it out as best he could with a spare sack. That reminded him to tuck one in his belt, which he did immediately after re-donning the boot.

His feet had gotten rather unsavory, he noticed; that came from sleeping shod, no doubt. He decided he owed himself a long, luxurious hot bath as soon as he could manage one.

Frima watched all this silently, her hand absent-mindedly stroking the warbeast's neck. At last, she asked, "Where are you going?"

"To the temple of Bheleu."

"To rob its altar?"

"Yes."

"Is that the last one?"

"No; I still have to rob the temple of death."

"But you can't! No one has ever come out of there alive!"

"Except the old priest, and what he can do, I can do."

She was plainly unconvinced. "What am I to do when you are killed?"

"Whatever you please."

"But the beast won't let me leave!"

"You need not worry about that; if I do not return within a day or so, Koros will go hunting. It's due for a feeding, and when it's hungry enough it will hunt, regardless of anything else. I would suggest you find a weapon; there is a stiletto among my supplies, and of course the dagger from the temple of Sai. You may be able to convince it that other food would be more easily obtained than you, particularly since it knows I don't want you harmed."

"He eats people?" She snatched her hand from the warbeast's neck.

"It; it's a neuter, not a male. And yes, it eats people. It even ate a wizard once."

"Oh." Her voice was tiny.

"I wouldn't worry; it seems to like you."

She made a small wordless noise, as Garth looked himself over. Finally satisfied with his preparations, he ordered Frima and Koros, "Wait here," and marched out of the stall.

Dugger was on duty, as he had expected. There was, therefore, no reason to go clambering around the roof; besides, he was pretty well over the anger that had made him so reckless earlier. Simply recognizing its existence had helped considerably, and he was better rested now—though he was slightly annoyed at having overslept.

He strode to the archway and asked the drowsing stable-boy, "Have you arranged to feed my mount?"

The boy awoke with a start, and said, "It's you!"

"Yes."

"You're the temple-robber!"

"Am I?"

"Aren't you? I . . . they said it was an overman, and you're the only overman I've seen around in weeks."

"You don't see every stranger that comes to Dûsarra, though, do you?"

"No."

"So you can't be sure I'm the one who robbed the temple."

The boy hesitated, and admitted, "I guess not."

"And that being the case, I think you should give me the benefit of the doubt. Now, I told you last night that I wanted you to feed my beast; have you done anything about that?"

"I forgot."

"It's just as well." It had occurred to Garth that anyone taking the beast its meal would see, and wonder about, Frima. An overman had no business with a human female, especially not keeping her penned in a stable. Dugger had seen her enter, but there was no point in reminding him and letting him see she was still there. "Is the street clear? Others might mistake me for the temple thief, and I'd prefer not to be delayed."

"Oh." The boy leaned out and looked both ways. "I don't see anyone."

"Good." He stepped past the lad, looking about for himself, and set out toward the Street of the Temples.

He encountered no difficulty; he was becoming familiar with the city, and knew which streets were diurnal, which nocturnal, and which seemed to have traffic around the clock.

As it had been the night before, the Street of the Temples was as silent as death, not a single thing moving on its moonlit pavement. He made his way quickly to the ruined temple, only to halt abruptly as he approached; a faint murmur disturbed the silence, coming from the shattered dome.

He hissed in annoyance. Another ceremony; it seemed as if no matter what he did, he was fated to arrive during some silly ritual or other.

At any rate, he could approach this one cautiously and watch, and then decide what to do; whether to wait until it ended or interrupt it or simply go away and try again later. He crept onward, slipping stealthily through the blasted gates, into the littered courtyard beyond.

The firewood was gone from the doorway, which now gaped at him like a toothless mouth; orange light shone from within. He stepped to one side, and peered cautiously around the broken frame.

The interior of the ruin was a single vast space; if there had ever been any internal walls, they were nothing now but part of the dust that served as a floor. The black stone walls and tattered metal frame of the demolished dome were lit by a great bonfire that blazed in the center of the temple, and around this conflagration danced a score or more of red-robed figures, prancing about and chanting eerily, casting long black shadows that writhed across red-lit walls and the deeper blackness of the cracks in the stone.

The scene had an odd fascination to it. Garth stared.

There was no sign of an altar, unless the bonfire could be considered that; it was certainly the focus of the worshippers' attention. Garth blinked, and studied the leaping flames more carefully. That was undoubtedly where the wood that had earlier blocked the entrance had gone. Logs of all sizes were heaped crudely together; in the center, a single slim, straight rod stood straight up, almost invisible through the flames.

He blinked again; the chant seemed louder. There was something about that single upright object that bothered him. It was not wood; it gleamed, it shone too bright a shade of red. There was a crosspiece near the top.

A dull rumble reached him, penetrating the chant that seemed to fill his head; distant thunder, he told himself. He glanced up, and saw that the stars had vanished, covered over by clouds. The brewing storm had blown up extraordinarily quickly, he thought, or else he had been watching the dance longer than he had realized. The moon was hidden, while it had been bright and clear when he entered the court; he had not noticed its loss in the brighter light of the fire. He loooked back at the ceremony, if such it could be called; it was lacking in the pomp and dignity of more familiar rites, though it certainly had a power of its own. The chanting filled his ears again, and his gaze was absorbed in the flames. As he watched, there came a second low rumble; as if in response, the central portion of the bonfire fell inward, leaving a ring of flame where there had been a cone, and revealing that strange upright object, which now stood dimly glowing behind the flickering curtain.

It was a sword. An immense two-handed broadsword was thrust through the center of the pile of burning wood. A great red gem blazed in its pommel. It was straight and strong, a good yard of bare metal showing between the quillons and where the blade vanished into the flaring coals; the hilt was black, and long enough to give even an overman's hands plenty of room. Assuming it to be properly proportioned, Garth estimated its full length at six feet or more.

A truly magnificent weapon; it made the sword he had shattered appear little better than a pocketknife. He stepped into the doorway to see it better.

The devotees of Bheleu paid no heed, but whirled on in their dance; it grew more manic now, and the chanting rose in pitch, split into two antiphonal voices pursuing one another in hypnotic rhythm.

Altar or no, Garth knew that this sword was what he had come for. This was what he wanted, of all Dûsarra. A sword like that would make him invincible. His gaze was fixed upon it in fascination.

The steel gleamed in the firelight and the chant merged with renewed rumbling, washing over him in a wave of close-packed sound. He saw nothing now but the bonfire and the glowing sword; the dancers flicked across his field of vision with no more meaning than the flickering of the flames. He would take that sword; he would wait until the dance had ended and the fire died, and tear it free.

No! Why wait? He would burst into the chamber while the dancers remained lost in their chanting gyrations and snatch it out red-hot from where it stood! Then he would flee, he thought at first, but instantly other thoughts crushed that out; he would not flee! Flee? An overman flee before humans? He would not flee; he would wield that splendid blade among the worshippers until it shone as red with blood as it did now with heat.

Somewhere a part of him knew this was insane, this uncontrollable craving for the possession of the sword; that part struggled vainly to restore calm. It revolted at the thought of wanton and unnecessary bloodshed.

It was brutally suppressed by the unearthly power that now dominated him, erasing his conscious self; his rationality was drowned in a flood of unreasoning blood-lust, like nothing he had ever felt. He had known the wild and involuntary passion that consumes an overman when he scents an overwoman in heat; he had known the roaring blind fury of battle rage that made a mortal warrior a berserker; this new lust was so strong as to make those mere shadows, trivial wisps of emotion, though it partook of both in flavor. He could contain it no longer.

An instant later the reeling, semi-hypnotized dancers were delighted to see the great dark form of an armored overman stride roaring into their midst, red eyes ablaze; they knew at once, with the absolute conviction of the fanatic, that this was their god who confronted them. They screamed with ecstasy, the chant collapsing into chaotic raving; the earth rumbled beneath them, and lightning forked across the sky.

Boldly, unhesitatingly, as if unaware of the flames and heat, the apparition marched up onto the verge of the holy pyre and wrenched the sacred sword from its place; his hands smoked with the heat of the hilt, and the stench of burning skin filled the temple. The overman paid no heed, but raised the blade above his head and whirled it about, so that it blazed and flickered in the firelight.

"I am Bheleu!" cried the monster in Garth's body; he thrust the blade upward at the heavens, to be answered by a crash of thunder and a blinding flash of lightning. The bolt struck, spattered, and sizzled across the spiderweb metal frame of the ruined dome; sparks showered upon the worshippers, who danced maniacally, scraming their devotion. A second bolt came on the heels of the first, leaping from the clouds to the peak of the dome, and thence to the point of the sword; it poured through Garth's body and blasted the bonfire apart at his feet, scattering burning wood.

The thunder was now a steady pounding as other bolts showered across the city; Garth's hands fell, the sword still clutched in them, and his eyes blazed crimson as the blade chopped through the skull of the high priest of Bheleu.

The worshippers screamed in frenzy, crying the name of their god.

The blade swung up, red with blood and gleaming gold in the firelight; lightning flashed, silver steel shone for an instant, and the sword came down, hacking through a man's neck, spraying blood into the scattered fire where it sizzled and stank.

"I am destruction!"

The worshippers cried hoarse approval, and surged toward him, forgetting their dance. The blade blazed upward, flashed down; blood showered unnoticed across fire, earth, and flesh. There was no trace of resistance; the eager worshippers flung themselves in the weapon's path as the earth shook and the sky raged, and the monster wielding it merely laughed.

For half an hour their god walked among his people, slashing aside all who approached him; for one insane half-hour he brought the total destruction their creed proclaimed holy. The priests of Bheleu had been warriors, for their faith required it. None shrank from the sight of blood, nor cringed away from the dismembered and disembowelled corpses of their comrades; instead they fought amongst themselves for the right to approach and be slain, their religious fervor blended with the old fighting fury, the death-wish of those who slay made manifest.

Throughout, the thunder rolled and roared, crashing arrhythmically about the ruins, and lightning blazed again and again across the open dome. Every so often a bolt would strike the exposed steel, and the temple walls would shake. With the agility of the warriors they once were, the worshippers kept their feet and pressed forward to the slaughter.

At last, as the dripping blade swung flashing upward for the final stroke, there came a crash of thunder like none before; the last devotee fell to his knees before his god, deafened and blinded, as the sword blazed red and silver against the sky, whirling about the head of the crazed overman-monster. It swooped down, like a hawk upon its prey, and struck the man through, entering the front of his throat and protruding between his shoulder-blades; no more metal showed, but only blood, red, brown, and black, coating the blade and spattered liberally across the temple floor.

The final lightning bolt's pealing echoed among the shattered walls, covering the sudden silence that fell with the death of the last screaming priest; overhead, the blasted dome sagged, twisted, and broke. Snapping sparks were strewn amid the dying remnants of the pyre, and drops of molten metal flew hissing downward. The framework continued to crumple, collapsing slowly, as the storm finally broke, whipping fat raindrops across the prostrate corpses and the upturned face of their slayer.

For long moments the overman stood motionless; rain filled his eyes and ran in cool streams across his face. The sword was still clutched in his hands, its hilt slimed with gore, its blade still thrust through his final victim. The madness was passing, fading, shrinking into itself somewhere within him; he blinked away the rain, and lowered his gaze from the storm.

He looked at the sagging, slack-jawed figure impaled on his sword, at the score of slaughtered men, at the scattered remains of the bonfire dying in the rain. His hands fell from the hilt, and sword and cadaver tumbled forward at his feet. He stepped back, appalled, and sank to his knees; then, for the first time in a hundred and forty years, Garth wept, as the shattered metal of the dome crashed to the ground around him.

CHAPTER NINETEEN

He came to as the first glimmer of dawn broke through the clouds; he was lying sprawled on the dirt floor of the temple, surrounded by tortured scraps of metal and ragged, red-clothed corpses. Ashes and charred wood were scattered at his feet.

Before him, the elongated hilt of the great broadsword protruded from the throat of his final victim; the gem set in the pommel gleamed as red as blood, but the blade had been washed clean by the rain. In the dim light the metal was dull gray.

He got slowly to his feet, and the events of the night seeped back into his mind; he grimaced in disgust.

Here was the destruction the Seers of Weideth had foreseen. What had come over him?

He found himself unwilling to admit that he had in truth been possessed by some higher power, acting as no more than a puppet; but then, the thought that he had within him such berserk savagery, so easily roused, was almost equally unacceptable. True, his rage and hatred of the Aghadites still smouldered, and his anger at the Baron of Skelleth likewise. Had the babblings of that senile old P'hulite suggested to his suppressed darker side that he take out his aggressions thus? Perhaps the dance of Bheleu had hypnotic properties designed to release a watcher's pent-up emotions; perhaps some mystic fumes, invisible and unnoticed, had affected him. He had heard that volcanoes produced such gasses, and Dûsarra was built on the slopes of a great volcano.

It really mattered very little; what was done was done, and could in no way be altered.

He recalled the roaring storm, of which nothing remained but puddles and dispersing clouds; the dome had been blasted away. He remembered the fiery lightning—had it actually struck him? That could not be. He looked at his hands; the palms were burnt black. He shuddered. Had he really pulled the sword red-hot from the fire?

No. He rejected that. The whole thing could not have been as he remembered; he must have been under some magical influence, whether hypnosis or hallucinogen or even actual possession he did not know. He had slain the entire cult of Bheleu, yes; there had been a storm, and lightning had destroyed the ruins of the dome; but beyond that, he refused to accept any of it. He had no idea how he had burned his hands, or how the bonfire had been spread about, but he rejected his memories of those events.

His hands were numb, he realized; the nerves might well have been destroyed. At the very least they had been temporarily overloaded. If they were intact, at any minute sensation might begin to return, and he was quite sure that the result would be pain like nothing he had ever suffered before—except possibly once, when he had recovered slowly from a wizard's death-spell. He cringed at the thought. *That* experience was not something he could bear to think about.

He still had one more temple to rob, and his escape to make good; he was a wanted fugitive. He could not afford to waste any time. If he waited for his hands to heal, he might be hiding and running about the city for weeks. On the other hand, if he moved quickly, perhaps he could finish his task before the pain began, and before any infection set in—if such were to happen. It might be that his hands were permanently ruined.

He did not care to consider that; instead, he snatched the sword of Bheleu from the final corpse and wiped the remaining blood off on the man's robe. He had not seen the temple of The God Whose Name Is Not Spoken, but he somehow thought he knew where it must be. The dead have returned to the earth, humans were wont to say; death is a part of the world. It was appropriate, then, for the god of death to have his temple in the earth itself.

Garth marched from the ruined shrine, across the rubble-strewn courtyard, and through the shattered gates into the street; it was still early, and none of the day-dwellers were yet about, so it stretched bare and empty from the overlord's palace to the blank stone of the volcano.

Garth turned right, toward the bare stone.

As he approached he made out what he had expected to find; at the end of the avenue, amid black shadows and black stone, was a deeper shadow. There was an opening into the mountainside that he knew to be the temple of the Final God.

It did not occur to him to wonder how he could now know, with such certainty, things that he had not even guessed at prior to the carnage in the temple of Bheleu.

The great broadsword was naked in his unfeeling hands; there was no way he could sheathe it, no other way he could carry it. Even had he still worn his old sword's scabbard, it would never have held the five-foot blade of this monstrous weapon.

He paused at the brink of the cave; it seemed very odd that such a cave would exist here within the city walls, but it undeniably did. He peered into the gloom, but could see nothing. He recalled what Frima had said of it, but paid it no heed; mere myths, to impress gullible humans.

A voice spoke from behind him, saying, "You broke your word, Garth."

He turned, but could see no one; the speaker was hiding somewhere. Garth made no attempt to locate him; he recognized the voice. It was the same one that had taunted him in the temple of Aghad.

"I gave no word."

"You gave assent by silence to our bargain, thief, yet you harmed no one in the temple of P'hul."

Garth marvelled at the perversity of this creature, criticizing him for not killing enough people when the Aghadite had surely seen the bloody havoc he had wreaked during the night. "Do not the many deaths in Bheleu's shrine more than compensate?"

"No. You were to slay a priest of P'hul."

"Who? The leper girl? The senile old seer? I gave no word, skulking liar; if I have failed of the terms you set me, what of it? Annoy me no further."

"You were to slay a priest of P'hul. Now you enter the temple of the Final God, yet the cult's priest is nowhere within. You scorn our agreement, and be sure that if you come alive from this cavern, you shall die nonetheless."

"In time, no doubt, I shall; but it will be none of your doing! When I emerge from this place I will depart this city, and I suggest that you not get in my way."

"Say what you will, but be aware that we can suppress information as well as disseminate it, and it is by our grace that the angry mobs gathered by the temple of Tema have not yet beset the stable at the Inn of the Seven Stars. Their agent who spied upon you and the owner of the house you so cavalierly broke open were kept from spreading the word by the followers of Aghad, but even now we are withdrawing our aid; the boy Dugger is being punished for his silence, and the good people of the city are no longer being held in check."

This speech caused Garth genuine concern for a moment; then he shrugged it aside. He had faith in the invincibility of his warbeast.

Still, there was no time to spare. Ignoring the further comments of the Aghadite, he plunged into the gloom of the cave, finding some slight gratification in the knowledge that the other would fear to follow.

There was no gate, door, nor guard; the reputation of the Final God was quite sufficient to keep out the unwelcome.

The gray light of early morning faded behind him as he marched down the smooth, sloping floor, but somewhere ahead of him he detected a faint, ruddy glow. He would not have to contend with complete darkness.

The entry passage gradually widened and the glow became more pronounced, until at last he found himself in a large chamber, where the natural cave had been artificially enlarged. The floor was smooth and level, the walls straight, but the central portion of the ceiling was the rough and broken surface of a cave, showing where the original opening had been, while the sides were lower and shaped into smooth vaulting, obviously the work of human hands.

It was impossible to distinguish any colors, for here the only light was the pure red of that mysterious glow that came from somewhere beyond the far side of the chamber; it seeped up from the continuation of the natural tunnel, which Garth could see sloped sharply downward. A dry warmth seemed to come with it. Shapes were plainly discernable, and Garth saw that the walls were carved into high-relief friezes of a grotesque and hideous nature, depicting twisted, semi-human creatures, cavorting obscenely, butchering one another while simultaneously engaged in a wide variety of perverse couplings. Garth wondered what manner of imagination had created such things.

In the center of the chamber stood the altar, high and narrow; it was scarcely a yard wide, but almost five feet in height, its sides smooth stone that blended seamlessly into the floor. Apparently, Garth thought, it had been carved from a column or stalagmite. The top was ornate and slanting; it was tilted up to resemble a reading stand, such as could be found in the best libraries, with elaborate decorative carving along either side and surmounted by a strange semi-human skull. The space where an open book would have stood, were it in fact a reading stand, was bare, smooth polished stone.

That meant the skull was what he had come for. He crossed to the altar and looked at it.

It was somewhere between human and overman in size and shape, save that it was impossibly tall and narrow, and two twisting horns thrust up from its temples; its teeth were gone, and its jaws leered open.

He put aside his sword and reached for it, and discovered that it was somehow anchored to the stone altar; furthermore, it was coated with some sort of slime, so that his senseless fingers slid from their hold.

Probably just drippings from the roof, he decided, though there was no discernable moisture in the warm air. He grasped and tugged at the skull, but it refused to yield.

A faint rumbling sounded, and he felt a vibration in the stone beneath his feet; he thought vaguely that it was unusual for a second thunderstorm to blow up so suddenly, and ran his fingers over the sides of the skull, wishing they weren't still numb.

They came away coated with slime; he peered at it closely, and realized that this was no dripping cavewater. The red glow dimmed slightly; he glanced up, then returned to his study of the skull.

The coating seemed to be some sort of ichor, though he had seen no sign of life in the cave-temple. The skull appeared to be firmly secured to the altar by a heavy rivet through the base of the cranium.

There was a faint tingling in his hands; the nerves were not wholly destroyed. He glanced down at them, and the red glow seemed to dim still further. There were blisters forming. He looked up in time to see the thing coming at him before its shadow covered him in darkness, shutting out the faint crimson light.

CHAPTER TWENTY

The thing was huge; its eyeless head seemed to fill half the chamber, and its gaping lipless maw appeared capable of swallowing an overman, armor and all, in a single gulp. It had no neck, nor in truth a distinct head, but only a long, segmented body reaching back into the farther tunnel and filling it so completely that the red glow, whatever it was, could no longer pass.

It was, in short, a monstrous worm.

Garth retreated instinctively, and feeling the weight of his axe upon his shoulder he reached up and freed the familiar weapon, forgetting for the moment about the more formidable sword he had left beside the altar.

He was in darkness, having been allowed only that single glimpse of his attacker; now he judged its location by sound and the feel of the moving air on his face. It was swinging its head about blindly in the area of the altar, where he had stood instants earlier, presumably groping for its usual sacrifice.

Cautiously, wary that the slightest sound might alert it—there was no knowing what senses guided such a creature—he inched backward toward the entryway.

Some part of his mind undoubtedly noticed the totality of the surrounding blackness; it was with only mild surprise that he found the entrance blocked by a solid metal barrier, which must have slid silently into place while he investigated the altar. He wasted no effort in battering at it; undoubtedly other victims had tried that, though perhaps none as powerful as himself, and it would leave him with his back exposed and inviting. Instead he turned at bay, and waited for the monster's attack.

The creature was not slow in obliging with an awkward lunge; he heard a slithering as it poised, and felt the rush of air toward him, giving him time to spring aside, hacking with the axe as he did so.

The blade bit into something with a sick, squashing sound, but there was no blood or ichor sprayed onto his hands, nor any sign of pain or injury from the monster worm. He wrenched the axe free and backed away, his left flank to the wall.

He wished his hands were capable of normal sensation; he wanted to test the edge of his blade, to see if anything had come away upon it, or if perhaps it was coated with the same slime as the altar. He was fairly sure this creature was the source of that substance, and somewhere beneath his wary attention to his situation he wondered whether it was an exterior lubrication or a saliva of some sort.

His palms stung, not from the impact the axe had made on the monster, but with the first twinges from his burns.

The head swung toward him again, and there was a brief flash of murky red as the creature's swooping lunge allowed a trace of light to pass; he saw the horny rim of its toothless mouth sweeping toward him and dove from its path, flailing with the axe. It sank into the thing's flesh, and was wrenched from his grasp.

He felt a brief second of panic as he realized he was virtually unarmed against this hideous pet of the god of death, then remembered the great sword that presumably still lay somewhere near the center of the chamber. He clambered to his feet, his twitching, stinging fingers clutching at the carvings that lined the wall without feeling them; when the worm reared back for another lunge, he took three running steps under its raised head and dove headlong, hands outflung.

The rattle of steel on stone told him that his hand had struck the sacred weapon. The pain in his palms was becoming a distraction, but he forced himself to ignore it as he groped for the sword.

Above him the worm's body twitched as it thrust forward, and a solid fist of air knocked him flat to the stones; it was scarcely a foot above him, writhing about in frustration, unable to detect him.

He forced his hands to close on the sword, though the motion of bending his palms sent a shudder of agony up his arms. The blade scraped across stone and the monster turned, twisting back upon itself, only to find the space within the chamber insufficient for such a maneuver.

There was a scraping sound followed by a rattling, as the axe he had left embedded in the creature was dragged along the wall and dislodged.

His unwilling hands arranged themselves upon the hilt of the sword, and a surge of renewed strength swept through him. Adrenalin, he told himself.

The worm was dragging much of its length back down into the tunnel; there was another brief flash of ruddy light. It was giving itself room, the room to move its head and get its hungry maw onto the reluctant morsel it knew was there.

He rolled aside, and felt the rush of air as it lunged; it missed, and he swung the great broadsword as he lay on his back inches from its flank. The blade cut deeply into the monster, but there was still no perceptible effect. Slime ran sluggishly over the quillons and across the back of his hands.

He struck again, before the thing could move far—vast and powerful as it was, it was also ponderous and, except for the swift lunges that used its own weight to drive its head forward, not capable of fast movement—and again the blade sliced messily into the yielding substance of the creature.

It was like cutting at mud.

He hewed again as it reversed direction, pulling back for another attack; with a ghastly sucking sound a sliver of its cold, damp flesh came free where this new cut met an earlier one.

An idea came to him as he rolled onto his belly and pushed himself further toward the wall. The thing's vitals were not within reach of his blade, it appeared; but he could cut the monster. If he could hack away enough of its insensitive outer layer at one spot, sooner or later he would injure it, perhaps inflicting enough damage to drive it back down into its tunnel, leaving him to deal with the metal door. No animal in Garth's experience, of whatever kind, could long survive having chunks cut away.

It would all be much easier if he could see what he was doing.

He flung himself sideways as the rush of air warned him of another lunge, chopping with the sword as he did so. The monster withdrew, a little more slowly than before; Garth wondered if he had already made himself felt. It paused; Garth knew from the sudden cessation of the slithering noise of its movement. He judged the head to be somewhere in the center of the chamber, perhaps hovering above the altar.

It was, he decided, time he took the offensive; with a bellow of simulated rage, intended to get his blood flowing more hotly, he lurched to his feet and charged the thing, the heavy sword swinging in front of him.

The blade struck the thing's horny jaws with a grating, scratching sound, without penetrating; the monster reared away nonetheless, and Garth flung himself beneath it. He found himself crouched beside the altar, and it occurred to him that that was a good place to be; obviously, the creature could not destroy the altar, or it would have done so years ago. It would be unable to come at him from above or behind if he kept his back to the stone column.

The head swooped down again, only to stop short as it struck the altar-top; Garth took the opportunity to strike two quick blows, at converging angles, and was gratified when the second blow left a chunk of pasty worm-flesh hanging by a thread.

The monster did not retreat this time but pressed forward unheeding, mindlessly trying to force its way past the stone altar. Garth had no intention of passing up such a chance, and followed up his first pair of blows with a series of chopping cuts, hacking more deeply into the wound he had made.

Slivers of flesh pulled away to hang loosely or fall at the overman's feet. The slime that coated the monster drooled sluggishly across Garth's hands and wrists, seeming to soothe the stinging agony of his burns—which he was ignoring anyway in the heat of battle.

He was striking from a crouch beside the altar, and

was unable to get the full force of which he was capable into his blows from such a stance; since the head was swaying back and forth he dared not stand up, as he knew that apparently gentle motion could knock him away like a leaf in a windstorm. Still, he knew that he could inflict more damage more quickly if he could get into a position where he could swing his blade freely, and where gravity was working with him rather than against him. If he were *atop* the worm . . .

His hacking had cut a ragged, oozing hole in the thing's side, a break in its smooth, slick surface; it served him as a foothold as he launched himself upward, scrambling madly with the great sword clutched in one stinging hand while the other hand and both feet scrabbled for holds on the thing's smooth wet flesh.

He realized he was not going to make it; he felt himself beginning to slide back, when the worm suddenly changed its direction, swinging toward him, apparently in response to his weight. For an instant he feared he would be smashed against a wall before he had time to leap clear, and he clung desperately, attempting to claw his way upward.

To his surprise, this panicky action was successful; the monster's motion had given him the additional traction he needed, and he was able to pull himself up astride the thing's "neck," using the sword as an anchor.

Now he only had to worry about being smashed against the ceiling; there was no way the thing could get at him here. He pulled his dagger from his belt and thrust it into the yielding flesh, to serve as a handhold, then set to the messy business of cutting his way through the monster with the great broadsword. He used both hands, pausing now and then to catch himself on the hilt of his dagger when he felt himself slipping.

Spraddled across the vast back as he was, he still was not striking with much power; it seemed to be sufficient, though. In moments he had carved out a trench, which he crawled into, ignoring the oozing discomforts of the omnipresent slime that seeped from every inch of the thing's flesh. Here he was much more secure, and could kneel while he wielded the sword, cutting his way deeper into the worm.

The monster was apparently unwilling to give up its prey; it did not retreat down its passage, but instead flung itself about the temple chamber, as if seeking the little pest that was now slicing deeper and deeper into its back; several times Garth thought that the violence of its movements might dislodge him, or that he might lose his grip on his sword.

Then, finally, he felt the blade bite into something more substantial than the creature's flaccid flesh; he pulled it free, releasing a spurt of viscous ichor and a ghastly stink. He had found the thing's vitals.

He had little time to appreciate his accomplishment; the thing went into wild convulsions that made its earlier movements seem like nothing, and he was flung aside like a bothersome insect. His head struck the stone wall; the sword flew from his hands, and the darkness that filled his eyes enfolded him completely. His last sensation was an eerie awareness of distant, barely audible laughter; something was pleased with him.

CHAPTER TWENTY-ONE

Frima was not happy with her situation. Still, while being penned up in a stable with a man-eating monster at the whim of an overman was scarcely a pleasant thing, she had to admit it was better than being sacrificed to Sai.

It had been some time now since Garth had marched off to rob the last two temples, and Frima was reasonably certain that he would not be coming back. All her life she had been told that nobody ever returned from the temple of death, and although Garth was plainly not the Unnamed God's ordinary victim, she did not think he could manage to defy one of the basic facts of Dûsarran existence. She was, therefore, stuck here until such time as Koros should give up waiting. The overman had said it would be a day or so; she had waited a night and a morning and half the afternoon, but the beast showed no signs of departing. It had allowed her to go through Garth's belongings, and she had found the stiletto he had mentioned; the knife did little for her self-confidence, however, as she had no idea of the proper way to use one, and found it completely inconceivable that such a puny little thing could deter a creature as magnificently powerful as the warbeast.

The monster was undeniably beautiful, and friendly enough; she found herself alternately petting it, and then cowering away from it as she recalled what Garth had said. It had once eaten a wizard! Wizards were the most powerful beings she had imagined prior to her abduction, yet this thing *ate* one as if he were no more than a mere mortal!

It did not occur to her to doubt Garth's words; his delivery had been entirely convincing, and she was a fairly trusting sort anyway.

She got up and walked toward the door of the stall, to try her luck at leaving once more; as always, Koros made no protest until her hand actually reached over toward the latch, whereupon it growled warningly. She withdrew her hand, sighed, and looked out at the empty stableyard. She was about to turn away when a movement caught her eye.

There was someone just beyond the arch; several people, in fact. She leaned out a bit to get a better view, and Koros growled again; she ignored it and continued to peer through the arch.

There was a great mass of people out there; not passing by, but gathering together. She wondered what they could want.

It occurred to her that perhaps they might rescue her; she considered calling out. After some thought she decided not to. Koros would undoubtedly take it amiss, and there might be bloodshed. She was not desperate yet.

There was a curious snuffling at her side, and she realized that the warbeast had come up beside her and was also watching the people outside the arch.

There was much discussion and shouting going on, but she could make out no words. A robe fell open for a moment, revealing that its owner wore a shirt of mail and had a sword on his belt. Thus alerted, she looked more closely and saw that several—perhaps *all* —of the men gathering wore swords, making curious bulges beneath their robes. Furthermore, all of the gathering crowd were men, as far as she could make out; nowhere did she see a beardless face.

Someone in a dark red robe had made his way to the center of the arch; now he turned and addressed the crowd, a fist raised above his head. She still could not make out much, over the shuffling and rustling of the crowd, but she caught the words "overman" and "defiler."

Beside her, Koros growled.

The man in red turned, and pointed into the stable —pointed directly at her, it seemed. The crowd surged, and with this apparent leader in the van marched into the stableyard.

Koros leapt from the stall in a single fluid motion and landed, feet braced apart, in the center of the yard. It roared a challenge that seemed the loudest sound Frima had ever heard, and the crowd's forward movement suddenly ceased.

Frima watched in astonishment; quite aside from the confusing events unfolding before her, she found herself wondering how a beast as large as Koros had managed to leap through the relatively narrow opening between the stall door and the overhanging roof. More of its height must be in its legs than she had realized.

Koros roared again and took a single step forward, toward the crowd of men; Frima saw that several had drawn swords, yet none dared approach any closer to the warbeast. In fact, they were gradually falling back.

Another roar and another step, and Koros sank into

a crouch, like a cat preparing to pounce. The crowd's backward movement accelerated, and in a brief moment all were once again on the other side of the arch. Koros rose again, stretched itself, yawned, and stood calmly awaiting whatever might happen next.

The man in red stood out from the crowd once again and spoke; this time Frima could distinguish his words, as Koros had frightened the crowd into relative stillness.

"Fellow Dûsarrans, we are not cowed by this unholy monster, but merely cautious! It is not with this beast that we quarrel, but with its blasphemous master! Let us then wait here for his return, when we shall strike him down in our righteous anger, slaughter his monstrous pet, and return the sacrifice he has stolen to her rightful place! We will cleanse our city of this filth!"

This speech was greeted with rousing applause. Frima, hearing the line about restoring the sacrifice, found herself very glad that she had not called out for aid. She suddenly saw Koros not as her jailer but as her protector, and found herself waiting eagerly for Garth's return—while simultaneously dreading it, lest he be butchered or prove in the end as bad as the cult of Sai—and still suspecting that he might not return at all.

CHAPTER TWENTY-TWO

Garth had no idea how long he was unconscious. When he awoke he lay sprawled on the stone floor, the sword of Bheleu at his side. The red glow shone unobstructed from the tunnel, lighting the gem in the sword's pommel with a murky crimson fire. Pools of gelid slime were scattered about, and his mail was thick with the stuff. He lay still for a moment, gathering his thoughts.

He reached out and grasped the sword; as his fingers closed around the hilt, he realized that they no longer hurt. He sat up, released the sword, and looked at his palms.

There was a slight puckering of the flesh, as of wounds almost fully healed, but no other trace of burns or blisters. Horrified, he wondered how long he had lain senseless.

He tested his sensitivity, pressing his fingers to various surfaces, and knew a moment of panic when his first trial, feeling the texture of his chain armor, seemed dull and blunted; it was with great relief he realized it was the coating of slime that deadened his sense of touch. Running his fingers across the carved walls he could detect no lessening of his tactile sense. He was fit, then.

But how long had he been here? What had become of Koros, who had been due for a feeding? Or Frima, who had been left with the hungry warbeast? Of the booty taken from the first five temples? Had anything come of the threats of the Aghadite priest?

He clambered to his feet.

As if on cue, as he turned his gaze toward the metal door that sealed the entrance, the barrier slid silently into the wall, and a stooped figure entered, garbed in a robe of such a dull black that it reflected none of the red light whatsoever. The man's face was hidden by his hood, as was customary for Dûsarran priests, so that in his almost invisible garments he appeared to be an animated shadow, deeper and darker than the others that lay about the cave.

No light entered with this apparition, and at first Garth assumed this to mean that it was night outside; he did not immediately recall that the passage was long and winding enough to admit virtually none of the sun's light whatever the time of day.

The robed figure was small and frail in appearance, despite the complete lack of visible detail. Garth thought at first that it might be a girl or young boy, despite the slowness and caution of age in its movements; but when the priest spoke, although his voice was high and broken, there was no doubt that he was an old man, despite his childish stature.

"I hear you breathing," he said.

Garth made no reply.

"Can you not speak? I know you are there, and alive."

"Yes, I am here. What would you have me say?" Garth picked up the sword as he spoke; the little old man appeared harmless, but he did not care to take any unnecessary chances.

"Whatever you care to say."

"There is nothing I care to say to you."

"Would you answer a few questions, from courtesy?"

"Perhaps. Ask what you will." Garth noticed that the priest had turned his head toward him only when he had spoken; that, and the man's words, made it seem fairly definite that, like the priests of Andhur Regvos, this feeble old man was blind. It seemed curious that such a decrepit and harmless person should be the sole servant of the most feared of deities—assuming that there was, as he had been told, only one priest of the Final God. Feeling that the priest need not occupy his full attention, he looked over the chamber, noting the already-rotting chunks and slices he had cut from the monster, the still-wet slime stains, the great pool of ichor where he had finally reached the thing's viscera, and the skull-topped altar that stood undamaged and unplundered.

"Have you seen what takes most who enter here, leaving no trace?"

"Yes."

"It did not take you."

"It tried hard enough."

"What happened?"

"It came up from the tunnel; I dodged. We fought, and I managed to injure it. I was struck unconscious, but its wound was severe enough that it preferred retreat to finishing me." That, he thought, was a succinct and accurate summary of his desperate battle; he guessed that such a simple account would serve him

better than any elaborate boasting, at least until he
fully understood the priest's attitude toward the monster. It might well be considered blasphemous to have
defended himself at all.

"What is it?"

"You don't know?" Garth's astonishment got the
better of him and was plainly revealed in his tone.

"No. I am but the caretaker of the temple; I know
nothing of the god's mysteries. The true servant of
the Final God has not yet returned. What was it you
fought?"

Garth was suddenly reluctant to speak, though he
knew no logical reason not to tell the man the nature
of the temple's inhabitant. "Tell me first more of your
cult. Are you not the high priest of The God Whose
Name Is Not Spoken?"

"No. I am a lesser priest. The books of prophecy
say that the one true high priest of death has not been
in Dûsarra in four ages or more, and will not return
until the dawn of the Fifteenth Age."

An uneasiness filtered into Garth's mind at this new
mention of the human system of numbering the ages.
"This is the dawn of the Fourteenth Age, I was told."

"Yes. When this new age grows old, the high priest
will return."

"If he has been gone for four ages . . . the Thirteenth Age lasted three hundred years. Your high priest
must have died centuries ago. Is it his heir you
await?"

"Oh, no! It is the one true high priest of the god of
death. It is in the nature of his service that he himself
cannot die."

There was a pause as Garth digested this information. He recalled mention made of immortality in the
King's Inn of Skelleth. An unpleasant theory crept
into his thoughts.

The Forgotten King had assured him that he sought
to fulfill the purpose that the gods had given him, but
which gods were they he spoke off?

He looked again at the unnatural skull that grinned
atop the altar. "What else do you know of your high
priest?"

"Oh, there are many legends! He was a king of old, in a land so ancient that its existence is forgotten; he made a bargain with the gods of life and death, whereby he shall live until the end of time, but he came to regret this and abandoned the service of his kingdom and his gods to wander the earth clad in rags. He will return when the Fifteenth Age, the Age of Death, begins, to complete his agreement. He alone has spoken to the Final God and lived; it is part of his task to be certain that The Name That Is Not Spoken is not lost. He commands all the world's ancient magic, but has no use for it. There is much more in the sacred texts—his name, which I cannot pronounce truly, and the records of his doings."

"Do your sacred books speak of the Sixteenth Age?"

"No, they cover only the current cycle, which ends with the Fifteenth."

"What do they say of the Fourteenth, then?"

"The Age of Destruction? It shall begin with the decimation and defilement of Dûsarra, and be an age of fire and sword. There is mention of a mighty servant of Bheleu who shall do the bidding of the Forgotten King."

"The Forgotten King?"

"Another name for the high priest of Death."

"The high priest of Death." Garth stared at the skull as he resolved that the prophecies would not come true.

"Yes." The old priest's voice sounded less certain.

"The thing from the tunnel was just a worm." Garth marched out, shoving the blind priest aside, leaving the horned skull on its perch.

The priest ran after him, calling for him to wait; Garth stopped and allowed the old man to catch up, as he had thought of another question he wanted to ask. He saw that the man's hood had fallen back, but took no notice.

"How long was I in there?" he demanded.

"The priest of Aghad said you entered at dawn; the sun is now almost setting."

"Only one day?"

"Yes." The priest's voice was now timid.

Garth stared at his hands. How had they healed so quickly? The sword of Bheleu was still clutched in his right fist; he had a momentary impulse to fling it away, but stopped himself. His dagger had stayed stuck in the monster worm; his axe was lost somewhere within; his old sword had shattered on the gates of Aghad. This infernal blade was his only weapon, and he had no intention of attempting to escape Dûsarra unarmed; after all, the priests of Aghad had promised to kill him.

He continued up toward the mouth of the cave, slowly enough that the priest could keep up with him; as the ruddy volcanic light faded behind him, a faint glow of a paler pink grew ahead.

The priest was babbling at him, asking question after question about the worm; he did not bother to answer most of them, but replied that yes, the slime on the altar came from the worm; no, he had not been able to see all of it; no, it had not all fit into the chamber; no, he did not think he had killed it; yes, it ate people, probably swallowing them whole.

At last the mismatched pair emerged into the gray light of gathering dusk; Garth kept the sword at ready as he stepped out onto the pavement of the Street of the Temples. He glanced at the priest, and saw the man's face for the first time.

His hair was pure white; one eye was gone, the other was pink under a frosting of cataracts; some sort of growth covered one side of the face. From one of the dead-black sleeves protruded the smooth stump of an arm, the loss of the hand long since healed over. He was the most repulsive human being Garth had ever seen.

That, of course, was appropriate for a priest of something as repulsive as death.

As Garth noticed these details the priest talked on, marvelling at the idea of a monster worm, speaking of all the people it had devoured, unmindful of the overman's scrutiny. Garth interrupted him.

"Old man, how were you able to read your books?"

"What? Oh. I was not always blind, and I have an

acolyte, who reads to me when I wish to be reminded."

"You have no powers of second sight?"

"No. I am just a caretaker."

That was, Garth thought, unfortunate; it would have been very convenient had the old fool been able to foresee the actions of the Aghadites. He had encountered enough seers on this quest that another would scarcely have been surprising; but as it was he would have to rely on his own abilities. He started to speak a farewell, to take his leave of the man, but was interrupted by a familiar voice from somewhere in the rocks behind him.

"We offer a final chance, traitor. Kill the old idiot and you may yet be allowed to live."

CHAPTER TWENTY-THREE

For an instant, Garth considered his position. His primary goal was to get out of Dûsarra alive; a secondary goal was to get Frima, Koros, and his loot out with him. It would be pleasant if he could also kill some Aghadites, both because it would discourage pursuit and because it would be enjoyable; he had no moral compunctions about that, since the cult was responsible for any number of murders. However, he was at a disadvantage here; the Aghadite was concealed, presumably in a good defensive position that he had had plenty of time to establish, and Garth had no idea of the number of his foes. There might be the single priest, or the entire cult, or even several cults. Direct battle was therefore inadvisable. Returning to his primary objective, he considered the best way to achieve it; the Aghadites could not have known *when* he would emerge from the temple of death, unless they

had oracles or seers available, and even then they'd
want confirmation. At this instant, messengers of some
sort were most likely carrying word across the city;
the Aghadites wouldn't rely on a single ambush. There
were probably people waiting for him at the stable and
at the city gates.

If he could reach them before the messengers did,
surprise would be on his side. Accordingly, he made
no answer to the taunting voice, and paid no further
heed to the ancient priest of the Final God, but took
to his heels, running full speed straight down the
Street of the Temples, ignoring the few startled pedestrians who scattered before him.

He had reached his decision in far less time than
required to explain it; by the time the Aghadite had
finished his second sentence, Garth was a dozen yards
down the avenue, the great broadsword still in his
right fist. The long blade was awkward, and slowed
him as he ran, but it was his only weapon.

It occurred to him that there might be enemies lurking in the temples along the way; at the first opportunity he turned right and dashed down a side street. He
had not forgotten his experience of being lost in the
maze of narrow streets that made up most of the city,
but considered the risk less important than being unpredictable. A person could not be ambushed or ap-
prehended unless his path was known in advance.

There was one very definite problem that he fore-
saw; the city had only the single gate, and he knew of
no other way past the wall. Also, of course, he wanted
to get Frima and his other booty. Koros could take
care of itself.

He turned left after he had put two blocks between
himself and the Street of the Temples, and found himself in a relatively straight lane paralleling the avenue;
he followed it as far as he could, and found himself in
a familiar alleyway, one he had traversed before. He
slipped from a full run into an easy jog, and headed
for the Inn of the Seven Stars.

Dûsarrans who happened to be out on the streets
gave him a wide berth; an overman with naked sword

in hand was nothing to argue with, particularly when he seemed to be in such a hurry.

The long run across the city tired him rather more than he had hoped; he had apparently not fully recovered from the battle with the worm and the blow on the head. His pace had slowed perceptibly when he turned onto the street where the house he had broken through faced.

He was not entirely sure why he had chosen to approach from this direction; the Aghadites would undoubtedly have it guarded. But they would also have the archway entrance to the stable guarded, and the route through the house would offer more cover and less opportunity for his foes to overcome him by sheer numbers. That it would also offer more cover for an ambuscade had not escaped him; still, he chose to risk it.

The street was not empty as it had been on previous occasions; a handful of men and women, in the usual dark robes and hoods, stopped and stared as he broke again into a full-speed charge toward the door midway in the block.

There was a hiss, and an arrow embedded itself in the hard-packed dirt of the street; it had not come anywhere near him. There was an ambush—but he had taken them by surprise.

He did not bother to try the door when he reached it; only fools would have neglected to lock it. He took the sword in both hands and hewed mightily, hoping the blade would prove sturdy enough.

Another arrow swished past his ear to shatter on the stone of the house's facade.

The sword struck the heavy wooden door and cut into it like a knife into cheese; the hilt suddenly felt hot in Garth's hands. He dismissed it as a trick of his imperfectly healed palms. He ripped the blade free and struck again.

The door exploded inward in shattered fragments, and Garth stepped through; he knew that something beyond his understanding was at work, as he had not the strength to so destroy the door with just two blows, but he had no time to worry about it. Two more arrows flew somewhere behind him.

The room inside was much as he remembered it—the stairway along one side, the archway to the kitchen at the back, the ceiling so low he was forced to stoop. There were details that were different, however; primarily a corpse that lay sprawled before the door, its skull split by a chunk of oak from the demolished door. It had been a man clad in helmet, mail, and breastplate, armed with sword and short spear.

The sword in Garth's hands twisted sideways, and he found himself chopping horizontally; there was a short scream as the blade cut through the belly of a second man who had lurked beside the door, a rattle as he dropped his sword, and a dull thud as he fell forward into a pool of his own blood.

The red gem in the sword's pommel blazed up as bright as a lantern in the dim room. Garth could no longer pretend that the weapon was nothing but simple steel; he had neglected to consider another ambusher at the door, and the sword had disposed of that possibility for him. The thing was not to be trusted. It was still his only weapon, though, and he still had no time for such considerations.

An arrow came in through the door and stuck in the leg of the corpse; Garth moved rapidly across the room. More cautious this time, he wielded the sword with his own will in sweeping around the corners of the kitchen arch and succeeded in wounding another man, who gasped and dropped his weapons as the blade cut his arm open.

Other men responded with attacks of their own; three men with drawn swords faced him, abandoning any attempts at stealth or surprise.

Behind him he heard steps descending the staircase; there was no time to waste. As his right-hand foe made a slashing feint, Garth brought the sword of Bheleu up from beneath; the man's sword was driven back sideways into his own forehead. The curving quillon snapped, leaving a ragged gash, and there was the crack of snapping bone as the thumb that gripped the hilt was crushed against the harder bone of the skull.

A second opponent's blade scraped across Garth's mail as he continued the upward sweep of the great broadsword, freeing it from the shorter sword of the man who was even now collapsing in agony; the tip of the weapon scratched a line in the wooden ceiling as it swept over the head of the central swordsman, its upward momentum too great to be checked immediately. Then it came sweeping down, and cut halfway through the left-hand man, entering his neck and chopping down into his chest.

The central opponent, seeing his comrades defeated in a matter of a very few seconds, made a wild lunge at Garth's unarmored throat; the overman dodged aside, yanking his blade free from the new-made corpse. Seeing his lunge unsuccessful, the man simply released his grip and let his sword fall, raising his hands in surrender; Garth checked his swing as best he could, but the sword cut deep into the man's side anyway, slicing through mail as if it were cloth. The Dûsarran's breastplate stopped it before the blade struck bone, and Garth hoped the wound would not prove fatal. The man slumped to the floor, and Garth stepped over him.

Ahead of him the doorway to the little yard was open; nothing had been done to replace the door he had ruined earlier. There might, he knew, be more men outside, waiting in a third ambush. Hoping to take them by surprise, he charged out, sword thrust out ahead of him, and whirled about when he reached the center of the tiny yard.

The little court was empty; unfortunately, the ones on either side were not. Men armed with crossbows peered up over the six-foot walls. Garth saw them in time to keep moving, to provide as poor a target as possible.

Bolts whirred and clattered against the walls as he stooped and dashed back into the kitchen, to find himself facing the men who had been upstairs. Two were archers, armed only with short bows, bent and strung but with no arrows nocked; they presented no immediate threat, and he ignored them. The others, three of them, were armed with swords. All five were bent over their fallen comrades, unready for combat; none made any threatening move when confronted with an angry overman holding a six-foot broadsword.

Taking no chances, Garth bellowed, "Drop your weapons!"

With varying amounts of reluctance, the five complied.

"Now, out of the house! Take your wounded and go!"

Hesitantly, they obeyed. Of the six men Garth had defeated, three were dead; the one who had been made to gash his own forehead was unconscious, but not seriously injured; the one who had been last to fall was alive but in bad shape, still bleeding despite makeshift bandaging; and the one who had had his arm cut while lurking in ambush was ambulatory but unarmed, the muscles of his right hand slack under rough bandages. The newcomers carried out the wounded, two to a man, with the man still on his feet aided by his remaining comrade. Garth watched them go.

He had lost the element of surprise; instead, he now had a defensible position.

There was a loud roar behind him; he whirled, sword ready, then recognized the sound.

Koros! The warbeast was fighting. Its battle cry was loud enough to be heard for half a mile, but by the volume Garth judged it to be much nearer; probably in the stableyard, defending Frima and Garth's supplies.

The roar sounded again, mingled with a human scream. Garth wished he were able to see what was happening, but he dared not venture out into the waiting crossfire again.

The roaring continued, and other sounds mixed with it: the clatter of weapons, hoarse shouts, piercing screams. With a start, Garth recognized the snapping of crossbow strings.

That could be serious; thick as the warbeast's hide was, at close range a crossbow bolt might pierce it. If a marksman got lucky and put a quarrel in the beast's eye or mouth it could do real damage. Garth did not want to let his faithful beast face danger alone. He peered out the door to the little yard, just to verify the continued presence of the crossbowmen on either side.

There was no sign of them. No faces or weapons showed above the walls. Startled, he took a cautious step outside, expecting the crossbowmen to reappear at any instant.

They didn't. The warbeast's roaring had died to a low growl, and the sounds of resistance had ceased; whoever it had been fighting, it had apparently won. Garth listened, and realized the sound was coming not from directly ahead, beyond the wall of the stable, but from his right. He turned and took a few steps, so that he could look over the stone wall that came to about the level of his mouth.

Koros was in the next yard, its head lowered out of sight; the warbeast's back was low enough that he had not noticed it before. Two crossbow bolts were lodged in its fur, but Garth saw no sign that it was seriously injured.

That explained what had happened to half the crossbowmen; the other half must have fled in terror, he surmised. It left the whereabouts of Frima and his supplies a mystery, though. He kept a cautious watch as he crossed the yard and leaned against the wall, watching his mount.

Koros was eating ravenously, and Garth remembered, with a trace of chagrin, that he had neglected the beast's feeding since arriving in Dûsarra. There were corpses or fragments of five or six men scattered at the monster's feet; Garth judged that that would be plenty, as it had not been all that long since it was fed. Ordinarily it would not have disobeyed his orders so soon. It must have been irritable with hunger, and became annoyed enough with the Dûsarran soldiery to forget its order to stay and guard.

It was quite likely still irritable, and Garth had no intention of bothering it until it had eaten its fill of its victims. He watched as it ripped apart sturdy mail with its fangs to get at the soft flesh beneath, and marvelled anew at the sheer power of the beast.

The sound of clanking armor from beyond the stableyard wall suddenly reminded him that his goods and captive were still unaccounted for; he vaulted up onto the lower wall between the private courts, the sword of Bheleu in his hand, giving himself a good view of the red-tiled roof of the stable and some sight of the stableyard.

Men were marching; he could see little more than their helmets, but it seemed clear they were heading for the stall where he had left Frima. As if in confirmation of his conclusion, his captive's voice called out, "Koros!"

Wasting no further time, Garth launched himself up onto the roof and ran clattering across the tiles. The helmetted men looked up at the sound to see a bellowing overman, spattered with blood, swinging a huge broadsword around his head.

It provided an excellent distraction; they stopped short, the leader a pace or two from the door of the stall. That foremost man even obligingly took two steps back, the better to view this newcomer.

A cry went up. "The overman! The overman!" There was a commotion in the street and more men poured through the arch in response. Garth bellowed again, shouting, *"I'a bheluye!* I am destruction!" He knew that the psychologically correct action at this moment would be to leap down into the men before him, slashing about with the sword; such an assault would almost certainly drive them all back out through the archway. Unfortunately, he could not bring himself to cause such unprovoked bloodshed, and instead merely whirled the blade about his head again, so that it flashed redly as it caught the last light of the setting sun.

The men stared up at him open-mouthed; none advanced—but none retreated, either, though there were some who shuffled uneasily. He was not going to awe them into flight unless he attacked, but he could not bring himself to do so. Quite aside from his aversion to such wanton aggression, it was a long leap down from the roof; even if he made it without injuring himself, which shouldn't prove too difficult, he would most likely stumble or fall upon landing, which would destroy his dignity and ruin the effect of his entrance by revealing him as merely mortal, leaving him open to a concerted counterattack.

The solution to his quandary arrived suddenly, just as the perfect moment passed and the men began to recover their nerve; in a single silent bound, Koros cleared the stable wall, rebounded from the roof with a spray of shards of tile shattered by its weight, and landed atop three of the Dûsarrans. They died without knowing what had hit them, as the warbeast's claws shredded robes, armor, and flesh; the crunching of bone was audible throughout the stableyard over the triumphant roar that Koros released as it struck. The swords the three men had held flew from their hands and clattered on the armor of their companions behind them; one laid open a man's scalp before falling aside.

Not satisfied with the single attack, Koros leapt again, a short, powerful pounce that smashed another man to the ground so suddenly that the man behind him went down as well, his leg trapped beneath the falling body even as he turned to flee. The first man was ripped open from forehead to groin by a slash of the warbeast's fangs, as the second lay screaming, pinned beneath the weight of the monster's forepaws on his companion's corpse. As an afterthought, one of those great velvet-padded paws licked out, in a motion identical with that of a kitten batting a ball of yarn, and the beast's curving claws snatched the screamer's head off, spraying blood across the heels of his fleeing comrades.

Garth stood on the rooftop, virtually forgotten, and watched as the crowd of warriors vanished back through the arch into the street. The huge broadsword hung loosely in his hands as Koros, with a brief gaze at the fleeing Dûsarrans, declined to pursue and settled down to feast on the five it had slain. It licked its claws daintily, cast a glance of its slit-pupilled eyes at its overman master, and began eating.

When a moment had passed with no further attention paid him and no sign of a renewed assault from
without, Garth tossed the sword to the ground, then
cautiously lowered himself over the eaves and
dropped down into the yard.

The gathering dusk had shrouded the stables in
semi-darkness, and he had no way of making a light;
he peered through the gray gloom at the familiar stall,
and made out the pale oval of Frima's face above the
door. He strode up to her, and found she was staring
fixedly, mouth gaping, at Koros as it chewed con-
tentedly on a human thighbone.

"We must get out of the city," he said.

She said nothing, but continued to stare. Her mouth
closed; her throat worked, making no sound, and her
jaw fell open again.

"Our best hope is to ride Koros. It can probably
carry both of us faster than we could move on foot,
and we need not worry about separation."

She was silent for a second longer, then blinked
and turned toward the overman. "Ride *that?*" Her
voice was hoarse.

"Yes. It is the same animal you petted yesterday,
and now that it has eaten, it should give us no trouble."

Her gaze turned back to Koros who, having eaten
its fill, was licking its paws clean, then travelled across
the fragmentary remains of its victims, to rest at last
on the severed head that had rolled, unwanted and
unnoticed, across the yard, to lie against the wall beside the arch. Her mouth twitched, and she turned
away to vomit on the dirty straw that floored the stall.

Garth waited patiently until she had finished, then
said, "It would be helpful if you would aid in loading
the supplies."

CHAPTER TWENTY-FOUR

Although it was plain from the rattle of armor, the mutter of voices, and an occasional quick glimpse through the arch that a considerable body of armed men lurked in the street in front of the inn, there were no further attacks nor attempts to enter the stableyard. Koros was completely docile once he had eaten his fill, and Garth had no trouble in loading and tying down all his remaining supplies and the sack containing the assorted loot from the first five temples—excluding Frima, who remained nervous and reluctant to approach the warbeast. When that was done, he found a place for the great sword, slipping it into the harness in such a way that its oversized blade ran along the beast's right flank, with the hilt at its neck. It would not be very accessible, but it would be secure; Garth was much more willing to trust their defense to Koros than he was to try and hang onto the awkward weapon while riding at high speed. When that was in place, he lifted Frima onto the back of the saddle, and swung himself up into position in front of her.

His current plan was simplicity itself; he and Frima would hang on as best they could while Koros made a dash for the city gate. The Dûsarrans had not yet had much opportunity to see the warbeast in action, and it was Garth's hope that they would be unable to do anything to stop such a dash. There was always the chance that a lucky archer would put an arrow through the beast's eye, or through his own throat, or through some part of the unarmored girl behind him, but he could see no way to avoid that risk.

He made a final check of the knots and buckles se-

curing everything, adjusted his own seat, and reminded Frima to hold on well; then he leaned forward
and spoke in the warbeast's triangular ear the single
word that meant, "Take us home."

It snorted, and padded silently out into the yard; it
circled once, studying its surroundings, and then, with
no warning, launched itself upward.

It landed on the now-familiar roof with a crunching
of broken tiles, continued forward with a shorter leap
to the brink overlooking the street, then dove over the
edge into the street, ignoring the crowd of humans.

Garth had expected the warbeast to take that route,
but the actual fact was nothing like the expectation;
never before had he been subjected to such sudden
changes in velocity and direction, such abrupt rising
and falling, and his firm grip on the harness seemed
suddenly very precarious. His stomach churned with
the movement; he had once been in a storm at sea—
or at any rate while aboard a ship, though technically
it had been in a sheltered bay and not on the high seas
—and the seasickness that had briefly overcome him
on that occasion was the only comparison he could
think of for this new and thoroughly unpleasant sensation. The seasickness had developed slowly and
gradually; this motion sickness was as sudden and in-
stantaneous as the motion that caused it. He leaned
forward, eyes closed, clutching at the beast's neck,
fighting the need to vomit.

Frima, behind him, was equally affected; her head
snapped back and forth with each leap, as she fought
to retain her hold on Garth's waist. Her just-emptied
stomach rebelled painfully, but was unable to expel
what was no longer there. Her eyes watered with the
pain.

Thus neither could see what was happening, which
was probably just as well. Unmindful of the puny humans, Koros had landed full in their midst, flattening
several, then bounded forward again, leaving half a
dozen dead or maimed. A shower of crossbow bolts,
fired far too late, tore through the spot where it had
first appeared on the stable roof, and a random spatter
of crossbow fire continued to follow in its wake as it

made its way through the crowd toward the market-place. At first its path was strewn with bloodied corpses and new-made cripples, but very quickly the mob vanished from in front of this unstoppable juggernaut, and it moved forward in its normal smooth glide instead of a series of violent assaults.

Garth recovered himself enough to marvel at the number of men his enemies had mustered, and at the incredible power and speed of his mount. He had seen the beast in action before and admired its fluid might and blurring quickness, but watching that velocity and being carried along were two entirely different things. When Koros moved at its full fighting speed, the wind in the faces of its riders was like a solid wall pressing them back; it was impossible to keep his stinging eyes open for more than a second at a time.

Koros had displayed more strategy than could be expected of a mere beast; instead of taking the short-est and most direct route to the marketplace it had looped northward around several blocks, and now entered the square from a totally unexpected direction. It had moved faster than the news of its approach, and burst unheralded into the broad plaza; for the first time since leaving the stable, it roared.

The market was still much as usual; the merchants' stalls ranged around the sides, lit by an abundance of torches, and surrounded a crowd of people. The crowd, however, was distributed in a most unusual manner, with squads guarding each entrance and a large mob on the street that led to the Inn of the Seven Stars. Someone was shouting, haranguing the mob.

There was another unusual feature, far more important: the city gates were closed.

The warbeast's roar echoed from the stone of the city wall and the wood and metal of the gates, and for a moment the murmur of the crowd ceased; the speaker broke off in midsentence and a brief silence swept the square, to be swallowed in renewed shouting and jabbering.

No one moved as Koros stalked across the market-place to the gates. It stopped a few yards away and looked up at the barrier, its golden eyes gleaming in

the torchlight. Garth, still dazed from the wild ride—
which had taken less than a minute—did the same.

The gates were iron-bound oak, towering up into
the darkness, black against the stars; they were at least
thirty feet high. Garth was unsure whether Koros could
leap such a height, and apparently it was unsure itself;
he was quite certain, however, that it could not do so
while carrying two passengers and assorted baggage.
He would have to dismount and get the portal open.

His head was clearing rapidly, but he did not feel
himself capable of walking yet; instead, he spoke a
soothing word to his mount and peered at the gate to
see how they were secured.

A heavy bar lay across a row of brackets; in the
shadows and flickering torchlight he could not see
what the bar was made of, but he supposed it would
be some sturdy wood, perhaps tarred to resist weather-
ing. Above and below it were masses of knotted rope,
apparently lashings around cleats on the two valves;
these, too, were dark.

A sound distracted him; he turned and saw that the
mob was approaching, apparently planning to overpower overman and warbeast by sheer numbers. He
saw an assortment of swords, maces, axes, clubs, and
other weapons brandished amongst the robes, and the
glint of torchlight on steel armor here and there where
robes had fallen open or hoods been pushed back. He
wondered why so many seemingly ordinary Dûsarrans
had such accoutrements available; did the city rely on
militia in times of war?

He recalled that he was unarmed at the moment,
and reminded himself that he did not want to be on
Koros' back during any fighting that might occur. Accordingly, before the foremost attackers could reach
him, he slid from his beast's back and pulled the sword
of Bheleu from its place in the harness.

It came free just in time; seeing his actions, the
Dûsarrans had broken into a run, hoping to kill him
before he could defend himself. Instead, the foremost
attackers, too busy running to properly defend themselves, had their bellies slashed open. The sword of
Bheleu cut through robes, armor, and flesh with equal

ease, and the overman's greater reach, combined with the length of the great blade, meant that the first Dûsarrans were dead before they could strike a single blow.

Behind them their comrades halted, momentarily deterred, and Garth grasped the opportunity for psychological combat.

"Scum! Is this the way of Dûsarra, to send hundreds against a lone warrior? Cowards all! Has any among you the courage to face me in single combat? True, I am more than a mere man, but I have already fought long and hard. I slew the abomination in the temple of death! I destroyed the cult of Bheleu!"

There was renewed muttering in the crowd; none approached. After a few seconds, a voice cried out, "You have defiled our temple!"

"I have defeated a monster that ate human flesh; I have slaughtered those who worshipped slaughter; and I have freed an innocent victim from a vile sacrifice! Does this defile your temple?"

"You slew the priest of Tema!" There was a rumble of response. There was no doubt that most of the mob were worshippers of the goddess of night.

"Who says this? I have fought in the temple of death; I have killed in the temple of Bheleu, and in the temple of Sai, and I have mocked and defiled the temple of Aghad, but who is it that says I have harmed a priest of Tema?"

"You defiled the temple of darkness!"

"Who says this thing of me? Let me face my accuser!"

There was an uneasy stirring but no further shout; a few took a hesitating step forward, only to retreat once again. Then a tall figure appeared at the edge of the crowd, pushing its way forward.

Garth stared at the approaching person; whoever it was, he stood head and shoulders above the majority of the crowd, his face hidden by a hood the color of drying blood. A path opened before him, and the last third of his journey across the market to face Garth was made in bold strides.

"Who is this that comes to meet me?"

"It is I, defiler; it is I who say that you slew the priest of Tema and robbed her altar, that you slew priest and priestess of Regvos. And I am he who will face you in single combat!" With that the hood was flung back, revealing the noseless brown face of an overman, yellow eyes gleaming in the torchlight.

It took Garth a moment to realize he faced one of his own species; he recognized that voice, and for several seconds was aware only that he was face to face with the high priest of Aghad. His enemy had delivered himself; here was the opportunity for a part of the revenge he craved. He raised the sword of Bheleu.

"Priest of Aghad! People of Dûsarra, you have believed the ruler of the cult of treachery, the high priest of lies and deceit, whose altar I desecrated in righteous anger! Let our duel decide my fate!"

The Aghadite grinned and flung aside his robe, standing upright; for the first time it occurred to Garth that he might not win this fight. After all, he was tired, while the overman priest was still fresh. Furthermore, when he abandoned his concealing crouch, the Aghadite was almost eight feet in height, a monstrous size even among overmen. He was curiously lopsided, his right shoulder much higher than his left; such deformities were common among the infants of the Northern Waste, but their victims were customarily killed at birth. That had been a reason for the slow rate of increase in the Waste's population, but necessary, due to the very limited food supply.

Silvery mail gleamed on the monster overman's arms and legs; his chest was adorned with a gleaming red-enamelled breastplate. A sturdy steel skullcap with chain-link earflaps protected his head, and blued-steel gauntlets covered his hands. Garth wondered for an instant where he had obtained the gauntlets, which were made to accommodate the peculiarities of an overman's double-thumbed, long-fingered hands; his own hands were unprotected.

Still grinning, the Aghadite reached up and slid his sword from a sheath on his back; its hilt was blood-red and its blade dull black—save for the edges, which gleamed silvery-red in the firelight. It was a magnificent weapon, a two-handed double-edged broadsword. It was in fact, to all appearances, the equal of the sword of Bheleu.

The creature was a priest, Garth told himself; he could have little real battle experience. His own greater skill should give him the advantage despite the monster's longer reach and presumably greater strength.

The black blade whistled; Garth parried the attack, only to find his enemy's weapon ducking downward unexpectedly, under his own silver blade. He dodged, and escaped injury.

The priest's grin remained, and Garth knew that the maneuver had not been the luck of a beginner. He made a feeble riposte, which was easily parried.

He felt a thin seep of despair as he reflexively met and countered the reply to his blow. This was not what he wanted. He was weary, his stomach hurt from his wild ride, his hands seemed weak and unfamiliar with scar tissue; this was not how he had wanted to face the priest of Aghad.

Of course, he had not known that the priest was an overman. One of his own kind! One of his people, serving—heading!—that loathsome cult! Despite his weariness, his despair turned suddenly to anger, and his next blow was faster, more aggressive than before.

He would not despair, he told himself; despair was the province of Sai, sister to Aghad. Of course, anger was the work of Aghad himself, and that realization angered him further. He would show this grinning monster his mistake, make plain to him his poor taste in employers! The sword of Bheleu flashed up, knocking aside the Aghadite's next blow, and whipped around and over, scratching enamel from the scarlet breastplate. The Aghadite's grin wavered.

Aghad! Aghad was nothing! His time had ended centuries ago; this was the Age of Bheleu! The red gem in the sword's pommel blazed.

"I am Bheleu!" Garth screamed.

The grin vanished. The black sword swung up into a parry, and with a long swooping blow the sword of Bheleu came down upon it, shattering it; splinters of black metal sprayed, ripping the silver mail, scoring the red breastplate.

The priest's face went blank with shock as he stared at the remaining foot of blade that protruded from the long hilt he clutched; instinctively, he brought the stump up to meet another blow that came sweeping toward his skull.

The sword of Bheleu went diagonally through blade, hilt, and hands; bones snapped and blood spurted, but the high priest of Aghad had no time to react. The blade travelled on, shearing through helmet and bone, and the brain that had devised so many taunts and trials was spattered in gory bits across the front of the crowd surrounding the battle.

The force of the blow was such that the corpse did not crumple, but was instead stretched out at full length upon the dirt of the marketplace, surrounded by gleaming shards of the black sword, a red-and-gray spray of blood and brain making an elongated halo about the ruined head.

The victor raised his sword in triumph, ignoring the baleful red glow of the gem in its pommel, and bellowed, "I am destruction!"

Koros roared in answer.

Then, abruptly, the spell vanished; Garth staggered and stared in horror at the dead form of his foe. He lowered the sword and looked about.

With the death of the Aghadite, much of the crowd had decided Garth had proved his point; the mob was shrinking steadily. The portion remaining, however, was the most militant group; when the berserk monster that had butchered their leader reverted to an exhausted overman, they began to advance toward him. Garth lifted the sword again.

The warbeast roared again, and stepped up beside its master; the advance halted. From the corner of his eye Garth noticed that Frima was no longer astride the beast's broad back, but he dared not divert his attention from the angry crowd to worry about her.

The sword felt unbearably heavy. Although the mob was reduced to a fraction of its former size, it was still more than Koros could handle unaided; not that the warbeast was likely to be killed, but it would be too bogged down by the enemy's numbers to defend Garth. He would have to defend himself, and he knew he couldn't unless the trance came over him again—and he didn't want that. He could never be sure it would pass.

And of course, he had no way of knowing what would bring it on; it had come twice now, once in the temple of Bheleu and once here in the market, but it had not touched him in the temple of death, so it was not anger or physical danger that triggered it.

Perhaps the sword itself would save him, as it had in the house behind the stable; he glanced at the pommel and saw that the glow of the gem had died away to a faint glimmer, which was not encouraging.

Perhaps he could talk the mob out of attacking; with sword and warbeast and strong words he might be able to deter them. He raised the blade above his head, with an effort he hoped was not visible, but before he could speak a low rumble sounded, as it had in the temple of Bheleu.

Recovering from his startlement more quickly than the Dûsarrans, Garth realized that the sound had come at the perfect moment for him; he took advantage of it by speaking in his deepest, most resonant tones, lower than any human throat could produce.

"Hold, scum! I have slain your champion in fair fight; would you still dare defy me?"

A tall young man in dark red robes answered him.

"You are still a blasphemer and defiler, a murderer and committer of sacrilege; the gods demand your death!"

"Fool! Which of your gods would dare? I am the servant of Dûs, Bheleu, the bringer of destruction; death and desolation follow me as hounds. What are you, to stand against me?" Even as he spoke, Garth wondered how he chose these words; although he knew his best hope lay in convincing his foes he was more than mortal, he felt that this eloquence was not entirely of his own making.

"You are Garth, an overman from the Northern Waste, sent here to steal by a third-rate wizard!"

This man was obviously another Aghadite, since he knew so much. Garth prepared to denounce him as such, but before he could speak a new voice sounded.

"This is Bheleu incarnate, come to herald the new age, whatever he may have been before! Let those who defy him know that P'hul and her servants recognize this her brother and serve his ends!"

The speaker of this proclamation stood behind the remaining mob and to one side, with a dozen gray-robed figures ranged behind him, all with hoods pulled forward and faces hidden. As he looked at them, it seemed to Garth that the light changed and the square became brighter.

Then it became brighter still, and he realized it was no illusion; some new flame had appeared behind him, but he dared not turn to see what it was.

There was a moment of near-silence as those who still stood against Garth muttered amongst themselves; the overman noticed that more had drifted away and vanished into the streets and alleys.

"The Lady P'hul your sister gives you greetings, my lord; what would you have of her?" The gray-robed speaker raised a staff toward Garth.

Before he could consciously decide upon a reply, Garth found himself shouting, "I am destruction!"

In a chorus, the priests and priestesses of P'hul replied, "Destruction!" Hands flew up, and a fine gray powder was scattered on the air, to be spread across the market by a sudden gust of wind.

"No!" cried the Aghadite. "The overman is a fraud and a thief! Slay him!" He drew a sword from beneath his robe and charged forward, a dozen others with him.

A black blur filled Garth's vision for an instant, followed by a flash of bone-white claws and gleaming fangs, and a spurt of rich red; but as Garth had anticipated, there were too many attackers for Koros to handle; even as half a dozen died screaming, others surged around and past the warbeast. Garth met them with a long sweep of the sword of Bheleu, disembowelling one, hacking open the side of another; a third came within reach and sent his own sword at Garth's flank. The overman twisted, and the blade scraped across his breastplate, bruising his flesh beneath despite his padding.

The sword of Bheleu came free. As Garth brought it around to run the point through the neck of his near-successful assailant, he saw that a new fire was kindling in the red gem. That threat disposed of, he turned to meet the next, and saw that the P'hulites were leaving, walking calmly away, without any opposition; he had hoped that they would aid him. A dozen allies, no matter how ill, might have turned this battle in his favor. What had been the meaning of their speeches, then?

His blade demolished a man's face. Blood now covered half its length, starting at the tip.

Where, he asked himself, was this Bheleu when he was needed? Garth's arms ached as he heaved his unyielding weapon about.

A face appeared before him, and he tried to bring his blade to meet it; before the blow fell, however, the face seemed to dissolve. The mouth fell open; skin cracked like dry mud, oozing pus; white gum filled the eyes, and the man fell mewling at Garth's feet.

The sweep of the sword of Bheleu met no resistance, the man having fallen from its path; Garth struggled to regain control and defend himself even as the shock of what he had just seen filtered through him.

New screams ripped through the square, added to those of the men Koros was slaughtering; a blade lightly grazed Garth's throat, the dying effort of a man whose skin was peeling in blistered strips from his flesh. Gazing around, looking for new attacks, Garth saw none; instead, men lay dying on the ground, their wounds seeping white ooze rather than the natural red of blood. Those still on their feet were fleeing in terror; as Garth watched, more fell as they ran, to lie whimpering in the streets for their last few seconds of life.

The sword of Bheleu fell unheeded from his hands. He had brought chaos and catastrophe to Dûsarra, despite his protestations.

A cry distracted him. "Lord Garth! Help!"

Recovering himself somewhat, Garth picked up the sword again and turned in the direction of Frima's voice.

She was at the gates, struggling to lift the heavy bar, a task obviously beyond her strength; the rope bindings were gone, leaving smouldering ash, and a torch lay on the ground near her feet. As he started toward her, he saw that the merchants' canopies on the eastern side of the square were ablaze; that had been the new light that had appeared behind him as he faced westward confronting the mob. He had no idea who had set them afire, or why; it was something he meant to ask Frima at the first opportunity.

He had intended to add his own waning strength to her attempt to lift the bar from its brackets; but as he approached, the sword hilt in his hands seemed to move of its own volition, and he found himself hacking at the center of the bar as he would hack firewood with an axe.

The sword, or whatever agency controlled it, seemed to know what it was doing; at the second blow the central span shattered, the wood reducing itself to splinters in a thoroughly unnatural way. The ends remained intact, but did not prevent the gates from being opened far enough to permit first Frima, then Garth, and finally Koros to slip through into the empty night beyond.

CHAPTER TWENTY-FIVE

The air was dry and warm as the trio moved down the tone hillside in an automatic effort to put some distance between themselves and the chaos of the Dûsarran marketplace; the orange glow that leaked through the gates paled until it was lost in the cloud-filtered moonlight. Somewhere behind them a faint rumbling sounded.

A few hundred yards from the city walls, Garth stopped and gathered Frima and Koros to him. He set about checking the straps and knots that had held his supplies and loot in place on the warbeast's back throughout the fighting as he asked, "How did the fires start?"

"I did it. With a torch from one of the posts."

"Why?"

"As a distraction; there were men sneaking around behind you."

"Oh." That was disconcerting; he had been totally unaware of any such maneuver. "Thank you. And the ropes on the gate?"

"They were tarred, to keep them from stretching in the rain; the tar burns well. That's why I had the torch when I saw the men coming."

"Thank you. You have been most helpful."

There was silence for a moment as he pulled tight a loosened buckle. A faint crackling came from the city; the fire must be spreading. Garth glanced up, but saw no sign of pursuit.

"I don't know *why* I helped you!" Frima burst out suddenly. "You're kidnapping me?"

"That's true," Garth replied. "But would you want to stay in Dûsarra at present? With fire, panic, and disease loose in the streets?"

"No." Her voice was flat and definite, all defiance gone.

"That disease—have you ever seen it before?"

"No, but I have heard of it. It is the White Death, which P'hul uses to dispose of those who have displeased her. She must favor you, as her priest said."

A few days earlier Garth would have dismissed that as more human superstition; now, he was less certain. The events of the last few days and nights definitely seemed to have involved powers beyond any he was familiar with. He slid the sword of Bheleu into the place in the harness it had occupied before, wishing he had some other more convenient and more trustworthy weapon.

"It may be," he said, "that the Forgotten King will have no use for you. In that case, you shall be free to go as you please; you may return to Dûsarra and to your family if you choose. I make no promises, however."

"I may just escape before that." Her tone had lightened.

"I hope to prevent that. Recall that you are unarmed and half clad, and that the city is a most unhealthy place just now."

"Oh, don't worry, silly." She petted Koros, who was licking blood from its claws.

Garth smiled. No one had ever called him silly before. At least, not for a century or so.

A blaze of red light lit the sky; Garth and Frima turned to see that one of the volcanic peaks was brightly aglow. A moment later the now-familiar rumbling shook the slope beneath their feet.

"I think it would be wise to depart," Garth remarked. He lifted the girl onto the warbeast's back, then swung himself up in front of her. He was weary and would have preferred to sleep, but it seemed quite clear that he would not be safe anywhere near the city.

When both were astride, Koros started forward in its customary swift glide, apparently unbothered by its recent exertions. As Dûsarra and the fiery volcano receded behind them, Garth contemplated recent events.

His life-long atheism he now suspected to be incorrect; there was something that had directed his actions since his acquisition of the sword of Bheleu. No other explanation was adequate. Whether it was in fact the god of destruction he did not know, nor did he understand the relationship between this power, himself, and the sword. Whatever it was, it had gained him powerful allies in the cult of P'hul, and it might therefore have made him enemies as well—something he would have to be watchful for henceforth. The enmity of the cult of Aghad he had earned himself, and it was plain that the cult had power in lands besides its own; that, too, he must be watchful for.

The sword itself he did not trust; were it not his

only weapon, he would have sworn never to touch it
again. As it was, he was eager to deliver it to the
Forgotten King and be done with it.

The Forgotten King—there was another matter for
consideration. The old man was the high priest of
death; it was not desirable, therefore, to serve him
any further. Garth would deliver the loot from the
various altars to him and then go his own way.

The vague promises of fame, of possible immortality, and of some great cosmic significance were, at
present, of little interest; his recent dealings with cosmic powers had left him far less enthusiastic about
such matters. There were mundane matters enough to
occupy his time. There was the possibility of trade
with the overmen of the Yprian Coast, should they
actually exist; there might well be repercussions from
the events just past to be dealt with; there was his
vengeance to be taken upon the Baron of Skelleth.
Trade or no, he was determined to have his revenge.

He rode on through the night, Frima hanging on
forlornly behind him as she left the only home she
had ever known, Koros padding smoothly along. His
mind seethed with schemes to humble the Baron, with
schemes to seek out and destroy the cult of Aghad,
with thoughts of great deeds to be done. None of the
three noticed the great red gem set in the pommel of
the sword of Bheleu, protruding from the warbeast's
harness alongside its furry chest, where it burned with
a murky flame the color of blood.

NOTES ON LANGUAGE
AND PRONUNCIATION

The reader should remember throughout that the characters do not speak English, but a language which, if pressed for a name, they would call "Eramman." All dialogue must be considered as translations from the Eramman, and all names as approximate transcriptions. An attempt has been made to keep all names as easily pronounceable for speakers of English as possible; since Eramman is an Indo-European tongue, reasonable accuracy is possible as well.

However, a rough guide to pronunciation seems advisable.

Accents: There are two different rules to be followed in regard to where stress falls; in Nekutta (including Dûsarra), Orgûl, Amag, Tadumuri, Mara, and almost all of Eramma, the accent always falls on the next-to-last syllable in any word, regardless of how many syllables there may be. In Orûn, the Northern Waste, the Yprian Coast, and in personal names but no other words in parts of northern Eramma (including Skelleth), the accent always falls on the first syllable, regardless of the length of the word. Thus Garth, being from the Northern Waste, pronounces the name of his home city OR-duh-nin, while the people of Skelleth or Dûsarra would pronounce it Or-DOO-nin.

The Plain of Derbarok, lying as it does between Eramma and Orûn, has no set rule; its inhabitants vary their pronunciation at whim, and there is no consensus as to whether the correct pronunciation is DER-ba-rock or Der-BAR-ock.

Phonetics: The Eramman language has seven basic vowels, which are represented in transcription by *A, E, I, Y, O, U,* and *Ü;* most have two pronunciations, depending on whether they occur in an accented syllable or an unaccented one.

A is always pronounced like the *a* in *era.*

E in an unaccented syllable is pronounced like the *e* in *get.*

E in an accented syllable is pronounced like the *é* in *passé.*

I in an unaccented syllable is pronounced like the *i* in *bit.*

I in an accented syllable is pronounced like the *ee* in *bee.*

Y is a sound which does not occur in English; regardless of accent it is pronounced like the Russian ы, best approximated as something between the accented and unaccented *I.*

O is always pronounced like the *o* in *got;* there is no long O in Eramman.

U in an unaccented syllable is pronounced like the *oo* in *book.*

U in an accented syllable is pronounced like the *oo* in *boot.*

Ü in an unaccented syllable is pronounced as in German; in an accented syllable it falls somewhere between the German *ü* and *ö.*

The use of a circumflex indicates that a vowel in an unaccented syllable is pronounced as if accented (e.g., Orûn and Dûsarra, pronounced OR-o͞on and Do͞o-SAR-ra). One-syllable words are always considered accented, but a circumflex may sometimes appear as a reminder.

Diphthongs are common in Eramman, especially *AI,* pronounced like the English word "I," and *EU,* which does not occur in most forms of English, but closely resembles the Cockney pronunciation of the long O-sound.

Consonants are pronounced much as in English, except *R,* which is trilled or "flipped" slightly (not rolled). The following combinations should be noted:

TH is always as in *thin,* never as in *there.*

DH represents the voiced *th* as in *there.*

BH represents a sound somewhere between *b* and *v,* as in the Castilian Spanish pronunciation of either.

PH represents a sound somewhere between *p* and *f;* in the combination *P'H* the apostrophe has no sound or value whatsoever except to indicate that the *P* and *H* are both pronounced individually and not as a single phoneme. *P'hul* is one syllable.

CH is pronounced as in *church.*

J is pronounced as in *jar.*

G is always as in *get,* never as in *gem.*

KH represents a voiceless gutteral, like the German *ch* in *ach.*

GH represents a voiced gutteral; it sounds rather like gargling.

SH is pronounced as in *sheep.*

ZH is pronounced like *z* in *azure.*

A final note on the names of the gods: Eramman is a declined language with seven cases; all nouns will ordinarily have an ending indicating their case and what part of a sentence they are. Names, however, do not have endings, ever. The names of the gods are, for the most part, simply words indicating their provenance with endings removed. Thus *aghadye,* the nominative form of the word for "loathing," becomes *Aghad,* and *bheluye,* meaning "destruction," becomes *Bheleu* (yes, it should be *bheleuye* or *Bhelu;* a few centuries earlier it was *bheleuye,* but pronunciations change).

Native speakers would not find this confusing, nor tend to identify a god too strongly with the single trait his name represents, because they are accustomed to names with root meanings that may not have much to do with the things named. For examples of similar attitudes among speakers of English, consider the names Grace and Victor; no one assumes that every woman named Grace is in fact graceful, or that every man named Victor is a successful fighter. How many people, upon hearing the name New York, even remember that there *is* an old York?

Furthermore, many of the root-words have changed meaning or dropped out of common usage; *regvosye*, meaning an unwillingness to understand, is extremely archaic, and no longer used as the ordinary word for blindness. That is just one example of many.

The first personated are usually referred to by
their attributes rather than their names, Life and
Death; they do have names, however. The role of
several gods of life as twice-born remains good. He

NOTES ON ERAMMAN
MYTH AND THEOLOGY

In the beginning, according to the myths of Eramma
and Nekutta, there was nothing at all except Dagha,
and a nothingness far more complete than is ordinarily considered. There was no time, no space, no matter, no energy, no life, no death, nothing at all.
Dagha, existing without these things, is therefore totally incomprehensible; it is customary to refer to
Dagha as "he," but actually there is no way of saying
whether he is male, female, neither, or both.

In some way, this incomprehensible being created
time and space; however, being outside time himself,
he could not directly interfere or manipulate anything
within the space he had created. For that reason,
there is no cult of Dagha, no worship, and no prayer
to him.

Not satisfied with an empty cosmos, Dagha also
created beings that could manipulate it, beings that
were within time and limited by it, but were still im-
mortal and unconfined by space. These beings were
the gods.

Since they were created from nothing, they were of
necessity created in pairs, each the negation of its
twin. In each pair there was a god dedicated to the
elaboration and ornamentation of the cosmos, and another dedicated to returning to primordial nothingness. Dagha created seven pairs in all; the seven
dedicated to creation are known as the Lords of Eir
(from an archaic word meaning both "tree" and "vi-
tality"), and their seven foes are known as the Lords
of Dûs (from *dusye,* meaning "death" and also "darkness").

The first pair created are usually referred to by their attributes rather than their names, Life and Death; they do have names, however. The role of Ayvi, the god of life, is frequently misunderstood; he is not in any way a preserver of life, but merely its bestower. He brings the first spark to each seed or embryo, but nothing more; and the Final God does nothing but remove that spark.

The next creation was of four gods rather than two: Aal, god of growth and fertility, countered by P'hul, goddess of decay; and Bel Vala, god of strength and preservation, countered by Bheleu, god of destruction. Aal is generally given precedence over Bel Vala, but P'hul is considered inferior to Bheleu; the reasons for this apparent contradiction are unclear.

The next creation was again of four gods, but this time there was no confusion in rank; Aghad, god of hatred, fear, and loathing, and his sister Pria, goddess of love, peace, and friendship, are universally acknowledged as mightier than Sai, goddess of sorrow and despair, and Gau, goddess of pleasure and delight.

These ten are the High Gods; their four younger siblings are considered lesser, but therefore more accessible, deities. The sixth pair is Leuk, lord of light and bringer of inspiration, and Andhur Regvos, the god of darkness and blindness.

The seventh and final pair of Eir and Dûs are Tema, goddess of night, and Amera, goddess of the day. With the creation of these two Dagha either exhausted his power or lost interest.

These fourteen gods amongst them created the world, to provide themselves with an arena in which to manifest themselves; and in the early days of their creation, in emulation of their master, they created lesser gods.

All the various cults of Nekutta and Eramma agree thus far, with the exception of a few outcast religions and followers of obscure deities; however, there is virtually no agreement as to the existence, number, and nature of these lesser gods, who are actually the objects of most worship, the Eir and Dûs being considered too powerful to waste time on mere mortals.

Most of the lesser gods are collectively classed as Arkhein, a word of unknown origin, and there are dozens, perhaps hundreds, of them, including among the more prominent Savel Skai, the sun-god; Mei, goddess of the moon; Eramma the earth-mother; Koros, god of war; Melith, goddess of storms and lightning, and her brother (or half-brother, or son, or cousin, depending on which cult one adheres to) Kewerro, the god of wind and air, particularly the north wind and storms at sea. Others range down through such minor powers as Eknissa, the fire-goddess, to the obscure and pointless, such as Quon, god of dogs, and Bugo, god of masculinity and petty aggression.

A popular pastime in some areas is to debate the pedigrees of the various Arkhein, a diversion not readily exhausted, since despite the sexes generally attributed to the various deities it is assumed that any Eir or Dûs can mate with any other and produce offspring, or that any one can by himself or herself produce a child. Furthermore, the Arkhein themselves are fertile; Eramma is generally considered the mother of most of the minor nature-gods, though their paternities (if any) are debatable.

It is no wonder that, confronted with such a tangle, most overmen prefer to assume that no gods exist at all.

ABOUT THE AUTHOR

LAWRENCE WATT-EVANS was born and raised in eastern Massachusetts, the fourth of six children. Both parents were long-time science-fiction readers, so from an early age he read and enjoyed a variety of speculative fiction. He also tried writing it, with little success, since he never finished a story.

Having survived twelve years of public school, he attempted to maintain family tradition by attending Princeton University, as his father and grandfather had done, but with rather less success than his forebears. After a year and a half of majoring in architecture, he flunked out as a result of too many parties and too few classes, and spent two years living in Pittsburgh (a city greatly underrated), trying to write for money and pretending to look for a real job.

At the end of this period he simultaneously sold his first story and was readmitted to Princeton. The story in question was one page of would-be humor; he returned to college and got through two successful years, majoring in religion. Leaving once again on an indefinite leave of absence, which continues to this day, he married his long-time girlfriend and settled in Lexington, Kentucky, where his wife had a job capable of supporting the both of them while he once again attempted to write. He also devoted considerable time to a hobby he had acquired three years earlier in Pittsburgh: collecting comic books. He spends his days keeping house, buying and selling comics by mail, and writing. Within a year of moving to Kentucky he produced a full-length fantasy novel complete with ending and, to the astonishment of all, it sold, starting a full-time career as a writer.